PRAISE FOR *THAT PINSON GIRL*

"*That Pinson Girl* is a beautiful novel about the destructive power of dark secrets. Gerry Wilson's prose shines as she breathes life into her characters and into the north Mississippi landscape. Leona Pinson, the young woman at the heart of this tale, is exactly the sort of heroine I long for in great fiction. I will not soon forget her. This book is a gift."

—Tiffany Quay Tyson, award-winning author of *The Past is Never* and *Three Rivers*

"I did not know Gerry Wilson's work before, but I loved *That Pinson Girl*. The book is both gripping and beautifully written, and the characters and setting quickly sprang to life. Though Wilson has her own voice, the novel calls to mind the work of one of my favorite writers, Elizabeth Spencer."

—Steve Yarbrough, author of *Stay Gone Days, The Unmade World*

"In Gerry Wilson's gripping debut novel, 1918 in North Mississippi becomes tangible again; here are the red hills, the suck of winter mud, the scrabble of subsistence living, and the intricately crossed lines of race and kin. Wilson's suspenseful threading of tales has lasting historical resonance. In confronting the tragedy of a broken family, she explores the weight of motherhood, the rich and betraying Southern landscape, and the body's intimate vulnerabilities. This story took me by the collar and shook me."

—Katy Simpson Smith, author of *The Everlasting, Free Men, The Story of Land and Sea*, and *We Have Raised All of You: Motherhood in the South, 1750-1835*

"Devastating and beautifully written, Gerry Wilson's *That Pinson Girl* is at once a heartrending tragedy and a testament to the indomitable human spirit. In her heroine, Leona, Wilson has drawn an unforgettable character buoyed by her determination to survive and to care for her child, even when confronted with violence, racial tensions, the horrors of a distant war, mounting losses from the influenza epidemic, and the lingering repercussions of murder. This historical tale about a hard-scrabble Southern farming family grabbed my attention and wouldn't let go."

—Clifford Garstang, author of *Oliver's Travels* and *The Shaman of Turtle Valley*

"The past of Gerry Wilson's riveting *That Pinson Girl* is far from dead as two families—one Black, one white—struggle to wrest a future from the unforgiving Mississippi hill country of the early twentieth century. A spellbinding story of murder, grief, and guilt with deeply sympathetic characters and a plot that takes you by the collar and won't let go. This is red-clay Faulkner country: the Klan rides, rivers overflow, crops fail—and yet its traumatized women and Black inhabitants find ways to salvage what's been lost and build new lives out of the rubble. Leona Pinson and Luther Biggs are two of the most memorable characters I've met in a long time. I want a sequel!"

—Minrose Gwin, author of *The Accidentals, Promise*, and The *Queen of Palmyra*

"In a richly textured and fearless first novel, Gerry Wilson creates a world that is lyrical at times and always unflinching. *That Pinson Girl* portrays the tension of biracial friendships and loyalties in the rural South, a reality that has rarely been depicted with such precision. A remarkable debut."

—Gale Massey, author of *The Girl from Blind River*

"Sixteen-year-old Leona Pinson grows up fast in this powerfully evocative story of resilience, triumph, and renewal. It's 1918. Every day, there's some scrap of news about the war in Europe, but where is Isaiah's father? And who murdered Leona's father out there in the woods? Transporting us to a rural American South not long past, Gerry Wilson delivers a timely debut novel, proving the importance of guiding principles, internal morals, and maintaining your own spirit light."

—Margaret McMullan, author of *Where the Angels Lived*

"There are scintillating glints that sparkle on every page of this novel. They are bright insights into the human condition which are expressed in the clear, uncluttered prose of Gerry Wilson's intrinsic art and craft of storytelling. Reading the conclusion of *That Pinson Girl* makes one want to begin again to delve even more profoundly into what informs and motivates the spirits of the characters who inhabit these pages."

—Nina Romano, author of *The Secret Language of Women* and *The Girl Who Loved Cayo Bradley*

THAT PINSON GIRL

Gerry Wilson

Regal House Publishing

Published by
Regal House Publishing, LLC
Raleigh, NC 27605
All rights reserved

ISBN -13 (paperback): 9781646034185
ISBN -13 (epub): 9781646034192
Library of Congress Control Number: 2023934861

All efforts were made to determine the copyright holders and obtain their permissions in any circumstance where copyrighted material was used. The publisher apologizes if any errors were made during this process, or if any omissions occurred. If noted, please contact the publisher and all efforts will be made to incorporate permissions in future editions.

Cover images and design by © C. B. Royal

Anna Akhmatova excerpt from "March Elegy" from *Complete Poems of Anna Akhmatova*, translated by Judith Hemschemeyer, edited and introduced by Roberta Reeder. Copyright ©1989, 1992, 1997 by Judith Hemschemeyer. Reprinted with the permission of The Permissions Company, LLC on behalf of Zephyr Press, www.zephyrpress.org.

Regal House Publishing, LLC
https://regalhousepublishing.com

Printed in the United States of America

In memory of my maternal grandmother, Lois Ellis Wood (1897 1994), whose life and stories continue to impact my own.

Who is wandering near the porch again
And calling us by name?
Who is pressed against the icy windowpane,
Waving with a branch-like hand?. .
And in answer a sunbeam dances from the mirror
To the cobweb in the corner.

—"March Elegy" *The Complete Poems*
Anna Akhmatova, trans. Judith
Hemschemcyer

Where is the dwelling place of light?

—Job 38:19

1

In the early, dark hours of the morning, Leona Pinson's aunt perched like a doll in the straight chair near Leona's bed, her short legs dangling. Sometime yesterday, Aunt Sally Pinson had put the sharpest knife they owned under Leona's bedstead.

"To cut the pain," Sally had said. "An ax blade would do better."

That knife wasn't helping Leona much.

When she cried out, her aunt slid down and went to the bureau where the basin was. She used a milking stool as a step, wrung out a cloth with her stubby fingers, came back to the bed, hoisted herself up. She tried to bathe Leona's face, but Leona covered her eyes with her hands. She didn't want to see Sally's large head and jutting chin, her bulging eyes, her stunted arms and legs. What if her own baby was born like that as a punishment?

Sally climbed down. Halting steps, the scrape of the stool, the clatter of the basin, the sloshing water, the creak of the chair. Then silence. After a while Leona opened her eyes. Sally slumped, dozing, her heavy chin resting on her bosom. Herbert Pinson's only sister, she had come after he died nearly two years ago, carrying all she owned in one satchel and a paper bag. She had never left.

The pain came and Leona's belly rose taut. She twisted the sheet and gritted her teeth against the sound that rose in her throat, against calling out the name she had vowed never to reveal. She drew her knees up and tried to take deep breaths that wouldn't come. After what seemed like a long time, the pain subsided. She could breathe again.

Leona had never seen a woman give birth, but she had helped her father birth calves. The first time, she was ten, maybe eleven. He said she could help, but when he saw the heifer was in trouble, he told her to get on back to the house. She begged him to let her stay.

He looked at her as though he were sizing up her mettle. "All right, then."

Leona almost turned sick when he plunged one arm to the elbow inside the heifer. He worked for more than an hour to turn that calf and pull it out into the world. It was the heifer's first, but you wouldn't have known she was giving birth except for her panting and the spasms of her belly. She had made no sound.

Leona wanted to be as strong as that dumb animal. She wanted to endure. But the pain possessed her. Was there a demon that possessed a woman giving birth? Was there a magic to make it go away?

Luther Biggs would know about such things. If only somebody would go for him, but sleet pattered on the tin roof and the wind moaned and shivered the house. Sally slept, and Leona's mother must have been sleeping, too, in her room. Her father would go, but he was dead. Her brother, Raymond, if he were at home, would scoff. But if Luther were there, he wouldn't sleep. He would take care of her and her baby. In her mind she called his name. She willed him to come.

ॐ

Luther Biggs came wide awake, all in a sweat, Leona Pinson's voice calling him out of a sound sleep. That girl, or the ghost or dream of her, had stood at the foot of his bed, her belly full to bursting, her eyes alight with tears and fear, and called his name, told him to get up and get going, to brave the icy road and come to her.

Wind rattled the shotgun house. Cold seeped through the chinks in the walls, between the floor planks. Luther's teeth chattered. He lit the kerosene lantern and set it on the floor beside his bed. Too cold to go to the outhouse; he would have to use the jar. He waited a full minute for his stream to come. He was fifty-two years old, not yet a very old man, but he felt like one. His life was too much waiting, remembering, regretting.

He shoved the jar under the bed. No time to empty it. He put on his only woolen shirt over the union suit he had slept in, then his overalls, two pairs of socks and his brogans, the broken shoelaces knotted back together. The mile walk to the Pinson house would not be easy. He took the lantern and went to the lean-to where his son, Jesse, slept.

Luther parted the curtain. Jesse curled on his side on a narrow straw mattress too small for him, face turned toward the curtain as though in expectation even in his sleep, hands clasped beneath his chin, knees drawn up like a baby. At fifteen, Jesse was tall, already a man. His skin was lighter than Luther's, whose own skin color had been the subject of talk all his life. Jesse had taken to going off on his own lately. All the colored and white folks close around knew him, but still Luther worried about leaving him by himself. If Jesse went out in this weather, he could freeze to death.

Luther said, "Jesse." A second time.

Jesse sat up, sleepy-eyed. "Pa?"

"I got to go down to the Pinson place. There's biscuits and buttermilk and coffee. You'll be fine for a while."

Jesse pushed back the quilts. "I'm going with you."

"Not this time. There's a thing happening over there you got no business with. I'll be home soon as I can."

"You'll be home," Jesse repeated, the way he did when he was trying to keep things straight in his head.

"That's right. You got plenty of wood. Keep the stove and the fire going. Don't let them die. And don't you go out. You go out, you get a whipping when I get home. You hear me?"

Jesse lay back down. "Yes, sir."

Luther would never whip Jesse, even if he still could, but he hoped the threat would do its work. He pulled the covers up, his hand lingering on Jesse's shoulder. How could he leave him alone to go tend that girl? But Leona Pinson was not just any white girl. She was Herbert and Rose Pinson's daughter.

Luther went to the kitchen, stoked the stove, and put on

coffee. He took a basket down from the top of the pie safe. His wife, Varna, had carried that basket with her whenever she tended the sick or birthed babies. He opened the cloth bags of herbs and smelled them, stuffing a few bags in his coat pockets. Varna had taught him which ones to use for a fever, congestion in the chest, gout, or infection. One to calm the heart, another to calm the mind. One to ease pain, another to stanch bleeding. She taught him how to make a tea to help a woman along in her labor and a poultice to put between a woman's legs after birth. "Varna," he had said, turning away, but he had learned, and now he was glad. Luther took out the crude figure of a woman he had carved for Varna from hickory, touched it to his lips, and slipped it in his pocket too.

Still black dark. He drank the scalding coffee. He needed the warmth.

When he went out the door, the cold struck him like a blow. In winter Pinson Road turned to sucking mud, pocked with craters dangerous for any man, and now it was iced over, the sleet still falling. Luther had brought a walking stick, but it didn't do much good. He had been on the road only a few minutes when his lantern went out. He made his way in the dark over the deep, slippery ruts to the side of the road and crouched against the red clay bank, pulling his coat close around him as best he could. Rose Pinson had given him that coat. It was too small, and threadbare.

He waited a precious half hour. With the coming of light, the world still seemed predawn dark, shrouded in gray, land and sky the same. Cold to the bone, he moved on. His chest hurt with each intake of sharp air. From time to time, he gripped his stick under one arm and rubbed his hands together and blew on them. His breath came in a freezing cloud. Death skulked in these woods and might step out from behind a tree, might put his finger against Luther's aching chest and say, "It's time," but Luther had faced Death before. He wasn't afraid.

The Pinson place sat low in the hollow against a line of bare trees, the house weathered gray as the landscape: on three sides cotton fields gone to black stubble, and beyond the house, the barn and the sheds, once whitewashed, now gone to gray too since Herbert was killed, and beyond that, forests of virgin pine, oak, walnut, hickory, and tupelo trees, older than Luther, maybe old as the land itself.

A crow swooped low, and Luther stumbled. The bird made another pass and perched on the fence only feet away. It ruffled, stretched its wings, and turned its black eyes on Luther. "Go on!" he shouted, waving his stick. "Go on now!" The bird flapped its wings in a fury and lifted into the mist.

By the time Luther reached the yard, the sleet had picked up and mixed with snow. Setting in. By night there wouldn't be any moving around. Jesse would be alone all day, all night. Would he remember to bank the fire? Would he remember to eat?

Luther crossed the yard and cut around the side of the house. He looked for some sign—a light, a sound—but saw and heard nothing until he reached the back where the land sloped steeply down and the brick pillars on which the house stood were almost as tall as he. From the kitchen windows, a flicker of light reflected on the frosty ground. He heard footsteps inside, the scrape of a stove grate. Who was up and about? Luther reached the steep back steps and tested the first. A skim of ice. He grasped the rail and climbed. He set his lantern on the porch and tapped on the kitchen door. He waited a minute, then knocked louder. The door creaked open.

Sally Pinson stood in the doorway, half Luther's height, owl-like circles under her eyes, her wiry gray hair undone. Her flour sack apron, tied above her breasts, dragged the floor. "Lord God," she said. "What're you doing here?"

Luther took off his hat. "I thought I might be of some help."

With the wind whipping through the open door, Sally seemed to consider it. "You knew."

Luther rubbed his stiff hands together. *Let me in.* "Yes, ma'am. I did."

"Well. You're here. You may as well stay." She turned away,

muttering. He heard the word *fool*. He didn't need to hear the rest.

He leaned his stick against the outside wall and stamped his feet to knock loose the crusted ice and mud. He stepped inside and shut the door. A flush of warmth, the smells of fried pork and coffee. The floorboards worn down to a smooth sheen, the same floor where he had slept all those years ago.

"How long you think it's gon' be?"

Sally shook her head. "Can't say. Been a day and a night already. Better be soon." She nodded toward the parlor. "Go in yonder by the fire, warm yourself up."

When he hesitated, Sally said, "Go on now. I got to tend to Leona." She tottered down the hall to the girl's bedroom, where Luther would go if he were allowed.

Luther knew every detail of the parlor. The entwined vine pattern of the faded wallpaper peeled away in places to bare wood, the horsehair settee, the worn hooked rugs, the ticking clock on the mantel. The straight chair where Herbert Pinson had sat and whittled on winter nights and tossed the shavings into the fire. The portrait of William Pinson staring down from above the fireplace, Herbert's father and Luther's, too, although Mr. William had never said the words out loud to Luther. The room had hardly changed since Mr. William brought Luther into this house when Luther was five years old. Luther had been inside the place only a few times since William Pinson died, so many years ago. The last time was when he had helped to carry Herbert's body into this very room and had sat the night beside the coffin with Leona.

The room was chilly, the fire diminished to embers. A kerosene lamp flickered on the table. Rose Pinson sat in her rocking chair, fully dressed at this early hour, her Bible open on her lap, her face halved into light and dark. The rest of the room was cast in shadows.

Leona cried out, and Rose flinched.

"Morning, Rose," Luther said. "How are you?"

Rose adjusted her spectacles, held the Bible to the light, and read aloud. "Then they shall bring out the damsel to the door of her father's house, and the men of her city shall stone her with stones that she die: because she hath wrought folly in Israel, to play the whore in her father's house, so shalt thou put evil away from among you." Rose closed the book but kept a finger at her place. "There's a bastard child being born in this house, Luther. How do you think I am?" She got up and left the room.

Luther crouched at the hearth and extended his hands, careful not to get too close. Once, long ago, he had held his nearly frozen fingers too near an open fire. He hadn't felt the blistering until he smelled scorched flesh.

Sally brought him coffee in a cracked cup. "I expect you could use this."

"Yes, ma'am, I could. Thank you."

"I told Leona you're here. She says she knew you would come. She says, 'Tell him to go walk the fence for me.' I said you aren't walking any fence. It's bad enough to send you to the barn."

Tears sprang to Luther's eyes. "I used to do that when she was a little thing. Mr. Herbert, he'd go off to cut timber. He asked me would I stay nights, look after Miss Rose and the children, so I did." He had slept on the kitchen floor, left his own, like now, only Varna was alive then. "Miss Leona, she'd be scared of the dark. Sometimes she would cry and cry until I'd take my light and walk all round the place, come back and tell her she's safe, there ain't no haints about. If they were, I'd tell her, I'd run them off!" He chuckled.

Sally said, "Seems like foolishness. That girl's full of foolishness, you ask me."

Luther said nothing. In that house, Leona had had much to overcome. No wonder she'd tried to find love somewhere else.

She had been seven or eight years old when Luther gave her the little lamp William Pinson had given him. Luther thought the light would give the child some comfort, but it was about more than her fear of the dark. Luther had seen how the girl drifted about the place, tormented by her brother, neglected by her mother who took to her bed for days, even weeks at a time. When Herbert was around, Leona clung to him, but he wasn't around much. He worked long days in the fields, and even in the winter, he was out tending to stock or repairing fences or turning over old soil or off working at the timber camp. He went to bed early and rose early too—the bone-tired life of a red dirt farmer. So Luther brought the lamp to work one summer morning, wrapped and cushioned in an old shirt. When Leona showed up at the barn, as she often did, he gave it to her, along with a tin of mineral spirits and some matches. He had not asked Rose or Herbert if it was all right. He doubted they would notice.

"Your granddaddy give the lamp to me," he told her, "when I was smaller than you. It's called a spirit lamp. You can keep it by your bed like I used to do, or you can carry it with you in the dark, light the way so you won't be afraid."

She picked it up, her eyes wide. "It's got spirits in it? Like ghosts?"

"No, ma'am. No ghosts." He tried to think how to explain it. He showed her the tin. "These is mineral spirits. It's what burns to make the light."

He taught her how to fill the lamp, trim the wick, and light it. It flickered and smoked at first, and then the flame steadied. Leona threw her arms around Luther and hugged him tight. She carried the lamp to the house on her tiptoes, like she carried something precious.

When Luther told Varna what he had done, she huffed and raised her eyebrows. "Seem to me your own daughter ought to have that lamp," she said.

"Alma don't need it." Alma had gone off to Memphis by then.

The night that Luther and the other men had built a coffin for Herbert and carried it into the house, Leona had sat alone on the porch with her lamp beside her, a frail light in all that darkness.

A wail drifted from the back of the house.

"Lord help us." Sally glanced over her shoulder. She wiped her face with her apron. "There's chores to be done, Luther. Raymond took off a week ago. God knows when he'll be back. The cow needs milking. We need firewood. And kill me a chicken while you're at it."

Who was that freak white woman to give him orders? But whatever he needed to do to stay close to Leona, he would do. He took the bags out of his pockets. "I got herbs. Sassafras, strawberry leaves, shepherd's purse." He chose a pouch. "You might brew some tea with this one. Tell her I say drink it. It'll help her along."

Sally stared at the pouch in Luther's hand. "We don't need none of your magic," she said. She left him standing there.

Luther put the bags back in his pockets. He wanted to brew that tea himself. He wanted to see Leona. It could get him killed if anybody suspected what he imagined, what he longed for: cradling that girl in his arms like she was his own, telling her she would be all right. Her long blond hair a mass of tangles, her green eyes bright with fear, her belly swollen to bursting.

When Luther went outside, he heard the raucous cry of a crow circling overhead. Was it the one he had seen on the road? Had that old bird followed him? A bad sign.

Inside the barn, he thought he could hear Leona's cries. He fingered the carved figure in his pocket. "Don't you be afraid. Don't you be," he said, his breath a vapor on the cold air.

෴

"Fix your eyes on a point," Sally said. "Don't look away. Breathe deep as you can."

Leona tried. A water stain the shape of a bear on the ceiling above her bed. A knothole in the varnished beadboard wall. The lamp Luther had given her burning on the bedside table, its flame unsteady. But the pain was everything, and she was so tired. She drifted into sleep and dreamed about her brother, Raymond, his sour whiskey breath.

She woke and Raymond wasn't there, but something rough

and hard probed and pushed inside her, twisted and pulled. Sally knelt between her splayed legs. Leona could see the top of Sally's head, one hand pressing on her belly, the other arm working, working, and then Leona knew it was Sally's hand inside her. Terror washed over her. She tried to push Sally away.

Sally said, "It's got to be done." After a last thrust and tug, Sally sat back, breathing hard. "Had to turn it. Baby was butt down. Won't never come that way."

Once when Leona was in the deep woods with her father, she had heard a sound not of this earth. She clung to him, but he said, "No need to be scared. It's a panther. Most likely it's birthing or it's dying." That same sound broke from Leona now, and for the next hour she rode the waves of pain, or they rode her, and somewhere in the distance, somewhere in the room, she heard Sally's voice *bear down, hold back, now push, push,* and the voice of another, her mother's low, drawn-out tone—was she praying?—while Leona's child tore its way into the world.

The baby was coated with blood and something yellow-white like curds. Underneath it, his skin was tinged with blue. Sally laid him on the bed and sucked the mucous and blood from his nose and mouth, turned and spat. Then she held him up by his heels and slapped his backside. He let out a furious cry. She cut the cord and tied it with a clean scrap, washed him and swaddled him and gave him to Leona. Her mother got up and left the room.

So small in Leona's arms, light as feathers. She searched for traces of the child's father in the shape of his brow, his nose and mouth, his coloring. The baby had dark hair like his father, but like her father and brother too. She wondered then if her father could see her. She had always been told that when people go to Heaven, they can look down and see the most secret acts. That thought had come to her the day she lay with the boy at Hawks Creek, but it hadn't been enough to make her stop.

Sally said, "Give him your breast. He won't take it at first, but you keep trying."

Leona bared her breast and held him to it, but he squirmed and made mewling sounds like a kitten, his little hands grasping at the air.

"Turn his face. My land, you never seen a woman nurse? Brush his cheek with your nipple."

The baby found the nipple, latched on, let go.

"That's right. Do that every little while." Sally looked at Leona's full breast. "You won't have no trouble."

The baby nuzzled, and Leona guided him back again and again. Soon, though, he fell asleep. Sally took him from her and put him in the cradle near the fireplace.

Leona had thought she was done with pain, but it came again.

Sally climbed on the bed and kneaded Leona's belly. Soon she felt the urge to push again, and the bloody sac slid from her. Sally wrapped it in a cloth and put it in a dishpan. She bathed Leona and packed clean rags between her legs, turning her to one side of the bed and then the other. She removed the soiled linens and made the bed without Leona's having to leave it. Sally's breath came in short gasps. Each trip around the bed, each tug of the sheets, seemed a labor of her own. She helped Leona out of her shift and into a clean nightgown. When she was done, she took away the afterbirth and the bloody sheets. Leona slept without dreaming.

She woke to the baby's lusty crying. She was alone with him. How was she to know what he needed? She pushed back the quilts and saw blood on her gown and on the clean sheets. Her first thought was that her aunt would be angry because she had just changed them. Leona sat on the side of the bed and waited for the dizziness to pass, but it didn't. When she stood, blood streamed down her legs and pooled on the floor. "Oh," she said. She called out for her aunt and her mother, but she heard only her little son's cries. Before darkness closed over her eyes like a drawn curtain, Leona looked out the window and saw snow coming down hard, the world transformed to white.

2

The sun was high above the pines when Raymond Pinson woke. It shone through a window crusted over on the inside with ice. The brilliance blinded him and he turned away. His head hurt, even his eyelids ached. It took a minute to remember where he was—in a cabin behind the bootlegger's house up near Sadie's Gap. The bed empty and cold, a moth-eaten woolen blanket cast aside on the straw mattress, the girl gone. He got up and peed in the jar. Cold, cold. He brushed ice crystals from the window and looked out.

Snow.

Raymond recalled drinking with that girl the night before, her nakedness, a pretty little thing except for her crooked teeth. She was warm in the bed but he'd had too much to drink to be of much good. He couldn't sleep unless he drank. When he dreamed, he saw the face of his father, half blown away, that one eye open and fixed on him. He saw it now without sleep, without dreaming, and the memory rose in him like bile.

He shook it off, sat on the side of the bed. He pulled on his britches, his boots, his shirt. The watch was still in his pocket. The only thing he owned that had belonged to his father, a bittersweet possession and reminder. Lucky that girl hadn't made off with it.

The door opened. The girl said, "I brung you coffee and some headache powders." She smiled. Those teeth. He remembered her name: Ramona. Her unwashed hair fell stringy around her face. His stomach churned.

When he left home a week ago, his sister, Leona, was ripe with that ill-begotten child. She could have had it by now. If their father were alive, he would rue the day Leona was born. Or would he blame Raymond for not taking care of her? He was always to blame for something.

3

Luther fed the chickens and the hogs and put out fresh hay for the cow and the mule. He made many trips from the barn, one with eggs, another with fresh milk, another with a chicken, its neck wrung. There was still the wood. The woodpile outside the barn had glazed over with ice, and now snow was falling. It took Luther an hour to move the wet logs aside and carry dry wood into the barn. The logs were heavy; whoever had cut them—Raymond, most likely—had not split them. He found Herbert's ax, set a log on end, swung the ax, set another, swung again. By the third log, he had broken out in a sweat. He concentrated on the heft of the ax, the lift, the swing, the rhythm of it, blocking out the pain in his arms and shoulders, the tight fist in his chest. Under his breath he repeated Leona's name like a prayer. He cradled as much wood as he could carry, piled it on the porch, and went back for more. Several times. Finally done, he went up to the house and tapped on the back door, but nobody came. He went inside.

The kitchen was empty. He sat on the floor close to the stove. He smelled of sweat and wet wool. He could hear voices coming from that back bedroom, and when he heard the baby crying, he thought, Thank the good Lord, it's over.

In a while, Sally came in the kitchen, her eyes red-rimmed, her apron bloodied. "Leona's bleeding bad. I can't get it to stop."

Luther knew then why Leona had summoned him. He got up off the floor. "My wife, Varna, she used to make a tea to slow the blood. She would make a poultice too." He couldn't say where the poultice might be used. If Sally had ever helped a woman birth a child, she would know.

Sally crossed her arms. "I told you. We don't—"

"There ain't no magic. It's plants right out of the woods."

He took the pouches out of his pockets and laid them on the kitchen table. "It won't hurt nothing to try."

Sally picked up the pouches, sniffed them, put them down. Luther imagined what she was thinking: What if he didn't know one herb from another? What if the herbs were poison?

She arched an eyebrow at Luther. "You don't have no reason to hurt Leona."

"Oh no, ma'am." Luther had sometimes seen Sally Pinson's eyes well up at the mention of her brother's name, had seen her face go slack with sorrow. He knew what to tell her. "Mr. Herbert, he would say do it. You know he would. Anything to save that girl."

Sally smoothed her hands over her apron. "All right. Make your tea."

Relief surged through Luther and warmed his blood. He soon had the water going. While he worked, he recalled other times when he had waited for children to be born in this house. Varna had brought Raymond and Leona into the world. The boy had come fast, but Leona's was a hard birth. Luther stayed and matched Herbert's every step while he paced the bare yard all night long. Just after dawn, Varna came out on the porch and told Herbert the baby had come, a little girl, and Rose was tired but doing all right. Herbert wept in Luther's arms, the only time since Herbert became a grown man that they ever touched.

One other time, Luther had waited there until he heard the wail of a child. He had seen Herbert Pinson come out then, too, slam the door behind him, drop to his knees in the bare yard, and raise his voice to Heaven.

꒰ঌ

Leona turned her head away, but Sally said, "Drink it. Luther says so."

The quilts thrown back, the shock of cold air. Something wet packed between Leona's legs. The smell of sassafras, like licorice. Leona gasped and opened her eyes.

"That's right. You stay awake," Sally said.

Heavy footsteps in the hall. Raymond? No. Leona recognized the sound of them. Luther.

And then there he was, standing in the doorway.

"Here's that wood, Miss Sally."

Sally covered Leona with a quilt. "Bring it in," Sally said.

He set the logs down on the hearth and stirred the low fire with the poker until it glowed and sparks rose. He added a dry pine knot that caught and blazed up, and last, the firewood, stacking it at angles to draw air. He stepped back as the flames crackled and licked at the new logs, the fire blooming and coming to life.

He came closer to the bed. "Don't you worry, child. You'll be fine. Just fine."

Leona reached out her hand, but Luther stepped away.

"Don't you have work to do, Luther?" Sally said. "Go on."

Leona's eyes closed. As the light dissolved, she heard Sally say, "Would you look at that. She's smiling. You'd think Luther was God Almighty."

❧

Near dark outside, although it was the middle of the afternoon. The snow still coming down heavy. Luther hoped he was done with going out in it.

Sally had given him the soiled sheets and the dishpan with the bloody bundle. "Use that big wash pot in the barn," she'd said. "Put them sheets in cold water to soak."

He knew what was in the dishpan. "What you want me to do with that?"

"Bury it on the north side of the lot."

"Miss Sally, that ground's frozen like rock."

She looked hard at him. "It's got to be done. Do it right."

He had dealt with the sheets, his hands so cold in the water he couldn't feel them, and then he'd taken a pickax to the frozen earth and dug the hole. It had taken a long time, and when he was done, his hands were cracked and bleeding. Twice he had brought in more wood and tended the fire in Leona's room.

Finally, when he crouched by the stove in the kitchen, when he couldn't stop shivering, he allowed himself to think about Jesse, wondered if he was cold, if he had eaten, if he had wet himself rather than disobey Luther and go outside to the outhouse. Luther missed Varna. Varna would have known what to do to help Leona, but Lord, she would have been mad at him for going off and leaving Jesse. She would take the broomstick to him for sure. He chuckled at the thought, and then he remembered the girl in the other room, her blood draining away, her little baby without a daddy. He imagined what it would be like to bury Leona in the frozen ground next to Herbert Pinson: the rough pine box Luther would build, the hard digging of the grave, the weight of the shovel full of red clay earth, the sound of dirt clods hitting the box. He got on his knees on that hard kitchen floor and prayed to the good Lord and to whatever powers there were over light and darkness, over life and death, to save her. He took out the carved figure and gripped it in his hands.

He woke with a start. Night. The wind whistled, and the fire had all but gone out in the stove. Sally Pinson stood over him, her face a fright in the shadowy light of the lantern she carried.

"It's stopped, but she's mighty weak. Can't afford to lose no more blood."

Luther squeezed the little figure in his hand, nodded. "That's good news."

Sally teetered, and the light swayed. "There's some cold cornbread in the safe and some milk. Help yourself." She left him, holding her lantern before her, its flame flickering and dying.

4

In her bedroom at the back of the house, Sally set the guttering lantern on the table and removed her bloodstained apron. She didn't bother to take off her clothes. She would lie down for a bit, but she wouldn't dare sleep. She couldn't leave Leona for long. Rose was sitting with her now, but all Rose knew how to do was pray.

Sally snuffed out the wick and climbed into her narrow bed. Jesus, God, the girl had nearly died. Sally had seen women die in childbirth and the anguish that followed. The grieving husband, the children crying for their mother, the newborn baby handed over to another woman to nurse, most likely a colored woman. New life the cause of death. By the grace of the good Lord, it seemed Leona had been spared.

Who would mourn Leona if she died? And what would happen to her baby? That child had a father. What of him?

Six months ago, soon after the United States entered the Great War, a young man had come to the house looking for Leona. He drove up in a shiny black car and got out but left the engine running. When he asked to see Leona, he fidgeted with the buttons on his jacket. Nervous, Sally figured. And well he might be, if Raymond had been there.

"I don't know where she's got off to," Sally said, a half-truth. Leona had said she was walking up to the Pratts to sew with her friend, Bertie, but the way she'd been going off lately, could Sally really know for sure? She stood on the porch with her arms crossed like a sentinel. The boy—that's all he was—didn't meet Sally's eyes, but then, not many people did. People mostly avoided looking at her.

He took a little box wrapped in brown paper out of his pocket. "I'm going to the war. I hoped to say goodbye to her and give her this." He offered the box to Sally. "Would you please see that she gets it?"

Sally made no move to take it.

The boy took two steps back, shook his head. "Well, all right. I'll come back later."

Sally held out her hand. "No need to do that. I'll give it to her." She slipped the gift in her apron pocket.

"Thank you." He started toward the car but stopped and looked back as though he might have second thoughts. Then he turned, got in the car, and drove away.

Sally intended to keep her promise, but the more she thought about it, the more it bothered her that Leona hadn't so much as mentioned a boy. She couldn't blame Leona for not bringing him to the house. No telling what Raymond would say or do. The boy hadn't offered his name, and she hadn't asked, but she knew the boys Leona's age who lived nearby and had gone to school with her. She had never seen this fellow before.

It bothered her too that his hands looked soft as a baby's. They were not the callused hands of somebody used to farm work. He was nicely dressed, and he drove a fine car; his father's, no doubt. Who around here could afford such a thing? Certainly not the farmers up and down Pinson Road.

He was too rich for Pinson blood, Sally reckoned, and Leona was too young and foolish to see it. They might be smitten, but that would soon pass, with him going off to the war.

Sally went to her bedroom and tucked the gift deep under her mattress. She had never had a child, but it was up to her to be like a mother to Leona. Rose was not capable of it.

Sally had put the boy out of her mind until she found out Leona was with child. She quizzed Leona about the child's father, but that girl was stubborn, stubborn. Sally had pieced it all together—Leona's going off on Sunday afternoons the previous winter and spring, the boy coming to the house last summer—but Sally didn't know who he was or how to find out.

She had decided to let well enough alone.

She got up now and felt under the mattress. The little package was still there, and there it would stay. That boy might not even come home alive.

5

Luther wondered how long it had been since Sally Pinson slept. He had never thought much of Sally, moving in the way she had after her brother's death, pretty much taking over the household. She had taken good care of Leona through the birth; there was that. Still, Luther found it hard to look at her, misshapen as she was. He pondered the unjust God who had made Sally in her mother's womb. Luther had no answer, just as he had no answer for the babies Varna had lost in the ten years before Alma's birth, or why the Lord had chosen to make Jesse forever a child, or why a good man like Herbert Pinson should have a troublesome son like Raymond. Luther had long ago concluded there was no explaining the injustice and suffering of this world.

Now Leona suffered. In Luther's mind he saw the girl and the man who had lain with her and her only sixteen, but the man's face was hidden in shadow. Luther shut his eyes and blinked away the vision of Leona, naked in a way he had never seen her. He pictured instead a child toddling around the yard, playing in a tin tub of water on a July day.

❧

Leona opened her eyes. The house was quiet, the windows opaque with darkness. She was alone. The baby slept beside her, this child born in sin, his round, perfect head, all that dark hair, his dark eyes. And then she saw it: the cleft in his chin. The cleft. His father's mark on him.

She allowed herself to think his name: Walker Broom. If only she could let him know he had a son. All these months since he went to France, there had been no letter from him. She had composed many letters to Walker in her mind, but she hadn't written any; she hadn't known where or how to send them without revealing who he was to her. Would he hear about her child now? There would be gossip around Sully.

Did you hear? That Pinson girl had a bastard son.

If only her daddy hadn't been shot.

Shame. But it's a good thing he was spared this abomination.

Let them talk. She didn't care. She had kept Walker's name close in her heart, borne the scorn and isolation, and waited. He would come home and claim her and the child. She knew it. No harsh words, not even her brother's taunting, could extinguish that hope.

She picked the baby up and held him. He nestled his little face against her neck. She would call him Isaiah, a good, strong name out of the Bible. It might protect him some from what she knew he would endure.

She tried his name out loud. "Isaiah."

&

On the third morning, after the snow had stopped falling, Luther set out for home. Sally Pinson had called him a stubborn fool for going, but she had given him an old pair of Herbert's gloves to wear. He walked straight into a biting north wind. Under the snow there was a glaze of ice. Even with his walking stick and picking his way over the treacherous road, he made it no more than fifty yards from the house before he fell.

He lay sprawled on the icy road, too far from the house to call out and be heard above the wind. He sat up and tested his limbs. His walking stick lay some feet away. He crawled to it, used it for leverage, and stood. His head throbbed. He touched the lump forming on his forehead, but there was no blood. "My good Lord, what to do?" he said aloud. He could ask to take the mule, but the mule might fall and break a leg, and that would mean more trouble. Or worse, that old mule might fall on him, and there he would be, weighted down and broken himself, unable to move. He would die for sure, and what would happen to Jesse then?

The sun had come out, a hard, cold ball of light. He would

go back to the house, get dry and warm, and try again. Sally met him at the back door with all the authority of her crossed arms. "What've you gone and done, Luther? Get in here!"

She sent him to the lean-to off the kitchen, a space that was all too familiar to him. She brought him one of Herbert's woolen shirts and a pair of trousers and made a great show of stalking out of the kitchen. The clothes were small on Luther, but they were dry. Herbert's old shirt smelled so strong of pipe tobacco that Luther half expected to see a haze of smoke in the air. When he put it on, his sadness over Herbert's death felt so fresh it made him weep. He pressed his fists to his eyes and waited for the feelings to pass. Then he stuffed his wet clothes in an empty croker sack and set it outside on the porch.

Sally came back in the kitchen. When he thanked her, she dismissed him with a wave of her hand. "You think I'd let you freeze? Go in yonder by the fire."

He crouched by the hearth, and Sally brought him coffee. She sat near the fire, too, sewing a baby gown. There was no sign of Rose. He heard Leona's baby crying for a long while. Luther wished he could hold the child in his arms and quiet him.

Sally looked into the fire like she was considering what it might reveal. "Wondering who that baby looks like. You got any idea, Luther?"

"No, ma'am." If he did, he wouldn't say. The trouble was, he had had no sign that such a calamity would befall Leona. On a Sunday afternoon nearly a year ago, he had seen her riding in an automobile with a young man. When Luther heard the clatter of the car, he stepped off the road into the trees to escape the cloud of red dust, but he saw Leona clearly when they passed, her hair all loose in the wind. Luther didn't see the driver well enough to tell who he was. Luther had been surprised, but he hadn't felt uneasy. What better thing could happen than for Leona Pinson to meet a nice young man who would marry her and take her away from here? After that day, though, Luther had thought it strange that he never saw the young man around the place. He should have known. He should have taken better care of her.

He stood up and felt the bruises from his fall.

"Where you going?" Sally said.

"May as well feed the stock."

"You can't make it to the barn." Sally nodded toward the window. "Sun's out. It'll thaw fast. Ain't nothing going to starve."

Sally set him to work peeling yams while she made cornbread. The smell of it baking soon filled the house and made Luther's mouth water. He ached all over, but his heart ached worse, thinking of Jesse alone, without food, the fire gone out.

By the middle of the afternoon, there were signs of thawing. Luther was about to set off when he looked out the kitchen window and saw Jesse round the corner of the house. Luther went out to meet him.

"Good God, son. What're you doing here?"

"Where you been, Pa? You said you was coming home. You *said.*"

"I know I did." Jesse was wearing a thin cotton shirt and his overalls, no coat, no socks. He smelled like he had wet himself. Luther hurried him inside. "Sit down by the stove. Let's get you warmed up."

"No, sir. You and me going home. Let's go now."

"We ain't going till you get warm. You gon' be all right." Luther's voice was firm but it wasn't loud. Raising his voice had never worked with Jesse. He took both of Jesse's cold hands in his own and rubbed them hard to get the blood flowing.

Jesse looked around the kitchen. "Where, where's Mr. Raymond?"

Sally said, "He ain't here. We ain't seen him in a week."

"Oh," Jesse said. "Oh." He sat on the floor near the stove, drew his knees to his chest, and rocked back and forth.

Luther sensed Rose's presence before he saw her standing in the doorway, a woolen shawl around her shoulders, her hair falling out of its pins. Not like herself, all undone like that.

Her eyes flicked from Luther to Jesse. "Oh my, look at you. You'll catch your death. Sally, get Jesse some coffee." Rose took off her shawl. "Wrap this around him, Luther."

And then Leona was there too, holding her baby. She eased herself into a chair. "I heard you all out here. Is Jesse all right?"

Luther nodded. "Soon as he warms up, he'll be fine." He remembered the dream, how bright with tear Leona's eyes had been. They were not so different now.

Jesse scrambled up off the floor. "You got your baby? Let me see it." He stroked the top of Isaiah's head with one finger. "It's a little bitty baby."

Luther said, "That's enough, Jesse."

"I ain't gon' hurt it, Pa."

"I know you wouldn't mean to, but babies are precious, like carrying eggs."

Rose took a tin plate of cornbread out of the pie safe and gave it to Jesse. Sally gave him coffee. He sat on the floor, stuffing pieces of bread in his mouth. And then his plate slid to the floor and he was on his feet. "Pa?"

Luther had heard it, too: somebody coming up the back steps, stamping his feet across the porch. The door swung open and banged against the kitchen wall. Raymond burst in, his hair and beard crusted with ice, his boots caked with mud.

Rose opened her arms wide. "Raymond. Thank the Lord."

He crossed the kitchen in three strides, into his mother's embrace. The baby woke and began to cry.

He let Rose go and turned. "What we got here? You all right, sister?"

"Better than you, from the looks of it."

He lifted a corner of the blanket, and Leona pushed his hand away. "Let him alone."

"It's a he? And what might his name be, I wonder. Named for his daddy?" Raymond reached for the baby. "Let me hold my nephew."

"No. Don't touch him."

"Aw, come on, Leona. You—"

"Raymond," Luther said. "She don't want you holding him right now."

Raymond's eyes narrowed. "You mean *Mister* Raymond."

"Mr. Raymond."

"And you're the one to stop me. Is that right?"

Luther smelled tobacco then, rich and pungent, and he knew if he looked at the shadowed corner by the lean-to, he would see the ghost of Herbert Pinson, his pipe clenched between his teeth. Herbert would nod as if to say, *Do what you can.*

Luther held Raymond's gaze. "I am."

"What did you say?"

Luther braced himself. "I said, I am."

Raymond stood there a second or two, his mouth agape. Then he laughed. "Well, damn. I'm gone a day or two, and the nigger starts giving me orders."

Luther saw Leona flinch at the sound of that word. She had never said it in Luther's hearing. Neither had her mother or father.

Raymond threw up his hands. "All right, all right. I got plenty of time to get to know the little bastard. Sally, what we got to eat?"

Sally said, "Go get cleaned up. I'll fix you something."

"Good. I'm starving." He stalked out with Rose right behind him.

Luther heard Rose ask, "Where have you been? And why so long?"

Luther glanced at the corner by the lean-to, but there was only shadow. He said, "Come on, Jesse. We're going home."

"You can't go yet," Leona said.

"Got to. It gets dark early."

Without asking, she gave Isaiah to Luther. "Hold him for me."

Luther had not forgotten how to hold a baby. He remembered holding Alma, and much later, Jesse. He swayed and hummed, and all the while he tried to see the likeness of the one who was to blame for the child's existence and Leona's shame. He saw Herbert Pinson in him, but he couldn't see the other. Not yet. Luther's visions came unbidden. He could not summon them.

Leona came back with two quilts. "Wrap up in these. You can bring them back the next time you come."

Luther understood that Leona wanted a promise. Her quilts, his return. He laid the baby in Leona's arms, took a quilt for himself, and wrapped the other around Jesse.

It took Luther and Jesse an hour to walk home. Once, Jesse brought the quilt across his face and breathed in.

"This quilt smells good, Pa."

Leona's scent. Luther worried about this son of his with a child's mind in the body of a man. Did he have need for a woman like other men did? When Jesse said, "It smells like Ma used to," Luther let out a breath on the cold air.

When they got to the house, Luther sent Jesse to fetch wood while he started the stove. Soon he had coffee going. He fried up some ham and made biscuits, and he and Jesse sat down to supper. Jesse cleaned his plate and looked at Luther's. Luther pushed it toward him. Tonight, he would take care of his son. Tomorrow or the next day, he would go back to the Pinsons'. There would be work to do, and Raymond wouldn't be the one to do it.

❧

From a front window, Leona could see Luther and Jesse, hunched against the wind, making their way over the slick road. What was it, a mile to Luther's house? Not far, but in this weather… She should have sent food with them. Baked yams, cold cornbread, a jar of coffee, anything.

With Isaiah asleep in her arms, she slipped past the kitchen where Raymond sat at the table, wolfing down whatever Sally had found to feed him, shut her door, and slid the bolt.

Raymond, home.

In Leona's earliest memory of Raymond, he towered over her. She must have been on a pallet on the floor. He bent down,

picked up a plug of her skin, and twisted it—she learned later
it was called pinching—and made her cry. He did things to her
when nobody else was around to see. When she was six and
he was eleven, he shoved her off the front porch. "You tell,"
he whispered when she lay on the ground, clutching her arm
bent at an awkward angle below the elbow, "and I'll break the
other one." Then he ran in the house to tell their mother that
Leona had jumped off the porch, which they were forbidden
to do, and had broken her arm. The summer she was ten, she
was raising three kittens after the mother cat died. She found
them one morning in the cow's stall, their little necks broken.
Raymond had denied it, but who else would have killed them?

There had been other times she would rather not recall. Since
their father died, Raymond had gone a little crazy, drinking too
much, going off for days at a time, raging at Leona and Sally but
never at their mother. He still seemed protective of Rose. He
had never been Leona's protector, though, not like some girls'
brothers were. Leona had always wished for that.

She heard Raymond come down the hall. She held her
breath and willed Isaiah not to wake and cry and irritate him.
He paused outside her door, moved on, and his own door
slammed. Isaiah startled at the sound but didn't wake. She laid
him in the cradle and stood looking down at him. It might be
blasphemous, but she thought she understood now what the
preacher meant when he said "a miracle made flesh."

When Isaiah was five days old, Leona came down with a fever
and lay abed for three weeks. Sally coaxed her to eat, and Luther brought herbs for tea to build her strength. It seemed that
carrying the child had sapped her body and her will. Listless and
weak, she nursed the baby and slept when he slept, and during
her waking hours, she tried to piece together all the accidents
of time and place that had brought Walker and her together. If
she hadn't gone to town with Raymond on that particular Saturday—she had not gone the week before, or the week before
that—if she hadn't stood on the square with her best friend

Bertie Pratt at a certain hour, if she hadn't gone for a drive, if she hadn't lain with him—there would be no child.

What she and Walker had done—was that love? Leona had believed it so. She thought about love and decided it was hard to define. She couldn't recall seeing any real affection between her mother and father. Whatever feelings they had had for each other seemed to have waned by the time Leona was old enough to notice such things. She had a deep affection for Luther. She might even say she loved him, but Luther was a Negro; she wasn't supposed to love him. She loved Isaiah. She loved her father still. She might burn in Hell for it, but she didn't love her mother or Raymond. Leona thought Raymond incapable of love. She imagined her brother's heart a shriveled thing, cold to the touch, relentlessly beating.

6

Raymond often couldn't sleep for the baby's crying. He would go outside for a smoke, or if there was a full moon and it wasn't too cold, he would walk the woods to clear his head and calm his thrumming heart, or he would go to the barn and drink his whiskey while he groomed his horse.

He had saved his money for three years to buy a spirited chestnut mare he'd named Belle. He liked the word, *spirited*. Like him. He loved to take her out on the road and ride her hard, but he also loved being in the quiet barn late at night. When Belle was restless in the stall, his touch calmed her. He told her about the girl over at Sadie's Gap. About what it was like to be left out of the war like a cripple or a loony. About his father, and how there had been no satisfying him, no matter how hard Raymond had tried. Belle shifted, switched her tail, and nodded as though she understood.

When Raymond got back to the house, sometimes it was too quiet. Other times, he heard sounds coming from Leona's room. When Leona was small, he used to crawl into her bed and curl next to her on cold nights or when bad dreams woke him. He remembered the clean smell of her hair and skin, and later, her body rounding and changing into a woman's.

No room for him now. His sister was no better than a common whore. If only Raymond could get his hands on the man, but Leona wouldn't tell.

With that thought his father's voice came to shame him. His father, who had no right, who everybody thought was such a fine man, but Raymond knew different. It had not been lost on Raymond that Luther's boy's light skin and eyes were unaccounted for. A sin is a sin, Raymond had heard the preacher say time and time again.

7

The end of March, on the second anniversary of her father's death, Leona settled Isaiah in a sling and set out walking to the family cemetery on Pinson land where her father was buried. The morning smelled of spring, and the trees, greening out, shone yellow against the washed-clean sky. The gravel road had been eroded down to red clay by the harsh winter. It was hard going, and Leona stopped several times to rest. Off the main road, the wagon track to the family grave-yard climbed a steep hill among pines, oaks, and sweetgum. It seemed the ground there, still cold and thatched with wintry brown, brittle weeds, had not yet heard of spring. No birds called, no squirrels scrambled in the branches. Halfway up, her legs trembled and the path threatened to fall away beneath her.

She stopped at the top of the hill, blinked at the hazy world, took deep breaths. An iron fence surrounded the cemetery. The gate stood open. Besides her father, her Pinson grandparents and great-grandparents were buried here. Some of the graves were marked with crudely carved stones, others unmarked. Her father's grave was overgrown with weeds, and the wooden cross Luther had made had fallen over. Before long, the cross would rot and disintegrate, and her father would disappear into time. Nobody would remember who he was or what had happened to him.

Leona swaddled Isaiah in the shawl and laid him on the grass. She dropped to her knees and pulled weeds with her bare hands until they were scratched and bleeding, but her effort was futile. With the spring rains, the weeds would spread right back. Like troubles, she thought, the way they seemed to overcome whatever joy there was.

She heard a rustling in the woods off to her left. She held her breath, listened. She didn't hear anything more, but she was wary. What if Raymond had followed her here? She didn't want to be alone with her brother, especially not in this isolated place.

Isaiah began to fret. She picked him up and walked among the graves, swaying him in her arms. She had nursed him before she left the house, so he shouldn't be hungry. It seemed not so long ago that she was playing with dolls, pretending to be a mother. That was nothing like the real thing. Sometimes he cried, and nothing soothed him. Sometimes she cried with him.

She sat on the ground beside the grave, unbuttoned her dress, and draped the shawl over her breast. What if the dead could see? The baby sucked like he was starving. She sighed. If only Isaiah could tell her what he wanted. If only her father could tell her what had happened to him that day in the woods.

Some nights, Leona dreaded closing her eyes, fearing she would see her father's destroyed face. No matter how many good memories she had, that was the way she remembered him. She had been home alone the day the neighbor men brought his body to the house. Her father had sent Raymond away by then; her mother had gone to a neighbor's house that morning; and Luther hadn't come to work yet. Leona sat on the porch and cradled her father's bloody head in her lap, felt his blood soak through her apron and her dress. He had been shot in the face, so he must have seen whoever did it. It broke her heart to think how terrifying his last moments must have been. And now, two years later, whoever had killed him was out there somewhere. A stranger? A neighbor? She wanted answers, and she had none.

Raymond blamed their neighbor, Tobe Sanders. Not long before their father was killed, he had sold a hundred acres to Sanders. The land lay along a high ridge that marked the end of the Appalachian range where it snaked its way down into Mississippi. The ridge was no good for farming, but it was heavily forested, and it teemed with deer and turkey in season. Pinson men had hunted there for generations. Her father had loved that land. Why Sanders wanted it was unclear to Leona, but he paid a good price, and they made a deal that her father could hunt there like he'd always done. But then Sanders found a

moonshine still on his land. It didn't take him long to figure out
Raymond had built it. Sanders destroyed the still and declared
no Pinson would set foot on the ridge again.

On the Sunday morning he died, her father had gone to
the ridge anyway. If Leona had gone with him, might she have
saved him? The thought wouldn't let her go. She knew those
woods better than most men. Her father had taught her well.

She had hoped if she came here, a memory or a detail she'd
missed would surface, an insight that hadn't occurred to her
before that would lead her to answers.

"Talk to me, Father," she said. "Send me a sign."

She waited in the quiet, but the sun shone down and the
trees whispered and Isaiah slept. There was no voice. There was
no sign. Only grief, like a fresh wound.

❧

Luther stood hidden in the trees. He had seen Leona leave the
house and told Raymond he needed to borrow a wire cutter
from the Caldwells. He had followed her at some distance. Now
he heard her talking, but he couldn't make out the words. He
had come to Herbert's grave many times at dawn or dusk, when
nobody else was around, but he had not come in a while. He
felt bad about Leona pulling weeds with her bare hands. For a
long time after Herbert died, Luther had gotten down on his
bad knees and weeded and talked to Herbert like Leona was
talking now, had told Herbert how things were going on the
place, how much he missed him.

A vision of Herbert Pinson rotting in the ground turned
Luther's stomach. He squeezed his eyes shut, but the vision was
still there.

The night before Herbert was killed, Luther had dreamed he
could fly. In the dream he skimmed the treetops. Barely dawn,
he saw through the blanket of mist covering the ridge, saw turkey and deer moving about, a bobcat in the brush, and Herbert
standing with his back against a tree, holding his gun. A man ap-

proached Herbert through the thicket, but before Luther could tell who it was, a mighty wind whirled Luther high in the air.

He awakened from the dream with the sensation of falling and falling. He got out of bed, dressed, and without waking Jesse, took his shotgun and headed for the ridge.

He climbed the hill by a back trail, careful to stay off Sanders's land. The sun was topping the hills in the east when Luther heard a gunshot. There would be other hunters in the woods, maybe Sanders himself. Maybe the shot only meant a turkey brought down, or a squirrel. Yet a fist of fear closed around Luther's heart. Luther's dreams never lied.

He left the trail and cut through the thicket. Limbs whipped his face and brambles snagged his clothes. Somebody came crashing through the brush toward him, but whoever it was veered away and into the thicket. Luther glimpsed a man, a flash of dark clothing, a hat pulled low, but he couldn't see who it was. Luther started to go after him, but when he heard shouts, he turned and followed the voices. He stayed low, careful not to be seen. Two neighbor men, Royce Caldwell and Carl Pratt, stood in a clearing, looking down at the ground. Even before one of them said, "Herbert? Lord God have mercy," Luther knew.

Except for when Varna died, Luther had never grieved for another person the way he had for Herbert. This grief, though, was rooted in shame. Luther owed it to Herbert to protect his child. He would do it with his life, if need be.

He watched Leona rise and wrap the baby in the shawl and wipe her eyes with the hem of it. He stepped deeper into the shadows while she crossed the cemetery, opened and shut the gate, and set off down the hill. He waited until she had a good head start, and then he trailed along behind her. When he passed the woods where Herbert was killed, he turned away from the road and climbed to the clearing. Luther closed his eyes and tried to empty his mind, hoping for a new vision of what had happened that day, but it didn't come, and the air, though freshened by the beginnings of another spring, still smelled of death.

8

When Leona got back to the house, her friend, Bertie, stood on the porch. Dear Bertie. She would remember what day it was.

Bertie took Isaiah. "You look done in," she said.

"I walked to the cemetery."

"Oh, Leona. I would have gone with you."

"I know you would have. I needed to go alone."

"I understand. I'm still sad about it all." She shifted Isaiah to her shoulder and patted his back. "Except for this little fellow."

They sat in the rockers on the porch and talked, almost like before. It seemed to Leona that her life had been divided sharply into two parts, before Walker and after, like somebody had taken an ax to it.

Bertie had gone quiet, her face clouded over.

"Bertie? What's bothering you?"

She ran her hand over Isaiah's dark hair. "Nothing."

"I know you better than that. Tell me."

"I can't. You'll be angry."

"Bertie Pratt! I could never be angry with you."

Bertie let out a long breath. "All right. Tell me, then."

"Tell you what?" Leona's palms went sweaty. Bertie had never asked about Isaiah's father, which Leona thought remarkable, the sign of a true friend. Now, Leona figured the question was coming, and she could never tell, not even Bertie.

Bertie's face flushed. "Surely you must see it. Other people will." Her voice dropped to a whisper. "Isaiah looks like Raymond."

"Oh, Bertie. That's an awful thing to say!" Leona got up and stood at the porch rail, her back to Bertie. It had never occurred to her that people might think that.

"I know, and I hate myself for saying it. But if it's true,

Raymond ought to be strung up. I don't know how you could live with a thing like that."

Wasn't it a relief, though, that Bertie didn't suspect somebody else? Leona turned and faced her. "Yes, Isaiah has dark hair and eyes like Ray. Both of them look like Father. Ray might be cruel, but he would never do such a thing." But he might have, if Luther hadn't stopped him. A lifetime ago, it seemed like.

"So somebody else is Isaiah's father, and you won't tell me who it is."

She and Bertie had always told each other everything, but those were innocent, girlish things, not secrets that had the power to ruin people's lives.

"I'm sorry. I can't."

Bertie gave Isaiah to Leona. "I'm the one who ought to be sorry. I ought not to pry." She wiped her hands on her skirt, as though she were done with it all. "I'm going to town tomorrow. Want to go? We could take Isaiah with us."

"I don't like going to town. I hate the way people give me room on the sidewalk like I carry a disease. Or they stare right through me, like I'm invisible." She glanced at Isaiah. "And he is too."

"It's terrible, the way people treat you."

"It's my doing. I deserve whatever I get, but Isaiah doesn't. People will be hateful to him because of me. I'm not sure I can stand that." She started to cry. What was wrong with her, all this crying?

Bertie wrapped her arms around both of them. "You're the strongest person I know. You'll be all right." She stepped away. "I told Mama I was coming to see you today. She didn't seem to mind."

"That's good."

"I think so. I didn't tell Pa, but I think he'll come to his senses."

When Bertie's mother and father had found out about Leona's predicament, they had forbidden Bertie to see her. Bertie had managed to sneak away from her house only a few times during the months before Isaiah was born. She had brought Leona the material and notions to make a layette, some hard candy, and sometimes, gossip from town. Bertie had made her laugh. She had not deserted her.

Bertie walked out of the yard and didn't look back. Leona wished she could tell her the truth. While they were talking, Walker Broom's name had rushed to Leona's mind, and she'd covered her mouth with her hand. She tried never to think his name, afraid she might say it aloud.

9

On a Saturday in the fall a year and a half before, Leona and Bertie had stood together on the square in Sully while some town boys cut the fool, climbing the Confederate statue and jumping down. One of them, Walker Broom, climbed higher than the others, crouched on the statue's shoulders, stood straight, and held out his arms like he might fly. When he jumped, he looked like maybe he could.

After the boys walked away, Leona dared Bertie to climb up on the statue.

"Not me," Bertie said. "I got to go. Pa's waiting."

Leona waited until Bertie had crossed the square and there was nobody else around to see her lift her skirts, grab hold of the statue's stone rifle, and pull herself up. The soles of her shoes were slippery, but she balanced on the base, turned, and leaned back and spread her arms wide like Walker had done. She closed her eyes, and when the wind lifted her hair, she remembered how her father used to brush it when she was small. Her father had done that for her, not her mother.

She opened her eyes. Walker was standing at the base of the statue.

"Jump," he said, grinning. "I'll catch you."

Now that was a dare. She took a deep breath and stepped off the statue. He caught her in midair and set her down with a flourish. Blushing furiously, she walked away.

"Wait, Leona," he said. "You ever ridden in an automobile?"

Her family had a mule and wagon, a buggy, and a horse that belonged to Raymond. They would never own an automobile. "No. I haven't."

"Would you like to go for a drive next Sunday?"

Leona doubted her mother would care, but her aunt would. "Pinsons are country people," Sally would say. "That town boy could have any girl in Sully." Raymond would give her the what for, if he knew. But would her father have allowed it? She thought he would.

She lifted her chin. "Yes. I'd like that very much."

"All right. I'll come to your house at two o'clock."

She couldn't let him come to the house, especially if Raymond was there. "No. I'll meet you at Hawks Creek." The old Hawks Creek settlement had been wiped out by typhoid fever fifty years ago. What was left of it—a ruined church, a cemetery—was past Luther's house and the Pratts', an easy walk for her. It would be a safe place to meet, isolated and abandoned as it was.

"I know the place," he said. "I'll be there." He didn't ask why. Maybe he figured she was ashamed of where she lived, or maybe he understood it was Raymond she worried about. Everybody in Sully knew Raymond.

Walker walked away, his hands jammed in his pockets, whistling a tune.

That night, Leona lay awake, imagining what it would be like to ride in an automobile. Didn't people have special driving costumes for going around in cars? She tossed and fought the feather pillows. Finally, she got out of bed, pulled a shawl around her, and went outside. There was no moon and the clear sky dazzled with stars. The bare ground was cold under her feet, but she didn't mind. What a show the heavens were! A night moth brushed her face, and she shivered.

She was about to go inside when she saw her mother walking along the fence line, near the woods. Barefoot and clad only in her nightgown, she stopped now and then and looked up at the sky. Strange behavior, but Leona had decided long ago that her mother was strange. Leona remembered a conversation with her father—she must have been eight or so—when she had asked him what was wrong with her mother. Her father hesitated, as though he were choosing his words carefully. "Your mother has a delicate disposition," he said finally, and Leona said, "I think she doesn't love me. She loves Raymond well enough, but not me." Her father had pulled her onto his lap. "She loves you both, in her way." His tone hadn't convinced her.

After a while Rose turned toward the house. As she came closer, Leona heard her thin soprano voice, singing. What the song was, Leona couldn't make out.

Leona went out to meet her. "Mama? Are you all right?"

Rose stopped singing. "Leona?"

"It's chilly out here. Let's go inside."

Leona draped the shawl around Rose's shoulders, and they walked into the house. When they got to Rose's bedroom, she went in and shut the door. Leona waited, listening to the floor's creak beneath her mother's footfalls. After a while, the sound stopped, but Leona lay awake with more on her mind than Walker Broom and automobiles.

Sunday week was a rare day with the chill of fall in the air and the sky the color of ice on the pond in winter. Leona told her mother and her aunt she was going to sew at Bertie's, took her sewing basket, and walked to Hawks Creek. She hid the basket in a patch of weeds beneath a big pine tree. Walker need not know she had lied in order to meet him.

When Walker was late, Leona felt foolish for having thought he might court her. All the girls who had gone to the Pinson Road School just down the road from her house had known who Walker Broom was, and most of them pined after him. He was four years older than Leona, taller than her father, with dark hair and brown eyes and a strong chin. He had graduated from high school, and now he worked in his father's store. Leona had finished the eighth grade at the country school. That was as far as she would go. She would be lucky to be courted by a boy like Charles Caldwell, Mr. Royce's son, a lanky boy with a shock of red hair and big, callused hands, who seemed kind but not smart. If Charles Caldwell were anything like his father, he would be a fine provider. Charles had come to her father's wake with his parents. When he expressed sympathy to Leona, he blushed and stammered. She had felt sorry for him. Leona couldn't see spending her life with a man so dull, so unable to speak his thoughts.

When she heard the car coming, she felt loose inside, as though only string held her together. The car came down the lane, bouncing over the ruts, and stopped. The engine sputtered and cackled like an old woman.

"Get in," Walker shouted. "If I cut the motor, I'll have to crank it again."

She climbed in the car, and he backed up, sped down the rutted lane, and swerved out onto Pinson Road, churning up dust. The car lurched along in fits and starts, not like the steady trot of a horse. Once she got used to the jostling and the noise, she enjoyed the rush of wind and the landscape passing by like a picture show.

He drove toward Sully, but then he took a road Leona wasn't familiar with and drove far out into the country, where the hills grew steeper and the road narrowed. From Leona's house these hills loomed beyond the ridge like a bank of blue-gray thunderclouds. When she was little, she had called them mountains. "Take me to the mountains," she used to ask her father, but he never did.

The car's engine struggled to make the climb. On the crest of a hill, he pulled over and stopped where the road overlooked the valley. There was Sully, in the distance. It seemed the town could fit in the palm of her hand. She had never traveled farther than Luna, fifteen miles past Sully. She had never had reason to come up into these hills only a few miles west of her home, beyond the ridge, which was the highest place she knew, but she couldn't look out from the ridge and get a sense of the world. The forests were too dense, the clearings walled in by trees like little fortresses. Now, looking out toward Sully and beyond, the horizon stretched long and flat, not curved like she would have expected, if she were to believe the earth is round as she'd been taught. If she could fly like a bird, could she see the curvature of the earth? But she could not fly, and her life so far was confined to the place where she was born, the old house, the land around it. She yearned for something larger.

He pointed. "Look, there's Sully."

"I see. It seems so small."

He laughed. "It is."

They sat for a while before he maneuvered the car around, and they coasted down, picking up speed.

Back at Hawks Creek, patterns of light filtered through the trees. Leona recognized the calls of mockingbirds, jays, cardinals, the bright, loud whistle of a wren. Any day now, the birds would fly south. Sometimes Leona wished she could go with them, but not today.

Hardly anything was left of the old settlement. The cemetery where many yellow fever victims were buried had been abandoned as tainted ground. The shell of the brick church remained. Holes gaped in the walls where windows and doors had been, the roof long since gone. Leona stepped across the threshold, her hand lingering on the rough wall. Slaves made these bricks, her father had told her. Luther's people.

"They say this place is haunted," Walker said. "Do you believe in ghosts?"

Sometimes she felt her father's presence and smelled his pipe tobacco. "I do."

She felt shy at first, but her words soon spilled out. She told him how strange her mother was, and how Leona believed she must be the cause of it. She told him about her dwarf aunt who had come to live with them right after her father died. She told him she believed her father had been murdered.

"Murdered?" His eyes widened. "Surely not."

"Well, it's what I believe."

He told her he didn't like working in his father's store. He wanted to read for the law, but his father expected him to take over the business. There was the war in Europe, he said. Who knew how that would turn out? She liked listening to him talk.

They followed an overgrown path beyond the ruins and down to the creek. Old water oaks formed a canopy of shade.

He took her hand, and they skidded down the steep red clay bank together. He removed his shoes and waded in.

"Coming in? It's cold!" She tied up her skirt in two big knots so it barely hid her knees. The water was so cold it took her breath. The bottom was shifting silt. She lost her balance, and Walker caught her and held her against his chest a little too long. She liked the way it felt.

Back at the ruins, he picked late-blooming bellflowers and tucked them in her hair. He offered to drive her home, but she said no, she would rather walk. After he got in the car and drove away, she got her sewing basket from the weeds, brushed it off, and walked toward home.

The next Saturday and the next, Raymond wouldn't allow Leona to go to town. She didn't believe he suspected anything; he was simply in one of his dark moods. She heard nothing from Walker. By the middle of November, the weather turned frigid, and in early December, the roads became impassable and stayed that way through January. Leona longed to see Walker again, but what if he wanted no more to do with her?

In late February Raymond turned sick with a deep cough. Leona offered to go to town for some cough remedy, and Raymond was too sick to protest. She took the buggy to Sully and went first to the drugstore. After she bought the cough syrup, she lingered outside Broom's Mercantile, pretending to window-shop. At noon Walker came out.

"I'm glad to see you," he said. "I've missed you."

"I'm glad to see you too." Her world seemed suddenly brighter. They planned to meet again at Hawks Creek the following Sunday.

That day, she told her aunt she was going to Bertie's to see some young people from town, but she went to Hawks Creek and waited for Walker. He took her to his family's fishing cabin on the Tombigbee River. Walker had brought his box camera. He showed Leona how it folded shut and how the wooden spool of film fit inside. He took pictures of her by the river. He gave her a bag of chocolate candies she would hide in her room later that day and eat one at a time, closing her eyes and savoring the chocolate more because it reminded her of him. He built a fire in the fireplace and they huddled together. She thought it was the cold that made them do the things they did. She let him unbutton her bodice and slip his hand inside it and then under her skirt while the fire burned their faces and the cold licked at their backs.

She didn't see him again until April. He showed her the photographs he had taken at the cabin of Leona standing on the riverbank, wearing her mother's coat with the fur collar, her light hair a halo around her face.

"Look how pretty you are."

She felt color rise up her chest and face. "You think so?"

"I do." He showed her three more pictures, all similar, except in one she was smiling. He tapped that one. "You can have the others, but this one is mine." He slipped it in his coat pocket. She took the rest. She looked, she thought, a little sad.

That day, there was more talk of the war. "We have to defeat the Huns," Walker said, "and free the Europeans from tyranny. If we don't, they'll be walking down the streets of Sully someday."

Leona didn't know that word. *Tyranny.* Where had he learned it? "Surely you don't believe that."

His solemn look chilled her. Did he intend to sign up?

She had brought cold biscuits, blackberry jam, and a jar of coffee. He slathered a biscuit with jam and ate it like he was starving. Her appetite was gone.

What she did, she did without thinking. She kissed him and licked the jam from his lips, his fingers. They lay on the ground and he kissed her in a way he had not before. They fumbled with buttons and tugged at clothes, elbows and knees sharp and in the way, and he was on her and inside her. She bit her lip to keep from crying out.

They lay in the shadow of the wall, a tangle of arms and

legs and twisted garments. Walker brushed tears from her face. "Did I hurt you?"

She shook her head.

"I'm so sorry. I shouldn't—"

She pressed her finger to his lips. "Please don't be sorry."

It was time to go. She straightened her clothes and pinned her hair up as best she could. She throbbed between her legs. She walked into the woods and pressed her handkerchief against herself, inside her drawers. The cloudy fluid mingled with blood surprised her. So this was what men and women did. She was surprised that the act was messy and crude, not that different from the animals she had seen mate on the farm ever since she was small. But the ache she felt was more than physical pain. She felt bound to Walker in a way that couldn't be easily broken.

When she got home, Raymond met her in the yard. "Where you been, Leona? I went to the Pratts. Bertie said you hadn't been there."

"I decided not to go. I went for a walk instead." A feeble excuse, she knew.

She started past him, but he grabbed her arm. "Don't lie to me."

"I'm not lying." She broke away and kept walking, conscious of the flush in her cheeks, her hair hastily pinned up.

"Don't turn your back when I'm talking to you. If Father were here—"

Leona whirled. "But he's not, Ray. He's not."

She went to her room and bolted the door. She hid the photographs in her bureau along with a stone from the creek bed and a handful of wildflowers. The chocolates were gone by then. She stepped out of the bloodstained drawers, rolled them and her bloody handkerchief up in a cloth she used during her time of the month, and hid them. She washed herself and hid the bloody washcloth too.

10

On a Sunday in April 1918, Leona, her mother, her aunt Sally, and Raymond were gathered around the dinner table when Raymond announced he had gotten a job with the railroad. Leona nearly choked on a bite of ham.

"Really?" she managed to say. Would he leave? For good?

Aunt Sally sniffed. "Doing what?"

"Rail inspector. I'll ride a handcar between Sully and Sadie's Gap and make sure the rails are safe." It was a good job, he said. He would get a room in Sully. He had wanted to enlist, but the army wouldn't take him because he was the sole breadwinner. "That's a hoot," he said.

Rose's hands fluttered around her face. "What will we do? You can't leave."

He knelt beside her and tucked a loose tendril of hair behind her ear. "I got to, Mama. But I'll be back." He stood. "Make the niggers earn their keep."

Leona said, "I wish you wouldn't use that word."

"What word? What?"

"You know very well. Father always said we ought not to."

"Well, Father ain't here." Raymond stormed out.

The following week, he kept Luther and Jesse in the fields from daylight to dark to get the plowing done. When Leona got up on Friday morning, Raymond was gone. She had thought he might be bluffing, but he had taken his clothes and their father's pipe collection. He'd taken his horse but not the buggy.

Rose sobbed at the kitchen table. Sally was stone-faced. Leona felt like dancing, until she thought about the farm. It was nearing the end of April, and Raymond had not planted the corn.

Monday morning, Leona was waiting for Luther when he parked

his wagon near the barn and climbed down. Watching him, she wondered exactly how old he was. She only knew that he was some years older than her father. She had heard the story about how Varna Biggs had brought Raymond and Leona into the world. Luther had told her other stories too. His mother was born a slave on this land, and when the war was over, his people had stayed. It seemed to her Luther could have left any time he wanted, but something had tied him to the place.

Dark clouds gathered to the north. She walked out to where Luther was slopping the hogs. "Morning, Luther. You all right this morning?"

He set the bucket down and came over to the fence, wiping his hands on his overalls.

"Moving slow. How y'all?"

"We're just fine. Raymond's gone." She crossed her fingers when she said the words. What if this were one of his cruel jokes, and he would come riding in the yard that very night?

"What you mean, gone? Raymond's always going off somewhere."

"He got a job working for the railroad. He's moved to town. I'm glad, but I don't know what to do."

A flicker of a smile lit Luther's face. "We do what we always done. Raymond ain't never been much help round here. Don't you fret. We'll be fine."

"I hope you're right."

Luther cocked his head and studied her. "That ain't all that's bothering you."

"No, I guess not."

"You want to tell me?"

She shrugged, said, "It's nothing." But then, why not tell Luther? He would understand. "I visited Father's grave the other day. It's been two years since—" Her voice gave way.

"Yes, ma'am. I know what day it was."

"His grave was all grown over. I pulled weeds the best I could. I talked to him. Do you think the dead can hear? Can they see us?"

"I believe they do. Sometimes I feel Varna's eyes on me. I hear her voice."

The clouds were closing in. Lightning flickered to the north. "Well, then. Do you think he's ashamed of me?"

"Oh, child, no. Your daddy's looking down on you and your little baby, and he's smiling. He might shed a tear because he can't be here to look after you. But he ain't ashamed. He loved you more than life." Luther looked south toward the hill where Herbert Pinson lay. His face changed; his eyes brimmed with tears. "When he was a little boy, I loved him, and he loved me."

"I know." The wind lifted Leona's skirts and whipped her hair around her face. "What happened between you two? Something did."

Luther cast his eyes at the muddy ground for a long minute before he said, "It ain't nothing for you to trouble yourself about." He picked up the bucket of slop and made his way among the hogs that nudged him for more.

Big, stinging raindrops began to fall. Leona ran to the house. The wind ripped clothes off the line, and the rain came, heavy as velvet curtains, and cut off her view of the barn. Standing there out of the pouring rain, she puzzled over Luther's emotions. She had no answers, just as she had none for her father's death or for what had happened between Walker and her. She went into the house. The moment she heard Isaiah crying, she forgot about all that. Her milk let down, and her whole body flushed warm.

❧

Luther wished the rain could wash him clean. He wished the burden of his heart were lighter. He stood in the rain until a jagged bolt of lightning struck in the woods south of the house, and then he retreated to the barn and waited, chilled and wet, for the storm to pass. He looked up at the house, empty of Raymond Pinson, only the women and the infant left. Herbert Pinson in the ground two years now.

Luther drew a long breath and let it go. "Lord, lord."

He had been five years old, his mother dead less than a week, when William Pinson had ridden into Luther's grandmother's yard. His horse whinnied and stamped and sent the chickens scattering. Luther knew who Mr. William was. He had come to his mother's house sometimes, late at night, when Luther and his brother, Benjamin, were supposed to be asleep. But that day, William Pinson might as well have been an apparition, with his tangled hair and wild eyes and his clothes in disarray.

Luther was in the kitchen eating supper with his brother when Mr. William stormed in and grabbed Luther up. Luther's grandmother begged him not to take the boy, but he nearly ran her down when he rode away with Luther clutched to his chest.

"Don't look back, boy," Mr. William said, "and don't you cry."

That night, he took Luther into his own house, made him a pallet in the kitchen, and left him there. Luther curled up, shivering and terrified. He missed his brother and his grand-mother and his mother most of all. In a while Mr. William came back, carrying a lamp no bigger than the candlestick Luther's grandmother burned by her bedside at night. He set the lamp down beside the pallet. "No need to be afraid of the dark," he said. "You be brave, now." Luther remembered lying awake, watching the flame flicker inside the clear chimney. Sometime before dawn, it sputtered and died.

Early in the morning, the Negro woman who cooked for the Pinsons came in and found him. She said, "Look at you, boy! What Mr. William gone and done? There'll be hell to pay round here."

The woman fed Luther a breakfast of cold corn pone and buttermilk. That morning, he heard raised voices in the house and the sound of a woman crying. In a while, Mr. William came and told the Negro cook to clear a space in the lean-to for Luther to sleep. "He'll be staying here," Mr. William said.

Luther saw little of William Pinson. A few times, he took Luther with him to ride the fields. Those mornings, Luther rode in front of him in the saddle, Mr. William's arm around his waist to steady him. They rode without speaking, and he showed

Luther no tenderness. Luther longed for his grandmother's house, but the only time he ever asked William Pinson to take him home, he slapped him. "Don't you know how lucky you are, boy?" he said. Luther didn't feel lucky. He heard the whispers of the other Negroes, withstood their taunts. As for William Pinson, Luther had no feelings for him one way or the other.

Mr. William's wife, Lucy, never said a direct word to the boy. She would say to another Negro, "Tell the boy this," or "Tell the boy that." Luther was told to stay out of her way, and he did. He was eleven years old when Herbert was born. Luther heard one of the Negroes say that Lucy had already birthed two dead babies. "Finally, she give him a living son!" the woman said. Luther felt sorry for Herbert and for Sally, born two years later, misshapen right out of her mother's womb. He knew the angers and jealousies of that house, but he didn't yet understand them.

He was fourteen when he first heard Mr. William's fits of coughing in the night. Three years later, he died of consumption and left Luther fifty acres, a mule, a plow, and his old hound. Not long after, Luther left the Pinson house to live in a shack on his own land. He carried with him the clothes on his back, a quilt, a pocket knife, and the lamp Mr. William had given him when he first brought Luther into that house.

When Herbert was old enough, he tagged along after Luther at his chores. "How do you do this, Luther?" he would say. "How do you do that?" Luther taught him all he knew about the land, taught him how to track and shoot. By the time Herbert was fifteen, he could birth a calf and plant and plow and shoot as well as any man. He didn't need Luther to tell him how anymore. Luther loved that boy like his own brother. Luther couldn't have said when he realized they were half-brothers, but he and Herbert never spoke a word about it. In time Herbert grew up and took to hunting with his neighborhood cronies and going off to Sully or Sadie's Gap. Once Herbert married Rose, he stopped coming to Luther's house altogether.

Luther could have left, but he had his reasons for staying.

He had his land and a house and a wife, Varna, a big-boned, handsome dark woman. He had Alma, and later on, Jesse. But Herbert had Rose, with her sweet-smelling hair, her small white hands that fluttered like birds.

11

Leona had done chores in the barn since she was little, but with Raymond away, she wished she'd gone to the fields with her father and paid more attention to the work that went on around the place. One thing she knew: it was May, and they were late getting corn in the ground.

The sacks of corn they'd laid by last year had mildewed where Raymond left them, around back of the barn, exposed to the weather. She took the baby with her to the feed store in Sully and bought new seed corn.

On her way home, she stopped to ask Mr. Pratt if he could spare any laborers. He stood on the porch with his arms crossed. He didn't ask her to come in. "What you need them for?"

"Raymond's gone off to work on the railroad. We need help besides Luther and Jesse."

He seemed to consider it. What would she do if he refused to help? But then he uncrossed his arms. "Well, all right," he said. He gave her the names of some young Negro men and told her where they lived.

"They're Sammy Hull's boys," he said. "Sammy used to be a good worker, but he's got heart trouble. These boys can get lazy. You'll have to keep an eye on them."

Half an hour later, she drove the wagon into the yard of a tenant shack on Mr. Pratt's land, a weathered house with the porch close to falling off. An old woman sat in a straight chair in the yard. Leona climbed down from the wagon with the baby in his sling.

"I'm looking for Jeremiah and Landry Hull. Mr. Carl Pratt told me they might be in need of work."

With difficulty, the old woman stood. "They my grandsons. I'll get them." She limped into the house. "Jeremiah, Landry! White woman out here to see you."

Leona stood in the bare yard, jiggling the baby, chickens pecking around her feet. It seemed like a long time before the woman came out with two boys who looked to be about Leona's age. A couple of barefoot children trailed after them. The older boys sauntered down the rickety steps. The little ones hid behind the old woman. "I'm looking for workers," Leona said. "At the Pinson farm. The fields are plowed, but we haven't planted the corn." When neither of them spoke or moved, she knew she had to talk money. "I'll pay you fifty cents a day."

The boys looked at each other. "I reckon we can," the taller one said.

"Good. You know where the Pinson place is?"

They nodded.

"I'll see you at seven in the morning."

She drove out of the yard without looking back. She didn't find those boys very promising, but without extra help, it would take too long to plant. Every day mattered.

When she got home, Luther was hoeing in the garden. She told him she had hired a couple of extra hands. He rested on the hoe and mopped his face with a handkerchief. "Don't see why we need nobody else."

"Well, we do. I'll need you to keep an eye on these boys. Mr. Carl says they're lazy. I expect you can fix that."

Luther nodded. "Yes, ma'am, I expect I can."

Jeremiah and Landry worked two days, got their pay on Saturday, and didn't come back to work on Monday. Luther, Jesse, and Leona finished the planting, although Luther wouldn't let her work in the field for long at a time. The sun shone, the weather warmed, and the corn came up. Leona thought, See, Raymond? We don't need you at all.

Then late spring rains flooded the fields and drowned the young corn. Bertie told Leona that the Baptist preacher had preached on the end times. The war and the flooding rains were all signs that the end was near.

Leona didn't know about the end times, but there seemed no

end to the war. July marked a year since Walker left. She had had no word, not a single letter.

She had last seen Walker on the fourth of July, 1917, at an ice cream social at the Caldwells', a party for boys going off to the war. That Sunday afternoon, Raymond had been sleeping off a binge, and Leona had slipped out of the house to go with Bertie.

The Caldwells' house was hot and packed with neighbors. Leona felt out of sorts and nauseated. Maybe it was the heat, or maybe it was the thought that Walker might be there. What would she say to him, if he were? She hadn't gone to town since that day in April when she'd bought the cough medicine, but Walker could have come to her. He could have written to her. Where had he been all this time? Why hadn't he tried to see her? When she thought about what they had done, she felt marked, as though anybody could look at her and know.

She got a glass of iced tea and went out on the front porch. Two neighbor women sat at the far end, fanning themselves. Some little boys played soldier in the yard, using sticks for guns. Even the children were infected with war fever.

A car that looked like the Brooms' turned into the long driveway, but most cars looked alike to Leona. It pulled over onto the grass and rolled to a stop. She held her breath, waiting to see who it was.

Walker got out. He wasn't wearing a uniform. He waved, and she waved back. She thought her heart might burst. A scenario of a life with Walker Broom flashed through her mind: a wedding in her little country church, a tiny house in town. And children. They would have children.

He crossed the yard, climbed the porch steps, and stopped beside her, turning his cap in his hands. She wanted to touch him. It might have been a good thing that she felt the old women's eyes on them.

She said, "You aren't going? I'm so glad."

He glanced away, and her hopes shattered. "Walker?"

He cleared his throat. "I am going. I volunteered." He lowered his voice. "I leave for camp in a couple of weeks. I want to see you before I go."

The old women had stopped talking. Leona set her glass of tea on the rail carefully, afraid she might drop it. She clasped her hands to stop their shaking. And then she laughed for the benefit of the women as though he had said something funny.

"Leona, please." He looked stricken.

Loud enough for the women to hear, she said, "Well, I wish you luck. I hope you come home safe and sound."

She went into the house, and he followed her, but a crowd of well-wishers surrounded him. Somebody put a bowl of ice cream in Leona's hands. She set it on a side table, found Mrs. Caldwell, and told her it was a fine party but she had to get home early. She told Bertie she had a headache. She didn't know if Walker saw her leave.

When Leona felt sick that day, she thought she had a case of nerves. When she skipped her time of the month a second time a couple of weeks later, she worried there was something wrong. Her mother's mother had died of a growth in her female parts when Leona was nine years old. Didn't Leona deserve to get sick and die? She had committed a terrible sin, and she wasn't sorry. Maybe that was the greater sin. She kept her fears to herself, and when she was sick, she ran to the outhouse to vomit.

When she got back to the house one morning, Sally was waiting for her in the kitchen. Leona walked past her, but Sally grabbed her arm.

"I been watching you. I been hearing you too. Sick every morning."

Leona stood there, shaky and pale, while Sally seemed to take stock of her. Then she laid her palm flat on Leona's nightdress, over her belly.

"How long since you bled?"

Leona shook her head. "I don't know."

"You must know. Think."

Leona closed her eyes. "Two months?" She started to cry. "Three? Am I going to die, Aunt Sally?"

"Die? Oh, girl, no. Oh, Leona. Who did this to you?"

"Who did what?"

Sally slapped her. "Don't you sass me. Who got you with child?"

Stunned, Leona stared at her aunt. "A baby?"

Sally climbed into a chair and sat, fanning herself. "Don't tell me you didn't know."

That last day at Hawks Creek. "No, ma'am. I swear."

Tears tracked down the lines of Sally's face. "Lord help us. I'm glad your daddy ain't alive to see this." She climbed down and went out the back door, the screen door slapping shut behind her.

Walker's child. Feeling weak and sick, Leona sat alone in the kitchen. Her mother was still sleeping, and Leona was glad she didn't have to face her yet.

She had known a girl in the seventh grade who got a baby with a boy who lived in Sully. He'd claimed it wasn't his and refused to marry her. The girl left school and had her baby, and now she was raising it, living at home, dependent on her family. Leona had seen people in town look the other way and not even speak to that girl. She had a right pretty little baby, but people ignored it. Such disgrace would fall on Leona and her family now. Some girls in her predicament were sent away, but Leona's family didn't have the money to send her to a home for unwed mothers, and they didn't have a relative far away who might take her in.

She got up and looked out the window. Sally was walking up and down the garden rows, talking and gesturing at the air like somebody was walking with her.

That afternoon, Leona went to Hawks Creek and sat with her back against the broken wall of the old church. She had heard that the Sully boys had gone to train at Camp Pike in Arkansas. After that, they would sail for France. She could think of no way to find out where or how to write to Walker. She resolved that nobody would know who this child's father was.

When Rose found out about the baby—Sally made Leona tell her that day—Rose wept and took to her bed. When Raymond found out, he raged.

"Tell me who the daddy is," he shouted. "By God, I'll see to it he makes things right. It's what Father would have done." Was it, Leona wondered? What would her father say and do? When she refused to name the man, Raymond slapped her twice, and it would have been worse if Rose hadn't stopped him. He stormed out of the house and stayed gone for days. Leona prayed he would never come back. But he did come back, a sullen, menacing presence.

Once her belly became obvious, Leona stopped going to her friend Bertie's house, to town, to church. One Sunday, Rose came home in tears from their little church down the road. "The preacher said he heard you're in trouble," she said. "He said it right there in front of people, Leona. I was mortified. He says you have to come to church and confess. You have to tell who the father is. If you don't, you're consigned to hell, and so is the child."

Leona didn't look up from polishing her grandmother's silver spoons. "You believe that?"

Rose's eyes were red and puffy. "You know I do. But you can—"

"No, Mama. I won't tell. Nobody can make me." She tossed the last spoon onto the table and hurried to her room and slammed the door.

That same preacher had presided over her father's funeral. He had baptized Leona in the creek on a June morning when she was ten years old. She wore a white cotton dress her mother had made for the occasion. The preacher took Leona by the hand and walked her waist deep into the water, stirring up the silt and turning the water murky. She remembered one of the questions he asked her. "Do you forsake the ways of Satan and all his works?" She said yes. The preacher told her to hold her nose, and he braced her against his left arm and leaned her backwards until she was submerged. He brought her up sputtering. "Praise the Lord! You are forever changed!" he said. But she hadn't felt changed. She'd felt chilled, and her dress had been stained with the red clay of the creek bottom.

Maybe she hadn't renounced the work of Satan that day. Maybe Satan was at work in her, but how could her love for Walker be the work of the Devil? So much for the love of God, if God turns His back so easily on sinners. And what about Walker? Wasn't he a sinner, the same as Leona? Would he burn in Hell too for what they had done?

12

Below deck on the great ship, Walker remembered the dark closet where his mother used to shut him away for being naughty. He thought of root cellars and graves. Twice during the first week at sea, he had clawed at his throat, gasping for breath, and his fellow soldiers had carried him above deck, up into the open air.

An army-issued Springfield rifle lay beneath his berth, a very different gun from the single-shot .22 his father had given him for Christmas the year he was twelve. The Springfield had a bayonet. At Camp Pike, Walker had hated the bayonet drills where he and the other men lunged at sacks filled with straw and jabbed the bayonets deep, aiming for what would be the chest or the belly of a living man. Walker couldn't fathom doing that to another human being, German or not. If it came to dying, to the choice between his own life or another's, he figured he could fire that rifle at a man's heart or his brain. But the bayonet—he wasn't sure he could drive it deep at close range, so close he could see the enemy's eyes, then pull it out and move on.

Walker was homesick. He couldn't erase from his mind his mother's embrace and her mottled, tear-streaked face the day he left. Nor could he put out of his mind what he and Leona had done and what had happened after. She had bled, and he'd known he was the first. When he had driven away from Hawks Creek that day in April, he'd looked back at her, standing in the middle of the rutted lane, a figure struck in gold in the late afternoon light. He'd turned his eyes back to the road and grasped the steering wheel, glad for the distraction of the car, its engine chugging, weaving over the bumpy road. He'd stopped the car outside of Sully, straightened his clothes, and run a comb through his hair. Would his mother smell Leona's scent on him and sense his racing heart? But when he got home, his parents weren't there. Relief had mingled with guilt.

In his berth at night on the ship, he closed his eyes and imagined Leona's light, abundant hair against his skin, her lips swollen from kissing, her green eyes. In his pack he kept the photograph he had taken at his daddy's fishing camp, the one of Leona wearing the coat with the fur collar. It wasn't a nice coat. When she became his wife, he would buy her a better one. Sometimes he showed the photograph to his army buddies. "My girl back home," he would say, and they allowed as how she was a beauty, all right. They slapped him on the back and winked as though they knew she was more than just his girl. Sometimes he took out the picture when he was alone. He tried to commit Leona's face to memory, whispered to her in the dark, promised he wouldn't forget her, promised he would make it back to Sully in one piece.

After that day at the Caldwells, he had intended to see her again. He'd looked for her in town, but she never came. He'd seen Raymond on the street or on the square, but he dared not ask about Leona. He was relieved—and ashamed—when Raymond paid him no attention.

A few days before he left for the camp, he drove to Leona's house. She wasn't home, or so her dwarf aunt said. The aunt looked him up and down and seemed to find him lacking. He almost walked away. Instead, he had left the wrapped present, a note tucked inside it, with the aunt and backed away like a cowardly hound.

Walker had plenty of time to puzzle over it all on board the ship. Maybe Leona had been ashamed to seek him out after what they had done. Maybe she'd worried that he thought her wanton because of the way she gave herself to him. It would be easier to believe that Leona tempted him—the way she had taken his fingers into her mouth, the way she'd pulled him down to her. Other boys bragged about what certain girls would do, especially country girls. They were known to be fast. Yet such thoughts made Walker ashamed. If anybody in this world had brought Leona down, it was he. And if he lived to go home, he would do the honorable thing. He would marry her.

And so, even though he had heard nothing from Leona, he wrote letters. He struggled to describe what it was like to live on the great vessel afloat on an ocean so vast there seemed no end to it. By the time the ship arrived at Le Havre, Walker had a dozen letters hidden away in the bottom of his pack. He could have mailed them once the ship docked, but he left them where they were.

13

Leona kept her vow of secrecy, although it was hard. Sometimes she wanted to say Walker's name at the dinner table or shout it on the street in town. As Isaiah grew and changed, she watched for some recognizable feature of Walker's to show itself. So far, nobody besides Leona seemed to have noticed the cleft in his chin. And who could make the connection? She breathed easier, but she longed for Walker and worried about him, especially when Bertie brought her tales about the war.

"Sometimes our boys get so close to the Germans they can see their eyeballs," Bertie had told her last week. She'd told Leona about Lonnie Simmons, a boy from town who had died. Three others had come home wounded, one missing his right leg below the knee, another an arm.

"Can you imagine?" Bertie had said.

Leona could imagine it. She remembered her father's shattered head, how his blood had seeped through her apron, her dress, and her undergarments, all the way to her skin, how she'd washed his blood away.

Leona wanted news besides Bertie's wide-eyed tales. She slipped money from the jar in the kitchen and gave it to Bertie to buy a newspaper in town. When Bertie brought Leona the paper, she brought gossip, as well.

"Pa saw Raymond Saturday," Bertie said. "Pa said he was hanging out with a bunch of ne'er-do-wells, and he looked like he was drunk."

Leona wasn't surprised. What else might Raymond do on a Saturday? The big news Bertie brought was that a gang of men who wore white robes like the old Klan had sprung up around Sully.

"It's terrible, the things they're doing. They've been burning

crosses, and last Saturday night, one of the colored families on
our place had their barn burned down. Pa's going to help them
build it back, but still." Even worse, that same night, Bertie said,
a colored family's house on another place was set on fire. "Five
people in that house, Leona. One little boy died. It's just pure
meanness."

Would Raymond ride with those men? Leona thought he
was capable of it.

The newspaper Bertie had brought Leona was two weeks old.
She locked the door to her room and moved the rocking chair
nearer the window where she could still see to read in the twilight. While Isaiah nursed, she read. A political cartoon on the
front page showed an American soldier, his face contorted and
fierce-looking, standing with one foot on a German soldier
lying on the ground. *Destroy the Huns!* the cartoon proclaimed.
Advertisements urged people to buy liberty bonds. Some news
alarmed her. The Germans had torpedoed a troop ship somewhere in the Atlantic Ocean, but none of the soldiers were
killed, and the German submarine had been destroyed. She
read a story about a young soldier who had taken his own life.

She saved the soldiers' letters to read last. The headline read
LETTERS FROM OUR BOYS AT THE FRONT. One was
from a boy she knew, Horace Craig, who had finished at the
Pinson Road School two years before Leona. She remembered
him as a shy boy, not one given to foolishness. When he wrote
the letter, he was still at the training camp over in Arkansas.
He missed his family, but mostly he was homesick for his girl.
Leona wondered if Walker missed her or if he was so caught up
in the soldiering life that he never thought about her.

Another letter made her weep. Leona didn't know Terrell
Anderson; he was from Luna. His mother had sent his first
letter to the paper to be published. That letter had also been
his last, the paper said. He'd been killed in the Battle of Belleau
Wood in June.

Dear Mama,

I hope this letter finds you well. We landed at a place called Le Havre in France on 22nd April, and they kept us there for a week while we were processed, is what they call it. Now we are on the march. My feet ain't been dry in a week. I sure miss your fried chicken. I want you to fry me up a platter full when I get home and I'll eat every bite. I wish I could tell you where I am, but they won't let us. France is a right pretty place in spite of the war. Some of the woods are so deep they remind me of our hills and hollows. Tell Pa his teaching me to shoot ain't come in handy yet. Please don't worry about me, Mama. I'm doing all right. Love Sissy and little James for me and tell them I say to help you with the chores I ain't there to do. I will write again soon.

Your loving son,
Terry

Leona folded the paper and laid it aside. She looked down at Isaiah sleeping and imagined him a young man like Terry. What must it feel like to get a telegram saying that your son—or your husband—was dead?

Luther failed to show up for work on a Monday in August. Because of the heat, Leona waited until nearly sundown to walk to Luther's house. Uneasy about what she might find, she left Isaiah with Sally.

Near Luther's place she smelled smoke, like burning wood or a grass fire. When she got close to the house, she saw a scarecrow-like figure of a man, ragged clothes stuffed with straw, a rope around its neck, hanging from a tree in Luther's clean-swept yard. The thing was only partly burned, like somebody had scared off whomever did it. She crossed the yard, calling Luther's name.

He came out on the porch. "You ought not to be here, Leona."

She looked up at the smoldering thing. "What happened here?"

"Ain't nothing but mischief."

"Luther, I'm not going until you tell me."

He sat on the top step, and she sat beside him. "All right. But it ain't for you to fret about. Last night, some men rode in here, wearing them white robes like the old days." He would know, Leona thought; Luther was old enough to have seen the Klan in its heyday. "They made a ruckus at first, cursing, calling my name and Jesse's. I made Jesse stay in the house." Beads of sweat stood on Luther's forehead. "By the time I came out, they was hoisting that thing over the tree limb and setting it on fire, such a whooping and hollering you never heard. One come up on the porch, he get right in my face, him wearing that hood with the holes in it. Too dark to see his eyes." Luther pointed at the hanging thing. His hand shook. "He says that'll be me and Jesse if we don't watch out. That's what he says."

Leona felt like something had taken hold of her heart and squeezed it. "They wanted to scare you. They won't come back." She wished she could believe it. "You and Jesse come down to the house, if you want to. It's mighty hot, but you could bed down in the barn." She didn't say, if you're afraid to stay here.

"No, ma'am. We ain't leaving this place. This place belong to us. Mr. William give it to me. I ain't going nowhere."

"All right, then." She stood. "Let's pull that ugly old thing down."

Luther put his hands on his thighs and rose too. "You're right. Why I been sitting in the house looking at it, I don't know."

The rope was tied to a stake a few yards from the tree. Luther pulled the stake out with no trouble, and the half-burnt thing fell to the ground and broke apart.

"Let's burn it all up," Leona said. "Let's get rid of it."

Luther nodded. "Yes, ma'am. Burn it right down to ashes. Let it blow on out of here." He got kerosene and matches, doused the straw and lit it, and the fire bloomed up and swirled in the hot wind. Jesse came outside and whooped and danced around it. Leona was sweating from the heat and the fire, but she felt good.

ॐ

Luther had not told Leona how scared he had been. He hadn't told her how the sight of those hooded men reminded him of another time, God Almighty, as clear to him now as when it happened so long ago.

Luther had been fifteen years old, staying a week in the summer with his brother, Benjamin, when one night they heard the sound of many horses. Benjamin told him to hide way back under the house, as far as he could get, and not come out. "Unless they light the house on fire."

Luther crawled under the house and lay where he could see out. A gang of white-robed men carrying torches rode into the yard. Benjamin went out to meet them, and three men dismounted, threw him to the ground, and bound his hands and feet. One of the riders dragged Benjamin up and down that rough road in front of the house while the others cheered him on. Above the din Luther heard the front door open, heard footsteps across the porch and down the stoop. Benjamin's wife, Millie, crossed the yard, carrying a piece of firewood and screaming at those men. One of them doubled back and knocked her down, but she got up and went after them again. Another rider hit her with the stock of his gun, and she crumpled to the ground.

Luther couldn't have said how long they dragged his brother. When the men were done with him, they left him lying on the road and circled back into the yard. Luther wished he were brave enough to come out from under that house and meet those men eye to eye. Instead, he scrambled farther back. The men went inside the house. Luther heard them stomping around, knocking things to the floor. He held his breath. Benjamin's two little boys were in there. He was sure Millie had hidden them, but still—

The men came out, and one of them yelled, "Wanna torch it?"

Luther's breath came hard, his face pressed in the dirt. Somebody said, "Naw. Leave it! He ain't gonna give us no more trouble!"

After the men were gone, Luther crawled out, picked Millie up, and carried her inside. He walked down the road and found his brother's torn body lying in a ditch. He managed to carry Benjamin back to the house. He was still alive, but he died the next day. Poor Millie, she was all broken up in body and in spirit. She was never the same. Luther had never known what Benjamin had done to make those men come for him.

Now men wearing the white robes and hoods were riding the countryside again. Why they had chosen him and Jesse, Luther could only guess. He knew one thing for sure. Those men were not finished yet.

❧

Leona hardly slept that sultry night. The windows were open, and more than once she got out of bed, thinking she heard shouts and riders. She felt better the next morning when Luther and Jesse came to work. "Any more trouble?" she asked Luther.

"No, ma'am. I expect there won't be."

Leona told her mother and Sally about the night riders. Her mother said nothing, but Sally said, "It's them Negroes that stir up the trouble. Maybe not Luther, but them others. And then there's consequences, if you know what I mean."

14

During the week, Raymond inspected the rails in the murderous heat. He saw things in the shimmer rising off the rails. His father, the way he looked that last morning, beckoning. A naked girl walking out of the woods, her eye sockets empty.

He lived for the paycheck that paid his rent and bought his whiskey. He liked wearing the hood and riding Belle on Saturday nights, the thunder of hooves on gravel or dirt roads, the dust, the wind. The men gathered at Hawks Creek or sometimes closer to town. They went into the woods to don the robes, out of sight. When they were finished with their mischief for the night, they split up and went different directions, stripping off the hoods and robes and stowing them in their packs.

That was what they called it: mischief. Raymond was as good at it as any of them. A few times since he left home, he had gone alone to Tobe Sanders's place at night. Once, he left a dead raccoon on the porch, another time a dead possum and her dead babies. He poisoned Tobe's flock of chickens.

Yes, Raymond was good at mischief.

In the beginning the riders stole a mule and a few chickens, destroyed eggs in a chicken house, killed a couple of hounds. One night, they were sitting around on the square in town with nothing to do. Raymond said they ought to burn crosses like in that picture show about the old Klan. "Scare the bejesus out of them," he said. The other men laughed. So they burned a few crosses, and one night a cross burning led to torching a barn.

The following week, they rode out Pinson Road to a Negro sharecropper's place not far from Hawks Creek. A couple of the men set fire to the barn. The weather had been dry, so the barn went up quickly. All the men rode around and around the house, hollering and carrying on. The little house was dark.

Jack Parker yelled, "Come on out of there! Whoeee! You better come out!" Nobody came. "All right then," Jack shouted. "Let's torch it!"

"Hold on," Raymond said. "Ain't no need to burn the house down."

"What's the matter, Raymond?" Jack said. "You turning yellow?"

"Naw. I ain't yellow. The barn's enough, that's all. Let's go."

Jack laughed. "You worried about them niggers? One whiff of smoke and they'll get out of there fast." Jack wheeled his horse around.

Belle shied and shimmied backward. "Easy now," Raymond said. He took the flask from his pocket and drank. He circled Belle out a ways. By the time he calmed her down and looked back at the house, Jack was pouring kerosene on the porch and the walls. He broke a window and splashed kerosene inside before he touched his torch to the old wood and backed away. Flames bloomed up, inside and out. It took only minutes for the fire to spread. Raymond clutched the reins so hard his hands ached. "Come on out, come on out," he whispered, wondering at the same time why in the hell he cared.

It wasn't long before the front door burst open and Negroes spilled out and scattered into the fields, hollering and crying. An old man with a walking stick stumbled down the porch steps and fell facedown in the dirt. And then on the porch there was a child, just a little tyke wearing a nightshirt. He—or she, Raymond couldn't tell—was bawling. A woman ran toward the child, yelling, "Johnny? Baby? Run! Come to me!"

"Aw, Jesus," Raymond said. He was of a mind to run in there and grab the child, but before the woman reached the porch, the house blazed up, the tin porch roof buckled, the front wall caved in, and the roof came down. The little house burned, sparks spiraling to the stars like a fireworks show, the woman on her knees in the dirt, howling.

Raymond leaned out of his saddle and threw up mostly whiskey. He and the others rode away, but down the road he could still hear that woman's wailing. In the sober light of the next day, he washed himself, but he couldn't get rid of the smell of smoke.

The Ridge Riders—by now they had a name—lay low for a while. A month later, they burned the Negro church at Luna clear to the ground. Nobody was inside it, so nobody got hurt. Raymond felt better about that. He didn't like the idea of killing women and little children for no good reason except that they were colored. The men—now that was different.

The night they burned the straw man at Luther's, Raymond went along but kept his distance from Luther. If Luther was scared, he didn't show it, and Jesse didn't come out of the house. The damp straw they had used to stuff the clothes put out a lot of smoke, and some of the men started to cough. Somebody shouted, "Let's go!" and they were off down the road.

It was almost midnight, but Raymond's home place—his place, he reminded himself—was close. He figured he might ride by. The house was dark except for a dim flicker in the kitchen window. Leona must be up, feeding the baby. Raymond had stashed away his robe and hood, but he considered putting them back on and riding into the yard, walking up on the porch, and banging on the door. What would his sister do if she opened the door and saw a white-robed man? But what if his mother came to the door? Shit, no, he could never do that to her.

Belle snuffled, strained at the reins, turned as though she would ride into the yard.

A figure moved within the deep shadows on the porch. Who could it be at this hour except his mother? Raymond held back tears. He wanted to walk into the house and sleep in his own bed, to wake up in the morning to the rooster's crowing, the smell of sausage frying, Sally's off-key humming in the kitchen, his mother's low voice, reading aloud from her Bible. But he could not abide his sister or the presence of her boy.

If anybody ought to raise a child in that house, it ought to be Raymond. Someday he would meet a pretty, nice girl, not like that girl with the bad teeth at Sadie's Gap, and she would love him. He would bring her home in the buggy, or maybe in an automobile, and when they topped that last rise, he'd stop and say, "There's the place. All ours." He would be the first man to bed her, and they would have many children. He'd die an old man, fat and prosperous, and pass the place on to them.

But here he was, twenty-two years old, and nothing to show for it but his horse, a couple of dollars in his pocket, calluses on his hands from farm work and that damned rail handcar, and a stain of guilt on his heart that wouldn't go away. He could drink it away for a while, but then the memory and deep down the relief would come flooding back. That was the worst of it—to admit he was glad his father was gone.

He felt in his pocket for his father's watch and took it out. He popped the catch with his thumbnail and held it so moonlight illuminated the face. Nearly one in the morning now. He put the watch back in his pocket just as the light in the house went out. He nudged Belle in the direction of Sully. He vowed to come and see his mother soon. "I will," he said to the night. "I will."

15

Rose's eyes hurt. Leona was in the kitchen with the baby. Rose gave up trying to read her Bible by lamplight and went outside and sat on the porch. She was dozing when a sound out on the road startled her awake. She got up and stood at the porch rail and looked up the road. There was a half-moon. Somebody on a horse came riding over the hill at a gallop. As the rider drew closer, he slowed, and when he came even with the dirt track into the yard, he stopped. Rose's heart played tricks in her chest. Was it Raymond? Three months now since he left. Leona had offered to take her to town to see him, but she had refused. Rose didn't like to go to town or anywhere else. Her world had narrowed until the four walls of that house were enough for her.

She wanted to call out to the rider, but she had heard about a gang of men riding around the county, causing trouble. Maybe it was one of them. She stepped back into the shadows. Whoever it was rode on, and the sound of the horse faded away.

Rose prayed for Raymond's safe return. He had always been trouble, even when he was a little thing, but he had gotten worse after Herbert died, so unhappy and angry. Going off drinking and carousing. He didn't think she knew, but a mother knew things. And the way he treated his sister. Well. When he came home, she would send Leona and her baby away. Sally, too. Sally should have left a long time ago.

Yet Rose was drawn to the baby boy. Sometimes, when Leona was doing outside chores and Sally was busy in the kitchen, Rose slipped into Leona's room and watched Isaiah sleeping. Her grandson. She fought the urge to hold him, to breathe him in, but she kept that longing to herself. How could she love another child? She had loved Raymond more than her own life. She would have been satisfied if there were no more babies after him, but then Leona came along, and they were even: a child for Rose and one for Herbert. And the other, the last one—Rose would not think of it: the cursed months of carrying it. The birth and after. The unbearable love, sorrow, loss, guilt, and finally, resignation.

16

September was the perfect prelude to fall: warm days, cool nights, and the promise of a small but decent cotton crop after the loss of the corn. Best of all, a traveling circus was coming to Sully. Bertie had seen the posters in town. "I'm going to take my brothers and my sister," she told Leona. "Why don't you come along and bring Isaiah?" When Leona hesitated, Bertie said, "Pa didn't want me to, but Mama says it's all right to ask you."

Leona's impulse was to say no, but it would be fun to forget about the farm and the war and everything else that troubled her. To be like a child for a couple of hours.

"Yes," she said. "I would like to go."

When she told Sally, Sally said, "Circus, my foot. Ain't it circus enough for you around here?" Sally stood on a stool in the kitchen and kneaded biscuit dough with a fury. "You ain't a child no more."

"You ever been to a circus?" Leona said.

Sally gave the dough a slap. "No. They put the likes of me in the circus. You know that."

It was true. She and Raymond had gone to a circus once. She must have been about six years old. The clowns, the elephant, the woman who walked the high wire seemed magical. A dwarf clown turned rolling cartwheels around the ring, so fast it made Leona dizzy.

"Aunt Sally could be a clown," Leona told her father that day. Raymond snickered.

"Hush," her father said. "You ought not to laugh about it."

Leona hardly knew her aunt then; Sally was living in Alabama, and Leona had seen her only a couple of times in her life. She didn't like looking at her aunt. She gave Leona nightmares.

"What made Aunt Sally that way?" she asked her father.

"The good Lord, I guess," he had said, which had frightened Leona. Why would God make such a creature?

Now Leona said, "I'm sorry. I didn't mean anything by it. But they have animals and clowns, and people swing high in the air and walk on wires." She shrugged. "It's an altogether amazing thing. I wish you would go with us."

Sally patted out the dough. "No. Thank you for asking, though."

But on the day of the circus, Leona was getting ready to leave when Sally came out, wearing her best dress. She had pinned her hair up neatly, and Leona detected rouge on Sally's cheeks. Either that, or her face was flushed with excitement.

"You think it's all right if I go?" Sally said.

Leona smiled. "I'm sure Bertie won't mind."

They waited on the porch for Bertie, who arrived with ten-year-old Matilda, Carl Jr., who was eight, and the four-year-old twins, Wayne and Winston, riding in the back of the wagon—all the Pratt children except for the youngest, Sarah, who was three months old. "Can I come along?" Sally asked.

"'Course you can, Miss Sally!" Bertie got down and unlatched the tailgate, and she and Carl Jr. gave Sally a boost up into the wagon bed. The twins were tussling in the back. "Settle down, boys!" Bertie said. "Make room for Miss Sally." Bertie climbed back up onto the seat, and Leona sat beside her with Isaiah. Bertie glanced back and gave the little boys another stern look. "They're a handful," she told Leona and Sally, "but everybody deserves to see a circus, don't you think?"

Leona agreed. Isaiah wouldn't remember, but she hoped he would take in some of it, that the smell of sawdust, the voice of the ringmaster, the sound of the calliope, the oohs and aahs of the crowd might be embedded in his memory. Leona hoped to get lost in that crowd. The circus was the attraction; maybe she wouldn't see anybody she knew.

They hadn't gone far before Sally had all of them singing, "Frog Went a-Courtin'" and "Charmin' Billy" and "Shoo Fly." Sally's voice rang out sweet and clear.

The circus had set up in an open field on the outskirts of Sully. It had rained the night before, and Leona's shoes sank in the mud. The tent leaned like it might collapse. Inside, there were only a few rickety stands. The clowns were shabby, their antics tired. Three of the clowns were about Sally's size. They locked their arms and legs together and rolled around the little dusty ring like a wobbling human wheel. The crowd whistled and clapped.

Leona, Bertie, Sally, and the children were sitting on the third row. On the clowns' second pass around the ring, they broke their circle and tumbled and danced right in front of them. The one with star-painted eyes and the biggest red smile climbed up in the stands and sat on Sally's lap and kissed her cheek. When Sally slapped him, the crowd roared, and the clown got down from her lap, knelt on one knee, and popped a red paper flower out of his vest and gave it to Sally. She blushed and laughed. He jumped down, and when he returned to the ring, he blew kisses at Sally. She covered her face with her hands, but she giggled like a girl.

The rest of the circus disappointed Leona. There was no high wire act, just a few acrobats who did handstands and back flips like most any child could do. The animals looked listless, half-starved, and moth-eaten. The elephant's skin hung on its frame like a hand-me-down coat. There was no calliope, only an old gramophone that somebody kept forgetting to wind up so the music played at a good pace and then slowed until it disappeared altogether.

The shabby circus didn't seem to bother the children. The twin boys cried to stay, but they all left after an hour and went into town and bought ice cream at Mr. Wall's drugstore. Sully was deserted. Leona walked across the square to the statue. Isaiah reached out and touched the cold stone. He shivered and buried his face against her breast.

Leona whispered, "This is where your daddy stood not so long ago." Isaiah set up a howl. She took him back to the wagon, and they started for home.

Leona and Bertie talked on the way about how sad the circus had seemed.

"Maybe it's not the circus," Leona said.

"What do you mean, Leona?"

"Maybe it's us."

17

Sally rode looking back toward Sully until the wagon topped a hill and she could no longer see the town. Leona and Bertie had called the circus shabby, not worth the twenty-five cents' admission, but Sally still felt the weight and warmth of that fool clown sitting on her lap. She touched her face where he had kissed her. He'd made her a part of the act, but wasn't it all in fun? The clown's eyes had sparkled with humor and mischief, like he enjoyed being a clown, and he had a nice smile on his painted face. She wondered what he was like without the paint.

There had been a man once, many years ago, who plied Sally with smiles and talk and shy kisses and then abandoned her. It was what men did. Remembering, her happy mood vanished, and her face flushed with shame.

Sally had left the home place on Pinson Road when she was twenty years old and caught a ride to Luna in a neighbor's wagon. Luna was only twenty miles from home, but it was far enough. She rented a room in a boarding house and took in sewing from town women who never looked her in the eye but paid her well. She was a fine seamstress.

She had been in Luna six months when a man knocked on her door. He was a man of normal size, though slight of build with a pockmarked face and thinning, slicked-back hair. He needed a suit coat altered, he said. He had lost weight after an illness. She didn't ask him what kind.

While she worked, she left the door ajar as the landlady required for Sally's male customers, as if they were gentlemen callers. The woolen fabric of the man's coat was worn to a sheen. With pins in her mouth, Sally stood on a stool and took up the seams at the shoulders, down the back, and at the sides.

While she worked, he talked. He was a government surveyor. He would be in town for a while, maybe permanently. He'd taken a room over the drugstore. He had no family. He hailed from Tennessee. When she was finished, he helped her down and took off his coat.

"When will it be ready?" he asked, and she told him three days. He smiled. His teeth were crooked and brown. "That will do."

When he returned for the coat, he paid her, and then he asked her to accompany him to the soda fountain for an ice cream. She said no, but he insisted. The next time he came to her room, he brought a shirt with a frayed collar and cuffs that needed turning. They sat with the door open and talked while she worked.

He asked her to go with him to the City Café for supper, and she accepted. Walking down the street, she was aware of people's stares. He rested a hand on her shoulder. She liked the warm feel of it. That night, they went to his room instead of hers. He shut the door. He was kind to her. He touched her shyly, tracing the line of her wide jaw with a finger. He held her hand and kissed her. Never more than that.

Surely the townsfolk noticed their going out to supper and returning to his room. Sally imagined what they said behind her back: that freak country woman, who does she think she is? He called for her every Friday evening for two months, and then one night, he didn't come. He didn't come the next Friday, either. She climbed the stairs to his bleak room over the drugstore, knocked, and got no answer.

When she inquired at the courthouse, a clerk told her the surveyor had moved on. "Is there a problem?" the clerk asked.

"No," she said. "No problem at all."

She had never heard from the man again.

"You disgust me," her mother, Lucy, used to say. "No man will ever have you."

18

Ten days after the circus, Leona was up at dawn feeding the baby when she heard a racket out front and looked out. The Pratts' wagon pulled up in a cloud of dust. The wagon had barely rolled to a stop before Bertie climbed down. Her hair was unkempt, her apron dirty, her eyes hollowed out.

Leona walked out to meet her. "What's wrong, Bertie?"

"I need help. Pa's gone, and everybody else at our house is sick. Can you come?"

"Of course I will," Leona said. She put Isaiah back in his crib, buttoned her dress, and pulled her hair back into a bun. She woke Sally and told her she was going to Bertie's. "I'll be back in a while. If Isaiah gets hungry, give him a sugar teat."

On their way, Bertie told her Matilda had gotten sick first with high fever and a cough, and one by one, the boys had come down sick too. "Now Mama and the baby have it. I've been up the last two nights with Sarah. Poor little thing, she can't hardly breathe."

"Where's your pa?"

"He's up at the Windham place, helping get their cotton in. He won't be back till Sunday." Bertie started to cry. "It's awful, Leona. I've never seen anything like it."

When they drove into the yard, Leona smelled the stench of livestock untended. No child played outside, no chickens wandered from the hen house. Martha Pratt kept a spotless house, but that day, it smelled like the jars hadn't been emptied in days.

"I'm sorry it's so bad," Bertie said. "I've been doing the best I could."

Matilda sat on the kitchen floor, playing with a doll with a porcelain head, its cheeks painted a pretty flush. One of its arms was broken off.

"Hello, Matilda," Leona said.

Matilda moved the doll's broken arm in a wave. "Hello."

Leona felt Matilda's forehead. Burning up. Matilda coughed, a deep, wracking sound.

"See?" Bertie said. "They're all like that."

Too weak to get up and use the jar, Bertie's mother had soiled herself. The baby girl lay in the cradle and made frantic attempts to cry. Carl Jr. and the twins lay in the middle bedroom. The coughing echoed like a chorus throughout the house. As Leona followed Bertie from room to room, she remembered a conversation she and Bertie had had weeks ago.

Bertie had told her the influenza was back after having subsided over the summer. "It's mostly up East," she'd said. "My pa says there's not much chance of it coming here."

What else could this be?

Leona went cold with dread. She wanted to bolt from the house and leave the Pratts to whatever might befall them, but she couldn't risk going home, not in an hour or two, not today, not tomorrow. If all the Pratts were sick, it was something terribly catching.

Damn you, Bertie, she thought, you are my only friend. She said, "You need to send for your pa. Right now."

Bertie looked blank, her eyes too bright, her cheeks flushed, and Leona knew that Bertie was sick too.

"Listen to me," Leona said. "Go to the Caldwells' and see if one of them can fetch your pa back here. And, Bertie? Don't go near them."

Bertie's hands flew to her mouth. "You think it's the flu?"

Leona shook her head. "I don't know. I hope not."

"Oh, Leona. You've got to go home, right now."

Isaiah in that house with her mother and Sally. Thank the Lord Raymond was gone. She fought tears. "I can't, Bertie. I can't go home."

Bertie reached for Leona like she might hug her, but Leona stepped back. "I'm so sorry," Bertie said. "I never thought—"

"Just go get your pa. Now."

While Bertie was gone, Leona helped Mrs. Pratt bathe. Afterward, Mrs. Pratt sank into a chill and a fit of coughing that brought up blood and pus. Leona piled on whatever covers she could find. The baby girl, Sarah, lay listless, her skin turning blue around the mouth, her little chest a spasm with every breath. Leona wanted to hold Sarah, but she was afraid.

Leona took the soiled bedclothes outside. She didn't know what else to do with them. She killed a chicken, plucked it, cut it up to stew. While it cooked, she cleaned. She gagged over the foul jars she carried to the privy. She began to worry about Bertie. It shouldn't take her this long to go to the Caldwells' and back.

When the chicken was done, she carried cups of broth to Mrs. Pratt and the children. She sat with them and encouraged them to drink. Mrs. Pratt refused it, and Matilda's came right back up with a fit of coughing. Carl Jr. took a little, but the twins refused to drink and curled around each other. Whenever one coughed, the other would start.

Twice, Leona heard a wagon on the road and went to the front windows and looked out, but whoever it was drove past. Bertie came driving in a little past ten. To Leona it seemed much, much later, a long day already.

"The Caldwells are sick," Bertie said. "I had to go all the way to the Robersons'. Mr. Roberson said he'd go and get Pa." Bertie sank into a kitchen chair.

"Come on," Leona said. "Let's get you to bed."

Bertie refused. She sat with the twins, bathed their faces, and gave them sips of water.

It was past noon when Mr. Pratt came riding in, his horse at full gallop. He stormed into the house but stopped dead still when he saw Leona. "Bertie? What's she doing here?"

"I asked Leona to come. I needed help, Pa. I—"

Bertie's pa pushed past her and went from room to room. When he came out of the bedroom where his wife and baby lay, his face was ashen. "Lord God," he said. He sank into a kitchen chair and covered his face with his hands. His grief, as

though he knew what was about to come, was so palpable that
Leona had to turn away. After a long while, he looked up. "You
did good, Bertie. And you, Leona. You can go on home now."

Leona shook her head. "Mr. Carl, I can't go home."

He looked stricken. "Oh. I guess you'd better not."

When Leona thought of Isaiah, her milk released and soiled
her dress. Who would take care of him? "Can you send Louvinia with a note to my aunt and my mother?"

Mr. Pratt nodded, but Bertie said, "Louvinia's sick. So are
two of her children."

"Write the note," he said. "I'll get it there."

Leona would recall the following days as a haze of endless
chores: making and applying poultices to relieve congestion, re-
moving fouled bedclothes and putrid jars of waste. Her nights
were sleepless and filled with longing and fear. Her breasts
ached whenever she heard little Sarah Pratt cry. Mrs. Pratt was
too sick to nurse her. Several times a day, Leona pressed her
milk into a basin to keep it from drying up.

One morning, she asked Mrs. Pratt if it would be all right for
her to try to nurse Sarah. "My milk's going to waste," she said.

"Oh, Leona," Mrs. Pratt said, "aren't you afraid?"

She was, but how could she not try to feed that baby? "Yes,
ma'am. But I figure if I get the influenza, it won't be from Sarah."

"All right, then." Mrs. Pratt turned away, as though she didn't
want to see.

Leona bared her breast and teased little Sarah's mouth with
her nipple. After a while Sarah latched on, sucked a little, let
go. She nuzzled Leona's breast, her mouth open, fighting for
breath. She didn't make a sound. Leona put her back in her
crib. Later, she tried feeding Sarah with a medicine dropper, like
she had fed baby kittens long ago. But the milk dribbled out of
the corner of Sarah's mouth. Leona sat and held her, rocking,
singing, the baby's breathing only a flutter.

At sunrise the next day, Luther arrived at the Pratts' house on foot. Leona went out on the porch to talk to him, but she wouldn't let him get any closer than the yard.

"You might could use these," he said, holding up some cloth bags.

Herbs. She thanked him, but she doubted that kind of medicine would do any good now, as sick as they all were. "Put them there," she said, motioning to the steps. "I'll get them after you've gone. Is Isaiah well?"

"There's sickness all up and down this road, but your folks is all right. Little Isaiah, he's fine. Don't you worry."

Isaiah is all right. Leona felt both guilty and jubilant that her own child had been spared so far, but it wasn't over yet.

Three days after Mr. Pratt came home, the baby died. Two days after that, the twins, within hours of each other. Each time, Mr. Pratt carried the burden of a dead child, wrapped in a sheet, out the back door. He buried them with the help of his hired man, Aaron, who seemed to have escaped the influenza but had lost a child himself. By the time the twins died, Leona knew what to do. She removed the bed linens, the few toys, the clothes, and took them to the barn. Mr. Pratt would burn them.

Images of the dead Pratt children often startled Leona in the midst of some mundane task. They wafted through her exhausted dreams at night. She had never seen such sadness as Mrs. Pratt's. Leona's own sadness at her father's death paled by comparison.

Nights, Leona and Mr. Pratt took turns sitting with his wife. As each took over the other's watch, they hardly spoke, but one night, in the midst of the darkest hours, Carl Pratt laid a hand on Leona's shoulder and offered to stay with his wife the rest of the night so Leona could sleep. She told him no, she was fine. When Leona finally lay down on a pallet in Bertie's room at dawn, exhausted, she found it hard to sleep. Carl and Martha Pratt and their children were good people. Why were they suffering so? Leona had not been in church in a long time, but a line from one of her father's favorite hymns played in her mind: *Sorrow and love flow mingled down.* That's the way it was in the Pratts' house. And what about her own? She'd had no more word. She wondered, too, where Walker was. Still somewhere in France? Under fire? He could be dead. She felt a strange detachment. She had no energy for pining or dreaming. She fiercely wanted to live to get home to Isaiah, to find him safe and well. That was all. That would be grace enough.

Every day that Mr. Pratt stayed well, Leona was thankful. Bertie had never been as sick as the others, and she and her father were able to help Leona. They made tea and applied poultices every few hours, day and night. Within a couple of days, Matilda's fever broke, and so did Carl Jr.'s. Even Mrs. Pratt seemed better. Leona had been at the Pratts' for two weeks. That she had not become ill seemed a miracle.

Leona and Bertie said their goodbyes at arm's length. Leona walked home, so tired she wasn't sure her legs would carry her. From far off, she saw Sally standing in the yard, holding Isaiah, as though she had known Leona was coming. Leona broke into a run. When she got to Isaiah, he reached for her, but she dared not touch him. She heated water and filled a tub in the kitchen, stripped off her clothes that reeked of sickness, scrubbed every inch of her skin, and washed her hair. She had gone to Bertie's expecting to return in hours, so she hadn't carried a change of clothes with her. She had worn Bertie's clothes while she was there, and now she put on a clean dress and carried the one she'd worn at the Pratts' to the barn. She would burn it later. She went back to the house and took her son in her arms.

19

Soaked and chilled to the bone, Walker Broom huddled under a canvas in a trench deep in the Argonne Forest near the Meuse River, a hundred yards from the barbed wire that marked the front lines. The hilly, rough terrain heavily forested with oak and pine, the wild gullies, the small streams all reminded him of home in spite of his fear and misery. His unit had slogged through mud and met the Germans at the river, but the Germans hadn't given way. Now the Americans were in retreat, waiting for orders.

At least he was out of the hell of the battle, where the living stepped over the wounded and dying and dead and kept right on with the task at hand, shoring up the walls of trenches where they threatened to give way, loading shells and reloading rifles and firing, firing, a steady barrage of percussion. Walker believed he had lost the hearing in his left ear. The tinny ringing never stopped.

So near the front, shells exploded around him and airplanes buzzed overhead like giant insects. Whose? he wondered. American? British? French? Or German? His body crawled with lice. His feet were rotting from the damp.

All the men had heard rumors that the Germans were ready to make a truce, and the war was almost over, but Walker didn't believe it. He didn't believe he would live to get home, and so he thought a lot about it. Only one letter from his mother had gotten through in the last three months. Walker supposed it was because the troops were always on the move that letters seldom caught up with them. His mother had written only the mundane news of home: his father had hired extra hands at the store, she had taken up knitting. He wondered why he had received no letters from Leona. Surely she could figure out how to write to him. Or maybe she had forgotten him by now.

By the light of a guttering candle, when he thought he wouldn't survive, he read the letters he had written and imagined what she might have written in return. He read them, too, after he had been with a French girl about Leona's age who was nothing like Leona at all.

20

Leona learned that the circus had brought influenza to Sully. Sally told her that by Sunday morning after the performance, half the troupe had been too sick to leave town.

"The sheriff quarantined them, but it was too late," Sally said. "The flu spread real fast. Not many folks escaped it like we have."

Within days, though, Sally got sick, and a few days later, Rose. Sally admitted to Leona that she had gone to town twice with Luther. "I stayed in the wagon with Isaiah. I didn't go nowhere."

"You took Isaiah?" Leona shouted. "You knew people were sick, and you took him?"

Sally rolled her head on her damp pillow. "I couldn't leave him with Rose."

"You could have stayed here. What business could you possibly have in town?" Leona fought off the image of Isaiah wrapped up like the Pratt baby and lowered into the ground. Such a small bundle. "The Pratt twins and little Sarah—they all died, Aunt Sally. You can't imagine how awful it was." Unable to breathe, Leona stood a moment longer by Sally's bed. The sickness was in her house. Sally turned her face to the wall and sobbed. Let her, Leona thought, but crying wouldn't do any good.

Yet Leona knew she was being unfair to Sally. Luther had gone to town, and he wasn't sick. Leona wondered if she had brought the sickness home, although she'd shown no signs of it.

For days she waited on her mother and her aunt, bathed and fed them, emptied jars. She moved about the house at all hours of the night, carrying the light Luther had given her.

Luther came to work as usual, but Leona talked to him only through the screen door. She told him she would be grateful if he took care of the outside chores, but he must not come into the house.

"I can't have you getting sick too," she said, but that meant there was nobody except her to take care of Isaiah. She considered asking Bertie to come, but Bertie's mother was terribly weak and devastated by the loss of her children.

Every time Leona came out of a sickroom, she scrubbed her hands and changed her apron. It seemed the right thing to do. Luther built a fire in the yard and boiled the soiled bed and bath linens in the big scalding pot they used for hogs. Leona boiled the cooking and eating utensils too. She felt Isaiah's ears a dozen times a day—a sign of fever in a baby, Luther had told her; his ears would feel hot to the touch—and every time his skin felt cool, every time he ate, slept, and laughed, Leona thanked God for sparing him.

On the seventh day, Sally's fever broke, and Leona's mother seemed better. Leona slept the night through for the first time in weeks and woke to sunlight slanting in her window. Isaiah was still asleep, which alarmed her, but he felt cool.

October now. Rain the night before had brought the chill of fall with it. Leona shivered while she dressed. She went to the kitchen, pumped water, splashed her face, walked out on the back porch, breathed in the cool, clean air. She took the change in the weather as a sign that they were finished with the sickness.

The following day, her mother's high fever returned. Her cough reminded Leona of the Pratt boys in their last hours. Leona's days and nights again became a blur. One night, sitting beside her mother's bed, she came sharply awake, frightened that she had drifted off. How could she keep going? She considered sending for Raymond, but he would be no help.

When Luther and Jesse came the next morning, Leona asked Luther to come inside. "Are you afraid?" she asked.

Luther shook his head. "I been round sickness more times

than you can count. We'll be all right. Me and Jesse, we can sleep in the kitchen. You need help in the night, we'll be close by."

Luther set Jesse to doing outside chores while he cooked and washed and cleaned. Luther wouldn't let Leona empty the jars. Her mother's waste was terrible now with bloody stool.

Leona gave her mother sips of water, tried to get her to eat, cleaned her up after she soiled or wet herself. She read aloud the Psalms and New Testament passages Rose had marked. Leona didn't know whether Rose heard or understood, but she read anyway. Leona sent Luther to town in search of Raymond, but Luther returned with bad news: a man in the railroad office had said Raymond was working up at Sadie's Gap. It might be a day or two before the man could get word to Raymond.

Let her live until he comes, Leona thought, a kind of prayer. Let her know I'm here.

Leona couldn't remember her mother holding her or expressing the least pleasure in her existence. Leona had hoped Isaiah would soften Rose, in spite of the circumstances. One day back in the summer, Leona had come upon her mother standing over his crib, patting the fussy baby and singing to him. The tune seemed familiar; was it possible her mother had sung it to her? In a little while, Isaiah quieted, and her mother came out. When she passed Leona in the hall, Leona saw in her eyes a tenderness that had always been reserved for Raymond. Rose went on to her room without a word, but Leona had seen it.

On the second night after Rose had taken a turn for the worse, Sally came in and stood by the bedside. "Let me sit with her."

Leona's lamp was the only light in the room. Sally's eyes looked like hollow sockets. How much weight had she lost, Leona wondered, and the guilt resurfaced: she had left her own family to nurse the Pratts. What a terrible risk she'd taken.

"No, Aunt Sally. If you feel like it, you can stay with her a while in the morning."

"Oh, child. I don't believe she'll be here in the morning."

Leona held up a hand. "Please. Go back to bed."

"All right. But come get me if you need me."

"I will."

Leona waited, listening to her mother's raspy breath. A shaft of moonlight crossed the ceiling and disappeared. An owl called in the nearby woods. Toward morning, Rose stirred. Opening her eyes seemed to take great effort. She hadn't spoken in two days.

"You," she whispered.

"Yes, ma'am. I'm here."

"Where's Raymond?"

Something deflated inside Leona. Her mother would want Raymond, not Leona. She held Rose's bone-thin hand. "He'll be here soon. You rest now."

Rose's grip tightened. She mumbled something Leona couldn't understand.

"What, Mama? What are you saying?"

Rose's eyes were glazed and fearful. "I'm not ready to die. I don't want to go to Hell."

If there had ever been a righteous woman, Leona thought, it must be her mother. All that Bible reading. All that praying. Leona was the one who should be afraid.

Rose started to cry, and the crying changed to coughing. Leona offered her water, but Rose refused it. Spent, she lay back. "I ruined everything, Leona. Everything. Raymond. You. Your daddy."

"Oh, Mama, no. Don't say such awful things."

Rose shook her head almost imperceptibly. "You don't know me."

Leona wanted to ask what she meant, but Rose closed her eyes. A trickle of blood appeared at the corner of her mouth. Leona wiped it away. After a while, Rose relaxed her grip on Leona's hand. The rattle in her chest was still there, and her breath came in gasps, far apart. After half an hour, her breathing quieted. More than once, Leona leaned closer to feel her mother's breath on her cheek.

So tired, but Leona couldn't sleep, not now, and yet she nodded off and woke to the brush of a hand on her shoulder.

Expecting to see Sally or Luther, Leona turned, but no one was there. The creak of a board, the wind like the echo of a fiddle's long note, and Leona came suddenly alert to the pale rectangle of the window, the light tinged with gray, the lace curtains moving. The room's shadowy corners, her father's hat still on a hook by the door, the smoky mirror over the mantel. Was she dreaming? No. Everything was still. Rose's eyes and mouth were open.

Leona had seen Mr. Pratt close his children's eyes. She closed her mother's eyes now, extinguished the light, got up, and walked to the window to open it. She didn't cry. She had lost her mother a long time ago. She looked out across the blue hills where a hint of color tinged the sky and a single star hung like an ornament, or a sign.

Leona stayed with her mother until it was good daylight. She went first to check on Isaiah and found him still sleeping. In the kitchen, Luther was up, setting coffee to boil. He turned from the stove.

"She's gone?" he said.

Leona nodded. She saw Luther, really saw him, for the first time in weeks—his stooped shoulders, the ashen cast of his skin—and she was full of love for him.

He opened his arms and Leona walked into them. "Your mama was a good woman. Maybe—" He didn't finish. He folded her in and held on for a long time before he stepped away. "Too warm in this kitchen," he said. He wiped his eyes on his shirtsleeve. "I sent Jesse to the barn to do the milking. What can I do?"

"Go ask Mr. Pratt to come as soon as he can and bring his mule." For her father's burial it had taken two mules to pull the wagon up the long hill to the Pinson graveyard.

"All right." Luther started for the door, but Leona said, "Eat something before you go."

"I ain't hungry. If Jesse comes up to the house, tell him where I'm gone."

Leona drank her coffee before she woke Sally and told her that Rose had died. Sally turned away and made no move to get out of bed. Leona bathed her mother's body, dressed her in her best church dress, and covered her with an old quilt they could spare. Mr. Pratt came with his mule and a double harness. He and Luther laid Rose in the back of the wagon. There was no pine box. The bodies of influenza victims had to be buried quickly and without ceremony.

It was nearly ten o'clock when they set out. Sally stayed home. Mr. Pratt drove, Leona and the baby beside him. Luther rode in the back of the wagon with Rose's body, and Jesse walked behind. Luther had suggested that Jesse come along.

"He's strong," Luther had reminded Leona. "We gon' need him."

Clouds were gathering, but for the present, the autumn sun cast golden light over the empty fields, the dried cornstalks, the cotton mostly stubble except for a few strands here and there. Along the roadside, a yellow carpet of coreopsis, and the trees—reds of every shade, pink to garnet to purple, fiery oranges and yellows—and beyond the fields, the hills clothed in a dazzling patchwork of color. Leona's mind strayed beyond those hills. Out in the world, all that living and dying, and somewhere, far away in France, either on the march or in a trench with shells falling all around, was Walker. She felt ashamed to think of him, but she couldn't help it.

The mules struggled up the long hill. The wagon creaked and swayed. Leona looked back at Luther, bracing her mother's body now with his own so it wouldn't shift and slide. Luther nodded to Leona, and she heard his voice from long ago: *Everything will be all right, little girl. You'll see.*

It took a long time for the men to dig the grave next to her father's. Leona sat in the wagon with the baby and watched. She examined her heart for feelings for her mother—love, sorrow, even anger—and found none of those things. What was wrong with her?

The sun disappeared behind the clouds, and she felt the chill. When the men were done, Leona climbed down with Isaiah and stood beside the grave while the men lowered her mother into the ground. How small her mother's shrouded body looked, lying at the bottom of that rough red hole. Finally, tears.

"Should we pray?" Mr. Pratt said.

She hadn't thought about it: no preacher, no last words. It seemed the least she could do, a prayer for her mother, but she couldn't do it. "Could you say one, Mr. Carl?" She bowed her head but didn't close her eyes while he mumbled the Lord's Prayer.

By the time the men filled the grave with the red earth, rain had begun to fall. Leona stayed by the grave while Luther loaded the shovels in the back of the wagon. He came and stood beside her. "You done all you could. Don't be troubled by it."

He put his arm around her and led her away from the grave toward the wagon where Mr. Pratt already sat, his shoulders hunched and shaking. Leona ached for all that poor man had lost. Luther helped Leona and the baby onto the wagon seat. He climbed in the back, and this time, Jesse rode with him.

Back at the house, Leona gathered up her mother's night-clothes and the sheets and quilts and pillows and carried them outside to burn. Luther helped her drag the mattress out to air. They scrubbed the furniture, the walls, and the floor with lye. When they were done, hardly a trace of Rose Pinson remained.

That night, after Isaiah was asleep, Leona went through the wooden box her mother had kept on her dressing table. Inside it, a string of pearls; an amethyst ring that had belonged to Rose's mother; a couple of monogrammed handkerchiefs; the watch Rose had worn pinned to her dress; a faded picture of Rose and Herbert when they were young. Creased down the middle from top to bottom, the photograph had been folded in half. Leona was stunned by her likeness to Rose: the same thick blond hair and light eyes, the full mouth. In the picture Rose wears a high-necked, light-colored blouse embellished with lace and a dark skirt, her small waist accented with a wide ribbon. Her hair is pulled back into a bun, but tendrils have escaped around her face. Herbert wears a coat but no tie. He looks straight at the camera, his expression unreadable, and Rose gazes off to one side, as though she were looking beyond the photographer. Leona turned the picture over, but nothing was written on the back. She tucked it inside her mother's Bible to keep.

She would keep the watch for herself and give the pearls to Sally. What would Raymond want? The ring, in case he ever married? Leona put the jewelry back in the case and set it on her dresser. She sat near the spirit lamp and opened Rose's Bible. Nearly every page had underlining and notes in the margins in her mother's handwriting. In the center of the book, she found pages of names, births and deaths and marriages going back three generations, the most recent in her mother's handwriting, the rest, in someone else's. There was Raymond's name, and Leona's. Even Isaiah's. It moved Leona to see her son's name recorded there. It meant her mother had cared enough to acknowledge him. Near the bottom of the page, an entry had been marked through with black ink. Whoever had done it bore down so hard that the pen had torn through the paper. Leona held the page up to the lamp, but she couldn't make out any letters. A mistake, she thought. Rose—or someone else—must have repeated an entry or misspelled the name. But why would anyone be so determined to blot out a name? Why not simply cross it out?

Dismay ran through Leona like a spark. An image surfaced, more dream than memory: around the time Leona was three years old, Rose had taken to her bed. One day, Leona went into her room without knocking, which she had been taught to do, but she'd pulled some daisies from the yard and wanted to give them to Rose. Rose was sitting at her dressing table, cutting off her hair. It lay like little clouds at her feet. She yelled at Leona to get out, and Leona ran to Varna, crying, and told her. Varna had gone in to Rose, and Leona had stood outside the closed door and heard her mother's crying. Leona had always wondered if she was the reason for her mother's sadness.

What if there had been another child who had died at birth? What if her mother had recorded the child's name in her Bible but couldn't bear to read it? Such a loss might explain her mother's behavior from that time on.

Leona was shaken by the memory, and Rose's words rang in Leona's mind: *I ruined everything.* Leona's mind swirled with questions, and no one remained to answer them.

Except Raymond.

The thought of her brother sent chills through her. He would come home soon, and she would be the one to tell him their mother had died. He was bound to blame Leona. And why shouldn't he?

She was too tired to think anymore, but every time she closed her eyes, she felt the grip of her mother's hand and saw her fevered, frightened eyes.

21

When Leona woke, bright sunlight streamed through the window. Isaiah wasn't in his crib. He had never climbed out of it, but she supposed he could. She got up and put on her wrapper and went looking for him.

She found him sitting on the parlor floor with Luther, playing with a little wooden car. Sally curled up on the settee, bundled in a quilt even though there was a fire going and the room was warm.

Luther said, "We decided you gon' sleep forever." He sent the car toward the baby, and Isaiah reached for it and laughed.

"Where'd he get that toy?" Leona said.

Luther picked it up and spun the wheels. They turned smoothly. "Carved it. Remember how your daddy used to make them little cars and animals? Mine ain't as good as his, but it'll do."

Leona was in the kitchen alone that afternoon when Raymond came riding into the yard. Leaving the horse untied, he thundered up the back steps and into the house. He was winded and wild looking. "I got word that Mama's sick. How is she? Is she all right?"

Leona's hand went to her throat. She shook her head.

"Leona? I said how is she?"

She braced herself against the sink. "Mama's gone."

"Gone? What do you mean, she's gone?"

"She got the influenza, Ray. She died yesterday morning. We tried—"

"Oh Jesus Lord." He dropped into a chair like he'd been punched.

"She was fine when I got home from the Pratts', and then she and Sally both—"

Raymond looked up. "What were you doing at the Pratts'?"

Dread settled in her stomach like a stone. She hadn't meant to tell him she'd nursed the Pratts. "They were sick. Bertie needed help. I didn't know they had the flu when I went."

"So you brought it home." Raymond came up out of his chair. Leona backed away.

"Raymond, don't you lay a hand on her." Sally stood in the doorway, her hair down, her face aged ten years since she got sick. "I went to town. I got sick first. If it's anybody's fault, it's mine. You want to hit somebody, hit me."

He looked at Sally with such contempt Leona thought he might strike her. Instead, he stormed out the back door, crossed the back lot, and disappeared into the woods.

Suppertime came and no Raymond. Leona worried about what he might do when he got back, but when he came in after dark, he walked past her in the kitchen, went into Rose's room, and shut the door. She heard him weeping.

Before she went to bed, she tapped on the door. When he didn't answer, she opened it. The room was dark. Raymond sat on the floor by the hearth. He didn't look at her. She couldn't help pitying him. Their mother might have been the only person in the world Raymond loved. When Leona approached, he wrapped his arms around her knees and buried his face in her dress.

She stroked his hair. "Mama loved you more than me, Ray. You know she did. She never even tried to hide it. She knew you loved her so very much. It's all right. It is."

He let her go. "Get out of here. Leave me alone."

Raymond wandered the house and the land and slept in their mother's room. Leona expected his anger to explode again. When it didn't, his silence frightened her more than the anger.

On the third morning, he came in the kitchen where she was cooking breakfast and sank wearily into a chair. She stole a glance at his tangled, filthy hair and beard, his red-rimmed eyes. The odor of whiskey exuded from his skin and clothes.

She offered him some eggs and biscuits.

"Not hungry."

"You need to eat."

He looked at the plate. "Well. Maybe a little."

The baby was still asleep, and Sally hadn't yet emerged from her room. This might be Leona's best chance to talk to Raymond alone. She didn't know how he would react if she brought their mother up, but there was only one way to find out.

She refilled his coffee cup, poured one for herself, and sat down across from him. "I want to ask you something. What do you remember about Mama when we were little?"

He kept right on eating, didn't look up.

"Ray?"

"What, Leona?" His mouth full.

"I asked you what you remember about Mama. I've been thinking about her, trying to remember things."

He shrugged. "Same as you, I guess."

"But you're older. You must remember more than I do." She got up and fetched her mother's Bible and put it on the table beside him. She showed him the family records pages. "Look at this." She pointed to the scratched-out name.

He took a swallow of coffee, belched. "Somebody marked something out."

"Yes, but it's on a page of birth names and dates. Look, there's your name. And mine. Isaiah's is on the next page. And then there's this line that's been crossed out. See how the pen broke through the paper?"

"Somebody made a mistake, it looks like."

"Maybe. But I've been wondering if Mama had another baby after me."

Raymond examined the page from both sides. He closed the Bible and laid it on the table. A muscle twitched in his jaw. "Maybe you ought to have asked her."

"I don't remember a little baby. You would think I'd remember something like that. But I know she took to her bed for a long time when I was about three years old. She was sick and sad, and I thought I was the cause of it. After I saw that ink blot, I started thinking maybe she had another child, and it died. It would explain why Mama was unhappy."

He set his coffee cup down so hard it shook the table. "What do you want to know for? It won't bring her back."

"I just— I've always thought something happened when I was born, or after, that changed her. I wondered if you knew more. That's all." She ran a finger over the page. "If this is a child's name, why would somebody want to make sure it could never be read? Maybe Mama couldn't bear to read it because it made her too sad. Or maybe there was—"

Raymond pushed back from the table and stood, nearly knocking over his chair. "Damn it, Leona. Let it alone. What if there was a goddamn child, alive or dead? What difference does it make?" He braced himself against the table's edge. "Did it ever occur to you that she was unhappy about something else?"

"What do you mean?"

"You ever thought about how light Jesse Biggs's skin is? Luther is lighter than most, but Jesse had a white daddy, sure as the world. I wonder who that might have been."

The idea was so ridiculous she almost laughed. "You don't think Father—"

"It's exactly what I think. And I ain't talking about it anymore." He took the plate of eggs and his coffee and went back to their mother's room and slammed the door.

Growing up, she had heard the story about her grandfather William taking Luther into his own house. Raymond must have heard it too. At some point, Leona had understood why her grandfather might do such a thing, but nobody ever talked about it. If Luther were her grandfather's son—her father's half-brother—it would account for Luther's color. Jesse's too. But her father and Varna? No. She would put that thought right out of her mind.

But if there had been a child who died, might that explain the blotted-out name and her mother's strangeness? The death of a child, Leona thought, must be the worst grief in the world.

What would it have been like to carry Isaiah inside her for all those months and give birth to him, only to lose him? Maybe Rose had been so deeply affected that she couldn't bear to see the name written there.

Raymond was right about one thing: If Leona had seen the Bible entries sooner, she could have asked her mother. But Leona had never seen the family records, not until now, when it was too late.

22

Raymond lay on his mother's bare mattress and imagined what had happened to her. Leona must have allowed Rose to suffer and die, and then Leona had erased every trace: her clothes, her quilts, the hand-crocheted doilies on the top of her bureau. Everything. Even her scent was gone. Only the smell of lye, the stripped bed, the bleached floor, and the cold hearth were left.

He blamed Leona, but he was the one who had gone off and left his mother. He hadn't even come to see her like he'd promised, not once since he'd been gone. He wondered if she called out for him as she was dying.

He had heard stories about the influenza. He imagined his mother lying in her own filth, her body wasted. He dozed and fought to keep his eyes open, and it was then, in the twilight between waking and sleeping, that he felt the warmth and pressure of a hand on his back. Rose was there. He dared not move; he hardly breathed for fear of sending her away. He remembered how he used to wake with terrible dreams when he was little, before Leona was born, and his mother would lie down beside him and rub his back until he fell sleep. He hadn't slept since he came home and found her dead and buried. He lay still and felt the weight of grief slip from his chest. His eyelids grew heavy, and his breathing deepened.

He woke at dawn, stiff, cold, and damp with sweat, his mother's presence gone. He slipped out of the house without telling anybody he was leaving. Not that they would care.

Sober, he had to admit Leona's curiosity the night before had piqued his own. He didn't know what to make of the crossed-out name, but he remembered clearly that when he was eight years old, their mother had given birth to a baby that died.

He remembered hearing her moans and cries all night long and hearing that little baby mewl like a weak kitten. At dawn, Varna, not his father, had come to his room and told him that the baby was dead. Raymond had begged to see his mother, but his father wouldn't let him. Leona had been right about one thing. Rose had taken to her bed for a long time after that, and she was never the same.

It was a hard memory, but it was his memory, by damn, and it had nothing to do with Leona. Rose and Herbert must have given the dead child a name. If that was the name in the Bible, why would somebody mark it out with such vigor that the pen tore the page? It looked like somebody had done it in a fit of anger. He had not thought about his childhood in a long time. He would rather not think about it now, but the look on Leona's face when he had suggested that Jesse was their father's child— that had been worth it.

He saddled Belle and rode out, stopping to look back to see the place, his place—the house, the barn, the orchards and fields beyond shrouded in the mist of early morning. He would come back and claim it. Soon, he told himself. Soon.

He met Luther and Jesse on the road. Luther hailed him. "Mr. Raymond. You going back to town?"

"I am. I can't stay at the house." Why was it that Luther got under Raymond's skin so? And that boy of his standing there, looking at the ground like an idiot.

"I'm sorry about your mama," Luther said. "Miss Leona done all she could."

"Maybe she did, but it wasn't enough, was it?" Raymond nudged Belle with his boots, and she skittered sideways. Jesse stepped off into the ditch. Luther didn't move.

"Take good care of the place, Luther." Raymond gave the reins a tug, and Belle reared her head and took off at a gallop. "I'll be back," he called out. "You can bet on it," he said under his breath. He slowed Belle a little and settled in with the rhythm of the horse. He breathed easier away from that place, haunted now by the ghosts of his mother and his father.

23

Raymond returned to the cheap room in a boarding house in Sully and went back to work on the rails. He tried not to picture his mother dead. As for the others—his sister, her boy, his aunt—he wouldn't think of them. Instead, he turned his mind to Tobe Sanders. Raymond's father might as well have given that hundred acres to Tobe. That was Pinson land going way back. It occurred to Raymond that maybe he could run Tobe off, and he began a campaign to do so. Raymond liked that word, *campaign*. Just like in the army.

He kept an eye on Tobe's place. One Saturday back in the spring, he had ridden right into the yard. One of Tobe's younger sons, a redheaded, freckle-faced boy who looked to be eight or nine, was playing with a ball and stick, and Raymond started kicking the ball around with him. They were making a racket.

Tobe's wife came out on the porch. "Henry? You come away from there this minute!"

Looking sheepish, the boy went to his mother.

Raymond said, "Evening, Mrs. Sanders."

She swatted her son on his rear. "Get in the house!" The boy went only as far as the porch. His mother ran toward the barn. "Tobe? Raymond Pinson's out here!"

Tobe came out, carrying a rifle. "Get off my place, Raymond!"

Raymond was already walking backward, but Tobe kept coming at him until he was so close Raymond could see one of Tobe's eyes twitching. Tobe raised the rifle and aimed it at Raymond.

Raymond held up his hands. "All right, Mr. Tobe. I'm going. I was just passing by." He couldn't wipe the grin off his face.

After work, Raymond's whole body ached. By November there

were days when, even with the exertion of the handcar, the cold numbed his feet and hands. It was hog killing time. He wondered how the women would manage without him. Sometimes he rode out to the bootlegger's and bought himself a bottle. He started taking a flask with him on the rails; he liked the way the liquor warmed him from the inside. Pretty soon, he was taking a nip first thing out of bed to get his blood going and throughout the day, whether he was on the rails or not. The bottle never lasted long enough to blot out his sister and her bastard child, his mother in the ground now, his father's face, half blown away. His resolve not to think about them wasn't working.

The day Raymond ran the handcar into the side of a wagon and injured a farmer, his wife, and their son, he'd had more than a nip or two. The railroad fired him straightaway, but he stayed on in town. The weekend after he lost his job, he holed up in his room, first drunk, then hungover.

On Monday, he slept until late in the afternoon and woke up with a headache, but hungry. He decided he would walk up to the square. Halfway there, he could hear shouts, and was that music? He met Jack Parker, one of the Ridge Rider boys.

Jack grabbed Raymond by his lapels. "You heard? The war's over! The Germans surrendered!"

"Naw!"

"No kidding," Jack yelled, moving on. "The news came in over the wire this morning!"

Raymond walked on, his head pounding. When he saw the square thronged with people hugging, crying, singing, waving flags, he had to believe it was true. Somebody had pulled down the faded red, white, and blue bunting on the courthouse, and a line of people snaked their way through the crowds with it, dancing and shouting, "It's over! The war's over!" He heard gunshots, some fools firing guns into the air. People gathered around a big bonfire in the middle of the square. Somebody had tacked a notice to a post outside the hardware store. ARMISTICE SIGNED, it said in big black letters. NOVEMBER 11, 1918.

The war had come and gone, and Raymond had not been part of it.

He crossed to the other side of the street and stepped around the corner by the drugstore. He stood with his back pressed against the cold brick wall, breathing hard, a ringing in his ears. He took a swallow from his flask. The whiskey burned good all the way down. A second big swallow. He capped the flask, put it back in his pocket, and climbed the stairs to the balcony over the drugstore. The balcony was crowded too. Looking out across the square, he could see more people coming in by the wagonload.

He went down the stairs and walked to the hardware store to buy a tin of kerosene, but nobody was tending the store. He took a tin and went back out on the street. He needed to meet up with some of his cronies. He could stand a little cheering up. He walked up and down the raised sidewalks. From the posters in the store windows, Uncle Sam still pointed his bony finger straight at Raymond: *I Want You.*

Then why the hell hadn't they let him go?

The full moon had risen when he met up with some younger fellows standing on the northwest corner of the square by the bank, jostling each other, passing a bottle and not caring who saw. One of them, a fellow named Silas Warren who lived with his widowed mother down the road from Raymond's place, elbowed him. Silas pointed up the muddy street. "Look yonder."

"What?" Raymond said.

"What?" the others echoed.

Raymond followed the pointing finger and saw Jesse Biggs coming toward them. Jesse, too, in town for the big party.

"Look at that boy strut," Silas said. "Ain't he something?" Silas jumped about, arms dangling. He made a sound like a hoarse dog barking.

Raymond said, "You ever notice how light his skin is? You reckon his mama's a whore?"

The boys all hooted, but Raymond had given the color of Jesse's skin serious thought. Varna Biggs was black as a moonless night. An image of Raymond's father with Varna formed in his mind: Herbert's pale, lean body atop Varna's black, full one. The thought made Raymond shudder, but in an intoxicating way. Luther was an ignorant fool. Couldn't he see what had been right in front of his face every day of Jesse's life?

By the time Raymond got back to the boarding house, the cold air had cleared his head. He could still hear shouts and music from the town square, those fools, celebrating in the streets over a war so far away it was not measurable except in terms of lives.

Raymond knew one thing: he had to get out of Sully. He owed his landlady three weeks' rent, and he owed Frankie Owen the two dollars Frankie had lent him a few days ago. Raymond's flask was empty. He had a few coins left, enough for a bottle. He needed a drink bad.

Near midnight, he folded his white hood and robe and packed them at the bottom of his satchel, under his clothes. He considered leaving his father's pipe collection behind—he had brought it from the house to spite Leona—but he decided maybe he could sell them. He blew out the lamp and slipped down the stairs and out the door.

The full moon was high in the sky now, the town quiet, only a random light in an occasional window. Raymond spurred the horse up the road toward the bootlegger's place and the honky-tonk at Sadie's Gap. He didn't know where he would go after that. Maybe to the bootlegger's daughter, but he had gotten a little rough with her a few weeks back, and she'd kicked him out. He doubted she would be happy to have him turn up on her doorstep in the darkest hour of the night. On the other hand, she might have a change of heart if he showed up with whiskey and worked his charms on her.

No matter. He knew folks. He would find a place. Anything was better than staying here.

24

Monday at dusk, Leona sat rocking Isaiah. He had the croup, his dry cough like a bark. Now and then, she looked out the front window. She had sent Luther to town to buy Vicks salve and cherry syrup. He had left their place at noon to go by his house and get Jesse. "We'll be back before dark," he had said.

When night fell, Leona stopped watching for Luther, more worried than irked. It wasn't like him not to keep his word.

She would try steam and add juniper berries to the water, a remedy Luther had taught her. She had started going to the woods with him to collect herbs when she was a little girl, but here was the juniper, right outside the door. She snipped branches from the tall shrub at the corner of the house, stripped off the berries, and added them to pans of water boiling on the stove.

She and Sally spent most of the night under a makeshift tent in the kitchen, taking turns holding Isaiah, keeping the steam going. A little after seven o'clock the next morning, she walked to Bertie's to see if they had any Vicks or cherry syrup she could borrow.

Bertie came running out. "Leona! I was about to come and tell you. The armistice is signed! The war's over, and you know what that means. Our boys will be coming home!"

Leona stumbled, stopped. "What did you say?"

"You heard me! The war's over! Aren't you glad?"

Leona laughed. "Yes. Oh Lord, yes! I'm glad."

"Pa heard about the armistice in town yesterday. He got home too late last night for me to come and tell you. He said there was a big celebration with a bonfire and—"

Leona stopped listening, caught up in a muddle of joy and

fear. He'll come home. What will happen then? She wiped her eyes with the hem of her dress. Bertie prattled on.

"Bertie, listen. Isaiah has the croup. I figured you might have some Vicks or cherry syrup."

If Bertie noticed the tears, she didn't let on. "I guess we do. Let me look." Bertie did a little dance. "Aren't you excited though?"

"I am." If only Bertie knew. If only Leona could tell her.

She followed Bertie into the house and waited in the kitchen. Leona could hardly keep still. Coming home.

Bertie came out with a jar of salve. "I found the Vicks, but we don't have any cough syrup." Her face clouded over. "I guess we used it all."

The influenza. It hadn't occurred to Leona that talk of coughs and remedies would bring back that awful time.

"I'm so sorry. I shouldn't have asked."

"Of course you should. I'd do anything for Isaiah. You know that."

Leona took the jar. "I have to get back. Thank you."

She pulled her coat tight around her and hurried down the muddy drive, bending against the wind coming out of the southwest. It started to rain. By the time she got to the house, she was soaked and freezing, but she put the Vicks on Isaiah's chest and wrapped him with a soft band of cloth before she changed her clothes. She sat by the fire, rocking the baby, her pulse rapid as a bird's. There was too much to think about. The war over. Walker coming home. After a while, Isaiah's cough eased. He nursed a little and fell asleep. She put him in his crib.

She told her aunt about the end of the war. Sally turned from the stove. "You mean it?"

"Bertie swears it's true. There was a big celebration in town last night."

"Praise the Lord!" Sally beamed, but abruptly her expression changed. She shook her head. "All those poor boys, dead and gone. I can't hardly imagine it." She brought a handkerchief out of her apron pocket and dabbed at her eyes. "The rest will be coming home now, I guess."

"They will," Leona said, keeping her tone matter of fact. She headed out into the cold to do the chores. She would go to town as soon as Isaiah was better. She wanted to hear for herself about the end of the war. Maybe she would hear something about Walker Broom.

25

Isaiah slept through Tuesday night without coughing. Early Wednesday morning, Leona dressed him in his warmest flannel gown that drew together at the hem. She tied it securely, even though Isaiah didn't like having his feet covered these days. She felt guilty, taking the baby out into the cold, but she couldn't bear to wait another minute.

When she told Sally she was going to town, Sally looked peeved. "What on earth for?"

"We need some things."

"We don't need nothing that's worth going out in this weather. And you ain't taking that baby."

"I may be gone all day. I can't leave him here."

"Leona, you have lost your mind."

Overnight, a heavy frost had turned the landscape silvery white. Leona hitched the mule to the wagon, drove it near the house, and tied up to a fence post. Inside, she warmed her hands and drank coffee. Sally slammed a pot on the stove, but Leona ignored her. She put two wrapped, leftover biscuits in one pocket of her coat, two dollars out of the kitchen jar in the other. She wrapped Isaiah in two flannel blankets, settled him snug against her body in a sling, and put her coat back on. Isaiah squirmed and fussed, but it was the only way she could carry him and drive.

Sally brought out two quilts. "You're determined to go, take these. Wrap up good."

Settled in the wagon, Leona took a deep breath and let it out as frost on the cold air. She whipped the mule and drove out of the lot and down the rutted lane.

Once she was out on Pinson Road, it was easier going. Her cheeks reddened in the wind, her nose ran, but she breathed in the cold air like freedom. When she passed the turnoff to

Hawks Creek, she yearned to show Isaiah that place. She had gone back a few times, sat in the ruins, and carried on imaginary conversations with Walker, whose name she still wouldn't speak aloud even in that solitary place. She had asked him what the war was like, what he ate, what the shells falling around him sounded like. If he was afraid. If he missed her. She listened as though she could hear him answer. *The war isn't a friendly place. We get rations twice a day. The shells sound like fireworks on the Fourth of July. No, I'm not afraid.* The last question—if he missed her— she had also imagined an answer for. *Yes,* he would say. *Yes, I miss you terribly.*

By nine o'clock, she was nearing Sully. The baby had slept the whole way, but as they approached town, he woke and struggled against the sling. Her shoulders ached from his weight. The sun had come out, and it was warmer. She stopped the wagon by the side of the road, nursed him, and drove on into town.

Bunting drooped from the courthouse pillars and the rutted roads were littered with trash. People were already out on the streets. Walker's father, Hiram Broom, crossed in front of the wagon and went in the front door of his mercantile store. Leona wanted to walk up to him and say, "This is your grandson. I'm his mother." She doubted he would believe her.

She tied up the wagon around the corner from the square, near Harrington's grocery. She gathered her windblown hair into a bun. Tossing aside the quilt, she climbed down with the baby. As she was hitching the mule to the post, somebody said her name. She turned. Fay Haney stood on the raised sidewalk, looking down at her. Leona and Fay had been neighbors all their lives, until the Haneys had moved to town a couple of years ago.

"Leona, I—" Fay paused, blushing. "How are you? I mean, are you okay? I wanted to come out to the house, or something, but I—"

"It's all right, Fay. Really, it is." Leona looped the rope around one more time, picked up her skirt, and climbed the high steps to the sidewalk. "I'm in something of a hurry, but would you like to see my little boy?" Leona folded back the shawl. "His name's Isaiah." Isaiah was awake and frowning, as though he weren't at all sure about Fay.

She looked at the baby. "He's a fine boy."

"Yes, he is. Come see me when you can. I don't get out much."

She left Fay standing on the sidewalk, looking bewildered. Why was it hard for people to grasp that Leona's life had changed, but she had not, at least not in the ways people thought?

The bell on Harrington's door jangled as Leona stepped inside. She had always loved this place—the high tin ceiling, the polished wood counters, the smell of coffee, the candy bin where her father used to buy her peppermint sticks and lollipops.

Mr. Harrington looked up, adjusted his eyeglasses, looked away. A friend of her father's, he had known Leona all her life. She gathered up what she needed—coffee, sugar, cornmeal, flour. She bought two candy sticks, one for Sally and one to share with Isaiah. He would have his first taste of peppermint. Mr. Harrington took her money, put the groceries in a cardboard box, and turned away. Bewildered by his rude behavior, she was wondering how she would manage to get the box to the wagon when Will Harrington, a year younger than Leona, came out of the back of the store.

Will said, "Let me take that out for you." He picked up the box and nodded toward the door. "If you'll open it, Leona."

She held the door open. "The wagon is around the corner."

Will hefted the box into the wagon bed and dusted off his hands. He chucked Isaiah's chin. "Good-looking boy you got there."

"Thank you." Yes, thank you. "So the war is over," she said.

He had a brother serving in France. "Yes! Can you believe it? There was quite a party in town."

"Your brother will be coming home?"

"He will, but we don't know when. He was wounded, you

know. We only found out a month ago. He's been in a hospital in England for a while, but he'll be all right." Will lowered his voice. "I think that's why Pa is so out of sorts. He's been mighty worried."

Leona figured that wasn't the case, but she said, "I'm sure it's been hard for all of you." She wanted to ask who else was wounded, who wouldn't be coming home, but Will turned and walked back in the store.

She wondered if Raymond was in town Monday night for the celebration. Knowing Raymond, he would feel cheated that the war was over. Things never worked out the way Raymond wanted. Leona figured he was out working on the rails today, so she wasn't nervous about running into him. But he had seemed so undone by their mother's death that she couldn't help feeling sorry for him. She decided to walk the three blocks to the rail yard. She would ask after him and leave a message.

Leona didn't know the man behind the desk in the tiny office. He stood. "Yes, ma'am? Can I help you?"

"I'm looking for my brother. He's been working for the railroad about six months as a rail inspector. His name is Raymond Pinson."

The man didn't offer her a seat. "Did you check over at Mrs. Barksdale's boarding house? That's where Raymond stays. I saw him in town the other day. I don't think he's moved on yet."

"Moved on?"

"Raymond had an accident on the handcar. Some folks got hurt. He was drinking on the job." The man crossed his arms. "There weren't no choice but to fire him."

Fired. "Oh. All right, then." Leona hurried out of the office.

She had passed the boarding house on her way to the rail yard. What if Raymond had been watching out the window and had seen her? As she approached the house, her pulse raced.

A tall gray-haired woman answered the door. When Leona asked for Raymond Pinson, the woman's face flushed red. "He's gone. Owes me three weeks' rent." As Leona walked away, the woman yelled, "You tell him to bring me my money!"

The sun was still high when Leona drove into the yard. She was almost to the barn when something made her look toward the house. Raymond stood on the back porch steps, smoking a cigarette. Leona broke out in a sweat. She climbed down from the wagon, opened the barn doors, and drove inside. She unhitched the mule and gave him water. She needed time to collect herself, but Isaiah started to cry. She took him out of the sling and hefted him onto her hip. She would come back for the groceries. She crossed the yard toward her brother.

Raymond dropped his cigarette and crushed it with his shoe. "Where you been?"

"I went to town for groceries. What are you doing here?"

"I thought it was time to pay the place a visit, see how y'all are keeping it up." He nodded toward the back lot and the fields beyond. "Garden ain't plowed under. The hog pen needs cleaning out. There's fences down. The place is a mess."

"We're doing the best we can."

Raymond sat on the steps, rolled another cigarette, lit it, inhaled. His hands were steady.

She felt small in his presence, standing at the bottom of the steps, holding her baby son. This was not the broken, sad Raymond who had left the house more than a month ago. "You're so worried about the place?" she said. "Maybe since you're here, we could slaughter a hog. It's past time we did."

"Don't know if I'll stay around long enough for that." He reached in his pocket and took out a roll of bills.

She looked at the money like it was poison. "Where'd you get that much money?"

"Let's say I got me some luck." He put the roll of bills back in his pocket.

She climbed past him on the steps and looked down at him. "I went to the railroad office. The man told me you got fired. He said there'd been an accident on the rails, and you were drunk. The landlady said you left without paying your rent. Now you show up here with a pocket full of money. Who did you rob?"

He scowled. "I didn't rob nobody. I had it coming."

"I'm sure you did." She crossed the porch, turned. "You're right, you know. The place is in bad shape. You want us to lose everything?"

He got up and stepped between her and the kitchen door. "I won't lose this place. It's mine."

Awake now, Isaiah reached for Raymond. He tilted the baby's chin up and looked at him until Isaiah twisted away. Then Raymond went ahead of them into the kitchen, letting the door slam behind him.

Leona didn't bother with eating supper. She took Isaiah to her room and locked the door. She fell asleep as soon as the baby did. When she woke, it was dark outside. She remembered the box of groceries, still in the barn. There was nothing that would ruin. Even if there were, she wouldn't venture outside that room as long as she could hear her brother roaming the house.

To Leona's amazement, over the next few days, Raymond mended fences and pulled in enough hay to last a while. He stayed sober. An uneasy peace settled over the house that kept Leona wary. She fretted over what he had said about the place being his. Their father had made no will. She supposed it was right that Raymond should get the farm, but it was her home, too—hers, Isaiah's, and Sally's. Sally had no other place to go. None of them did.

Early December now, and they still had not butchered a hog. Every year they sold some of the meat. The rest carried them through the winter. Leona pressed Raymond to get it done.

"Oh, all right. But Luther and Jesse ain't worth much. We need more help."

"We can hire some other colored men," Leona said.

"We ain't hiring nobody. You want it done, do what I say. Ask the Pratts and the Caldwells if they can come Saturday. They won't turn you down."

26

Saturday came, a bright, cold morning. Just after dawn, Leona carried hot coffee out to Raymond, where he was stacking wood for the scalding fire. Leona's old coat was no match for the cold. She turned to go back inside.

"Where you going?" Raymond wiped sweat on his coat sleeve in spite of the cold. "I need you out here."

"What for?"

"You'll see."

She stayed, pacing the yard to try to stay warm.

Luther and Jesse came to help with the butchering. Jesse's strength would be a handy thing. Mr. Carl Pratt and Mr. Royce Caldwell came, too, with their wives, who went up to the kitchen to help Sally. Ever since Leona was big enough to stand on a stool without falling, she had helped her mother in the kitchen with the meat. Not until two years ago had she seen the kill. She had not flinched when her father put his .22 rifle against the pig's snout and angled the shot so it would spare the brains. He'd had a fondness for the brains, cooked in an iron skillet and served up with scrambled eggs.

When her father butchered hogs, Raymond had mainly stood around. Today, he bossed everybody like he knew what he was doing. Mr. Carl and Mr. Royce exchanged looks. They had been butchering hogs since before Raymond was born.

Raymond, Luther, and Jesse rolled the heavy black iron scalding pot out of the shed and Luther filled it with water. Raymond lit the fire. It took all the men to rope the hog, drag it out of the lot, wrestle it to the spot where it would die, and tie it down. Raymond took their father's deer rifle, aimed it at the animal's head, and fired. When Leona looked down at her blood- and brains-spattered coat, the earth gave way under her feet. She grasped for something to hold on to, but there was only air. She ran behind the barn and threw up.

"Leona!" Raymond shouted. "Get back here!"

Bile burned her throat. She walked back in time to see the men lower the hog into the vat of boiling water. After the scalding, they tied its back legs and hung it from a sturdy tree limb. Mr. Pratt and Mr. Caldwell scraped at the bristles. Luther poured more boiling water over the carcass, and the white men kept scraping. When they deemed the carcass clean, Luther slid a pan under it. Raymond took a long knife out of a sheath tied to his belt. He pointed the knife at Leona.

"You do it, sister."

"No." She looked past him, toward the house where Isaiah was.

"Come on, Leona. It's time you learned."

"I said no." She felt sick again.

Mr. Pratt reached for the knife. "I'll do it."

Raymond glowered. "No, sir. I will." With one smooth stroke, he slit the hog's throat. Blood spurted into the vat.

When Leona started toward the house, Raymond called after her. "Hey! You ain't done yet!"

She ran, expecting him to follow her, but he didn't. Maybe the presence of the other men stopped him.

By the time she got to the back steps, she heard Isaiah crying and felt her milk release. She looked back at the men gathered around the carcass, and Jesse, sitting on his haunches off to himself, all of them waiting for the blood to drain out so they could carve it up. She heard Raymond's voice, holding forth about something.

27

After the hog slaughter, Raymond fell back into his old ways: he would stay home a few days and then he would go off on a bender. When he was home and sober, he worked all day and went to bed early, so Leona couldn't complain.

As Christmas approached, she wished for a tree for Isaiah; not that he would remember, but he was old enough to notice the shiny baubles. She worried it wouldn't be right to celebrate, so soon after her mother's death. She talked to Sally about it, and Sally said, "I don't know about your mama, but I think it's what your daddy would want, for sure."

They had not had a Christmas tree since her father died. He had always gone out into the woods and cut down a big cedar tree and brought it home. Sally couldn't help, and Leona wouldn't ask Raymond, so on Christmas Eve, she went to the woods alone and cut down a small cedar and dragged it home. By the time she got back to the house, she was freezing and her nose was streaming and her back ached. She leaned the tree against the porch steps and stood back. It was a little thin on one side but fine otherwise. It was right pretty, she thought.

Raymond walked out on the porch. "I wondered where you'd gone. I could have cut a tree."

"I didn't think you would want to."

"Well, I can make a stand. I know how Father did it." He hefted the tree over his shoulder and carried it to the barn. He came back with two pieces of wood nailed to the bottom and brought the tree into the house and put it in the parlor. It stood a little crooked, and Raymond got on his knees and leveled it.

That evening, Leona went into her mother's closet and found the box with their few decorations: three clear glass balls Rose had treasured, a dozen crocheted snowflakes and stars, a couple of strands of gold garland that was coming to pieces, a box of tinsel. There were little candles, too, but Leona wouldn't use those because of Isaiah. She had bought a few sheets of colored paper in town, and she and Sally made paper chains. Even Raymond helped hang things on the tree, and when they finished and Leona held Isaiah up to see, he laughed and clapped his hands. They didn't have presents for each other, but it seemed all right.

The last day of the year, Raymond left and stayed gone for two weeks. He came home hungover and haggard and slept for twenty-four hours straight. The little tree had long since been thrown out.

One morning in late January, dark clouds rolled in out of the southwest like a wall suspended above the earth, trailing whirling wisps of wind. The air went deathly still and the turbulent sky took on a green cast. Just as the blinding rain came, Leona grabbed Isaiah up and she, Sally, and Raymond ran across the yard to the storm cellar. They waited there for an hour, listening to the roaring winds and the thunder and the pounding rain.

When they ventured out, they saw that the house had been spared, but the barn roof was gone. The lot around the house had long ago been cleared except for one old beau d'arc and two sweetgum trees. Those still stood, but a couple of massive limbs had fallen, and smaller ones littered the ground. Crumpled tin from the barn roof tangled high in the trees. The storm had cut a path through the woods that bordered their land, snapping trees in half or lifting them and dropping them like a game of pick-up-sticks.

"Goddamn bad luck," Raymond said.

"I don't know," Leona said. "Seems like we were lucky."

"Shut up, Leona." Raymond got his slicker and took the wagon to town to get roofing supplies. He didn't get home until late afternoon. After he had unloaded the tin and nails for the roof, he came in for supper, shedding the slicker and dripping water everywhere.

"There's damage up the road," he said. "The Pratts got a big tree down on one corner of their house. Looks like they got the worst of it, except for the Sanders place. Lots of damage up that way."

"What about Luther?" Leona said.

Raymond looked up. "What about him?"

"You went by there. Was his house all right?"

"Looked all right to me." He stuffed half a biscuit in his mouth. "The big news is, I ran into a couple of fellows in town, Sam Murphy and David Witherspoon. They been home from France about a week. They said everybody's back except for Harry Sowell, Walker Broom, and Dickie Nix. And—let's see— Perry Streeter." He counted on his fingers. "Yeah, that's all."

Leona clasped her hands in her lap to keep them still. "Why aren't those boys back?"

"How would I know?"

Bertie might know. Leona wanted to get up from the table and run up the road in the dark to Bertie's, but she would have to wait. Tomorrow, she would find out more.

The next morning, Raymond walked in the kitchen as Leona was pulling on her coat. "Where you going?"

"Bertie's. Maybe they need help."

"There's plenty to do here."

"But you said—"

"They can take care of themselves. You ain't going nowhere."

Raymond had hired a couple of colored boys to help with the roof, but it rained hard again that morning and stopped the work. He paced and cursed the Negroes, as if the rain were their fault. Leona kept out of his way. When the rain stopped, he sent the colored boys back up on the roof and put Leona to work sawing up the broken limbs in the yard. Raymond allowed her to go in the house at noon to nurse Isaiah and eat, but he made her go back outside and work until all the limbs were cleared except for a couple of large ones.

"I'll cut those," Raymond said. "They're too big for you."

Was he mocking her?

While she worked, she imagined Walker lying in a hospital bed, his legs blown away, or buried in that foreign soil without so much as a rock to mark his grave. Surely if he were wounded or missing—if he had been killed—folks would have heard. By the time she finished clearing the limbs, her hands were blistered, and her heart was sore with worry.

Toward the end of the week, Leona hid the last of the coffee and told Raymond they were out. "I need to buy some."

"No, you don't. I'll go. What else do we need?"

"Besides coffee? I need some things I expect you'd rather not buy. Female things."

He frowned. "Well then, hell. Go on. What do I care?"

She didn't want to leave Isaiah at home with Raymond there, so she took him to Bertie. Leona had another good reason not to take the baby with her. Her errand involved more than buying coffee they didn't need. She needed to go to Broom's Mercantile, and if Mr. Broom was there, she didn't think she could ask about Walker without telling him about Isaiah. "Here's your grandson," she imagined saying. She hoped Ella Harmon would be there. Miss Ella, who worked in ladies' goods, had a son, Boyd, who had come home from the war months ago with a leg amputated. Mrs. Harmon was a gossip. If anybody knew about those other boys, she would.

In town Leona found it helpful to pretend to be invisible. That way, she could go about her business immune to the stares and whispers she believed still followed her.

She bought a little coffee at Harrington's before she summoned her courage and walked into Broom's. She browsed the fabric and looked at a display of toys. Christmas had come and gone, so there weren't many toys left. Mrs. Harmon was busy with another customer. Mr. Broom didn't seem to be there, and Leona was glad.

After the other woman left, Mrs. Harmon offered to help Leona.

Leona pointed to a high shelf. "I'd like to see that little fire engine, the one up there."

Mrs. Harmon smiled. "For your little boy?"

"Yes, ma'am. He has a birthday coming up."

Mrs. Harmon got the sliding ladder, climbed up, and handed the shiny red tin truck to Leona. She ran it back and forth across the counter. "How's Boyd doing?" she asked.

"He's getting better all the time, thank you."

"I hear there's others coming home."

"Why, yes." Mrs. Harmon named half a dozen boys who had returned in the last few weeks.

"So there's some who aren't back yet?"

Mrs. Harmon shook her head. "They say Harry Sowell is missing. His mother has took to her bed. Dickie Nix isn't back yet, either. I don't know why. The only other one I know of is Mr. Broom's son. Walker got the influenza right when he was supposed to leave France. Last I heard, he was in a hospital in New York. The Brooms have been real worried about him."

Leona breathed in, breathed out. He's alive. He's coming home. "That's awful about Harry," she said. "I'm sorry to hear it." Her heart pounding, she turned the little truck over in her hands. "How much does this cost?"

The toy fire engine cost fifty cents. She paid Mrs. Harmon, thanked her, and walked out into the cold. She stepped around the corner into the alley where she burst into tears. She stood there for a few minutes, struggling to calm herself, before she headed back to the wagon.

When Leona started home, her head was full of fantasies. She and Walker would talk about what happened before he left, how they had been stubborn and mistaken in their understanding. They would say they were sorry. He would hold Isaiah. He would confess his love for her, no matter what anybody said. He would ask her to marry him.

By the time she was halfway home, she was chilled by more than the cold drizzle that had begun to fall. She didn't know what Walker would do. He must have heard gossip about her and the baby in letters from his mother or father or friends. How could he not know the baby was his? Still, he hadn't written. She didn't know for certain he would get well. He was staying a long time in the hospital, so he must have been very sick. She had heard tales of her great-grandfather who was never in his right mind after the War Between the States, after all he had seen and endured. What if Walker were like that?

By the time she stopped off to get Isaiah at Bertie's, she could hardly breathe. That night, she lay a long time in the dark, trying to recall Walker's touch, but she was unable to do so.

28

Walker was weak from the influenza he had suffered before he left France, and the crossing home was harder than the first. The day the ship docked in New York, he was running a fever, and the army doctor feared a relapse. Instead of boarding a train to Mississippi, he was dispatched to an infirmary on Long Island. He wrote his parents and told them not to worry, he was getting well. But he was impatient. He had hoped to be home for Christmas. He wondered about Leona, whether she was all right, whether she might have married by now. He didn't know those things because he had never mailed any of the letters he wrote her, and she had not written to him.

One bleak afternoon, a young woman brought him hot cocoa. Snow was falling. Snow, something Walker had so rarely seen in his life, and there it was, piling up in great mounds. Edith Brewster was fair with auburn hair, big brown eyes, and natural color in her cheeks and lips. The first time he spoke, she laughed. "What's so funny?" he asked.

"You. I've never heard a Southern boy speak. It's true what they say."

"What's that?" He was feeling a little peeved.

"That you could melt butter with that voice."

At first, she brought him coffee and left. When he asked her for news, she brought newspapers and read to him. He turned his good right ear toward her and asked her to speak up and slow down. Not only was he having trouble hearing her, he couldn't understand her clipped Yankee accent. Sometimes he fell asleep while she read. He would wake and find her gone.

She began stopping by his room after she had finished with her rounds of books and papers and treats. He told her about the rolling hills of north Mississippi, the red earth, the hard-scrabble life some people led. He described Sully, built around a square with the county courthouse on one side. He told her about his daddy's mercantile store, waiting for Walker to take over someday. He didn't say anything about Leona.

Edith had lost two brothers in the war, one in France and the other to the influenza on the troop ship, going over. She told it clear-eyed and matter-of-fact, but he saw the trembling of her lower lip and wanted to reach out and touch her.

"I'm sorry," he said.

Here he was, so damned weak he could hardly get up to relieve himself, but he was alive. He wondered why. What was he meant for? Soon it would be time to leave. He didn't look forward to days and nights on the train, first to New York City, then Chicago, and from there down to Memphis. Even if he left within the next week, he would still miss Christmas. It made him feel mighty low.

A couple of days before he was supposed to be discharged, Edith came into his room empty-handed and sat down beside his bed. "Spend Christmas with my family," she said. "My parents said it's fine to ask you. We hate to think about you on the train, going all that way alone, over Christmas."

He accepted her offer without a pang of guilt about his own parents, waiting and worrying at home, without a thought of Leona. He wrote his parents and confessed he had had influenza, but they were not to worry. He was recuperating and would spend Christmas with a nice family who had offered to take him in.

When he was discharged from the hospital, Edith picked him up in a car with a driver. Walker and Edith sat in the back seat, a wide expanse between them. He was bundled in an overcoat she brought him that had belonged to her brother and a lap robe. There was still snow on the ground, such a bright white in the sunlight that it hurt his eyes. They drove through stone gates and down a winding drive. The Brewsters' house was built of red brick, two stories, with massive front doors and tall windows. He'd had no idea Edith came from such wealth.

Robert and Miriam Brewster were friendly enough, but Walker sensed a certain hesitation. Maybe that was their Yankee way, or maybe they looked at him, remembered their dead sons, and wondered why he lived and they didn't. He learned over dinner the first night that they had brought other soldiers to this house who were waiting to get transportation home. The last was a young man from Illinois who had lost a leg in the war.

Edith's mother offered Walker shirts and trousers that had belonged to one of her sons. When Walker told her no, thank you, he couldn't accept them, she said, "You need some regular clothes. You're just our Martin's size." Her face went solemn. "He would want you boys to have them."

You boys. If Walker thought Edith had singled him out because she was drawn to him, he lost that illusion. Maybe he was just another charity case.

The Brewsters gave him warm socks and a scarf for Christmas. Practical things. He had nothing for them. At dinner, Walker watched to see which fork Edith used. How meager his parents' Christmas meal would seem compared to this. He had written to them again, but he'd given them no date to expect him home.

As though Edith knew, she asked him to stay on. "The train trip will be draining. Give yourself more time."

So he stayed. One day, Edith took him for a drive to the shore. Walker had seen the ocean from the decks of ships where its vastness had frightened him. The horizon had seemed like the end of the earth, and once the ship reached it, they would surely drop into oblivion. Maybe it was Edith beside him, holding on to his arm, but when he stood high above the sea and looked out at the curvature of the earth, when he looked down at the waves crashing on the rocks below, he drew strength from them. He knew then that he would get well, but his life would never be what he had expected.

He wanted to walk a bit on the sand, but Edith rushed him back to the car. "It's too cold. We'll come here again soon." She stood on tiptoe and kissed his cheek.

29

The days dragged by, and Leona heard no more about Walker. She might have lost her mind if not for Isaiah. A year old, he was walking. He called her "Ma." He knew "light," "bye," and "night." He made clucking noises at the chickens, toddling after them in the yard. He was a beautiful child with dark hair like Walker's, her father's, and Raymond's, too, only Isaiah's had some curl to it. He had Leona's green eyes, a fine nose, a mischievous smile that made it hard for her to tell him no. He already loved the outdoors. As soon as he was old enough, she would take him to the woods the way her father had taken her. She would teach him to hunt. The thought brought a catch to her throat. It was a father's job, not a mother's.

The first time her father had awakened her before dawn to go to the woods with him, she was seven years old. He'd handed her a pair of her brother's old overalls and his outgrown brogans. "Put these on. It's cold. I'll wait in the kitchen. Be quiet."

She got up and pulled on her woolen leggings and two pairs of socks, stuffed her nightdress into the overalls, and rolled the legs up. Her brother's shoes were still too big, even with extra layers. Last, her coat that was getting too small. She tiptoed to the kitchen. Her father was wearing his long woolen coat and a hat. "Come with me."

He took his shotgun down from the rack, and Leona shivered. She knew she was going hunting, something that had been reserved for her father and Raymond until lately, when Raymond had stopped going, and Leona didn't know why. Her father opened the kitchen door and leaned his full weight against it so the hinge wouldn't creak. He led her out into the cold morning.

The moon, not quite full, hovered in the western sky. The grass in the pasture looked like somebody had painted the tips with silver. Halfway across the pasture, he picked her up and carried her. She rode easily in his arms, her head on his shoulder. His breath was like little bursts of frost. When they came to the thicket, he set her down and took her hand. They walked into the woods. She didn't know how far, but it seemed a long way. The spot where he stopped didn't seem at all special, but her father sat down, his back against a tree. He motioned for her to sit. She felt the damp, cold earth through her clothes.

"Now," he whispered, "we wait until it's light."

The trees loomed dark overhead. She was cold and a little afraid. Her bottom went numb and tingly from sitting still, but when she wriggled, he said, "Be still. It won't be long now."

In a little while, she heard a warble in the thicket. "What was that?"

"Turkey," he whispered. He cupped his hands to his mouth and made a sound much like the one she had just heard. The bird called again, closer this time. It was light enough now to make out the trees, their branches like bare arms reaching to a cold gray sky. They were at the edge of a clearing. The warble again, her father's answering call. A rustle in the underbrush, and a big gobbler strode out of the woods. He stood still for a full minute, stepped out of the foliage, stopped. He spread his wings, lifted off the ground a few feet, and landed closer to them. He called, but this time her father was quiet, and from the woods came a less raucous call. A smaller bird appeared. It didn't have the red wattle of the other. The gobbler spread his tail feathers and strutted around the clearing.

She was surprised when her father didn't shoot. A hawk swooped low and back up into the trees with a great flurry of its wings, and by the time she looked again at the clearing, the turkeys were gone.

She and her father stayed to see the dawn come. Leona could still hear those birds calling. She was glad he hadn't killed them, but she wondered why. Finally, her father stood up and brushed off his clothes. He helped her up and brushed her off too. He took her hand again. This time they could see to make their way back to the pasture and on to the house.

"Why didn't you shoot them?" she asked.

"They're God's creatures. I only take them when there's a need."

Back at the house, Leona's mother scolded him for taking Leona out in the cold and her for going, but it didn't matter. Leona felt a warmth inside in spite of the cold, a fullness in her heart she would never forget.

For her twelfth birthday, her father gave her his pump-action twenty-gauge shotgun. A good gun for a woman, he said. She became a good shot, but she never liked to kill. At the last second, she would fail to pull the trigger. Her father often hesitated too before he shot and grimaced when he did. He would turn away when they stood over a turkey or a deer, its body still warm and quivering.

Leona would want Isaiah to learn that lesson: when to kill, and how to do it with mercy.

The middle of March, they were all sitting at the supper table when Raymond said, "I heard Walker Broom is back. He's brought a Yankee girl with him. He done married her."

Sally said, "Ha. Wonder what Hiram and Nell Broom think. Not much, I reckon."

Leona dug her nails into her palms while Raymond went on. "They say her name is Edith. I heard she talks so fast you can't hardly understand a word she says."

When Isaiah started to cry, Leona snatched him up. "All right," she said, "it's time for you to go to bed." She said it harsher than she meant to. She carried the baby to her room with him shrieking all the way.

Long since dark. She lit Luther's lamp and lay down on the bed with Isaiah. She held him until he stopped crying. She was trembling. Walker, married? She didn't believe it. Yet Raymond had said it was so. He wouldn't make up such a thing.

"Poor little boy," she whispered. "It's not your fault."

Isaiah climbed over her and gave her sloppy kisses. "Ma," he said, patting her face. He tugged at the buttons of her dress, and when she told him no, he howled. She gave in and let him nurse until he fell asleep.

She was far from sleep. She might as well have been slapped; her head still spun from the blow. She got up and looked out the window. In the light of the full moon, she could see the line of ruined trees along the north fence and the woods beyond. She wanted to walk out into the chilly night and keep walking, but here she was, and here she would stay. If only there was somebody she could tell who wouldn't condemn her.

And then she knew. She could tell Luther. Her secret would be safe with him. In her mind she turned the words over, tried them out, whispering them into the quiet of her room.

30

The day after Raymond brought home news of Walker and his wife—his wife; the word stuck in Leona's throat—Leona took Isaiah and struck out for Luther's place. The urge to tell was strong, now that it was too late and would accomplish nothing.

When they got to Luther's, he hurried them inside, out of the cold. She waited for her eyes to adjust to the dimly lighted room before she put Isaiah down. He stood, a little wobbly, looked up at her, then Luther, and then Jesse, who sat by the hearth. He took a few steps.

Luther said, "Look at him. He's walking good."

The baby tottered to Jesse, glanced back at his mother as though he were asking permission, and reached for Jesse's hand. Jesse took it and they walked to the window. He picked Isaiah up and pointed to something in the yard. "Look, baby. That's a squirrel. See it?" Jesse made a noise that sounded like a squirrel's chatter, and Isaiah laughed. Jesse jiggled him, humming a tune. Leona wondered if it was a song Varna had sung to him a long time ago. Isaiah wriggled in Jesse's arms.

Luther said, "He wants down."

When Jesse set him on his feet, Isaiah walked to Leona and threw himself at her skirt, tugging at it. Jesse went back to his chair by the fire. Isaiah said, "Go bye."

Luther chuckled. "He's a smart one."

Leona picked him up and buried her face in his hair. "I believe he is." She was close to tears. The words, the truth, threatened to come out.

"You want to sit? You don't seem yourself."

She said, "I'm all right," but she knew Luther saw she wasn't. Last night, she had thought she could tell him. Now, she couldn't. "Oh, Luther. There's nothing right or fair about the world, is there? Tell me one good thing about living."

Luther held out a finger to Isaiah, and the baby grasped it. "You're right. Life ain't fair. I don't know what's worrying you, but you holding your reason for living right there in your arms. Long as you got this boy, you keep on going."

Leona felt selfish. Here Luther was, burdened with Jesse, his wife dead, his daughter, Alma, moved off to Memphis long ago.

Luther's arms closed around her and Isaiah. She smelled copper and lye soap and remembered the little girl she had been, walking across the back lot to the orchard, holding Luther's hand. He had lifted her up and let her pick apples off the trees. She ate one right then and wanted another, but Luther wouldn't let her have it.

"Give you a stomachache, then I'll be in trouble with your folks," he had said. He'd looked after her in ways nobody else ever had, except her father.

She wished she and Isaiah could stay with Luther, but even if he said they could, Raymond would never allow it.

❧

Luther watched Leona walk down the road until she was out of sight. She carried that baby boy like he was the weight of the world. He was sure she had come close to telling him something.

When he went back inside, Jesse was standing at the window, looking out, his hands pressed against the glass. Something was troubling Jesse, too, but Luther didn't know what it was. "Come on, Jesse," he said. "Let's make us some supper."

❧

The following Saturday, Leona and Isaiah came out of Harrington's and ran into Walker and Edith Broom. Leona felt cornered, with no place to run.

Walker said, "Leona. Hey there."

He was too thin, his olive skin sallow, his dark eyes too big for his face. She shifted Isaiah to her other hip. "Walker. Welcome home."

"Thank you." He put his arm around the woman. "Edith, this is Leona Pinson, a friend from over near Hawks Creek. And this little fellow is—"

"Isaiah." Leona took in Edith Broom: taller than she, a slim, almost boyish figure, not exactly pretty, clearly older than Walker. Leona said, "How do you do, Edith."

"It's nice to meet you," Edith said. Isaiah smiled and tucked his head like he was flirting. "What a handsome boy. Isn't he, Walker?" Edith gave Walker a look so full of intimacy that Leona thought she might be sick.

Walker's eyes met Leona's, flicked away. "Yes, he is."

"Excuse me," Leona said. "I have to get home. I'm glad you're back safely, Walker." She couldn't bring herself to congratulate him on his marriage.

Hurrying down the sidewalk, feeling weighted down by Isaiah and so much else, Leona didn't hear what Walker said to his wife as Leona walked away. She barely got outside of town before she stopped the buggy and began to sob. Isaiah patted her face. He settled against her and sucked his thumb. Finally, when she was all cried out, she gathered up the reins and started for home again.

How could Walker see Isaiah and not know?

31

A few days before, when Walker and Edith had come into Sully on the train, he had seen Sully through her eyes: a backwater place with unpaved streets, a handful of stores, wagons parked around the square with men in overalls and women in flour-sack dresses selling their wares. It couldn't be more different from what Edith was used to. Speechless, he had squeezed her hand.

He reached for her hand under the dinner table now, as his mother lapsed into local gossip. He paid her little mind until he heard her say "that Pinson girl."

"What about her?" Walker said.

"She had a baby, maybe a year ago. God knows who the father is. She won't tell." His mother folded her white linen napkin and placed it beside her plate. "Some folks say it's her brother's child."

Walker's father said, "That's enough, Nell."

"Well, it was the talk of the town, Hiram."

Walker's left ear rang, a high, tinny sound. He swallowed to try and clear it. "Edith and I ran into her in town today."

Edith added, "The little boy is beautiful."

His mother put down her fork. "You know them, Walker?"

"I used to see her and her brother around town." Walker broke out in a sweat. He hoped nobody noticed.

"Well, it's a pity," his mother said. "That girl lost her father in such an awful way. They say he was murdered, Edith."

Walker pushed back from the table. "Edith, I'm really tired. Aren't you?"

She looked bewildered. "I'm fine." She had not yet finished her apple pie.

"Well, I'm going to bed. You'll excuse me, Mother?"

His mother said, "Goodness, I'm sorry. How thoughtless of me to keep you here."

He kissed his mother on the cheek and he and Edith went upstairs to the room still marked by his boyhood: the single beds, the desk where he had carved his initials, his favorite caps hanging on a rack by the door, and on the wall above the bed he'd always slept in, an embroidered sampler his mother made when he was a baby: a kneeling boy wearing a blue romper with God Bless above him and Walker's name below. There was the trunk that had gone to France and back, the photograph of Leona he'd carried and all the letters he'd written her but never mailed buried deep inside it.

Neither of them looked at the other while they changed into their nightclothes. Edith got into bed first. The night was unseasonably warm, and Walker opened a window. He lay with Edith in the small bed and hoped she wouldn't notice his rapid heart. He stroked her hair. "We'll get our own house soon."

"I know." Her voice was muffled against his chest. "It's going to be all right."

Walker wished he could believe that was true.

After she fell asleep, he lay down on the other bed and waited until he heard his mother and father come up the stairs and go to their bedroom at the end of the hall. He got up, put on his robe, and went downstairs and out the back door. His hands shaking, he lit a cigarette. He had picked up the smoking habit in France. The doctor had advised against smoking while he was recuperating from the flu, but tonight, he needed a smoke.

Leona had a son. He paced the yard, trying to reconstruct those last weeks before he left, all the things that had conspired to keep him from Leona.

He had been sitting on the back steps a while when his father came out and sat beside him. "Son? Are you all right?"

He swiped at his eyes. "I couldn't sleep."

"I can imagine, after all you've gone through. But that pretty bride of yours might wonder where you are."

"Don't worry. I'm fine." He wished his father would go back to bed.

The silence hung heavy and awkward between them. Finally, his father clapped him on his shoulder and stood. "I'm glad to have you home." His voice cracked. "Come on inside. Your mother would have a fit if she knew you were out here in the night air." His father went in the house and closed the door quietly.

Walker crushed out his cigarette and waited a few minutes before he went inside. He got in bed and lay awake into the gray hours of dawn. Unless Leona had been with another man around the same time—and Walker didn't believe that was true—the baby was his. He dismissed the idea that the child could be Raymond's. Raymond was mean, but Walker didn't believe him capable of such a terrible thing. The cleft in the little boy's chin had not escaped Walker. Raymond had no cleft.

He looked over at Edith, sleeping. He slipped in next to her, and she nestled against him. She sighed but didn't wake. He despised himself when he felt his arousal. He slipped her nightgown up. When she woke, he was fast and rough with her. Afterward, she rolled away and pulled the covers up. She was crying, but he made no effort to comfort her.

32

The fields were plowed for corn by the end of April. Leona helped with planting and later, as the corn grew, with hoeing. The backbreaking work helped to keep her mind off Walker, although sometimes when she straightened to rest her back and shoulders and looked off toward the tree line, she thought she saw him standing there.

By July they had as fine a corn crop as Leona could remember. It was a wonder to see her brother work until dark, come in and eat, and go straight to bed. Leona didn't understand the change in him, but she hoped it would last. In the middle of the day, she took him a lunch of hard-boiled eggs, ham, biscuits and jam, and a big fruit jar of water. Raymond would be behind the plow, urging the mule on, sometimes cursing him, but getting the work done. Leona carried a bell, and when she rang it, he came to the end of the row and unhitched the mule to graze. Sweat-soaked and sunburned, he would pour some of the water over his head, then gulp the rest down, sit in the shade, and eat.

Raymond boasted about how well the farm was doing now that he was in charge. If the crops were good enough, he said, and they just might be, he would buy Tobe Sanders out.

"The Sanders place is for sale?" Leona said.

"No, but it will be."

&

Raymond could put up with Tobe Sanders only so long. Tobe had held fast in spite of the storm damage, a mule shot dead in the pasture, and the disappearance of his dogs. The time had come to convince him to go. Raymond talked the Ridge Riders into paying Tobe Sanders a visit, though some of them were doubtful.

"He's a white man," somebody said.

"Don't matter," Raymond said.

The men rode out to the Sanders place on a Saturday afternoon near sundown. The evening had not cooled at all. Raymond sweated under the hood. They rode into the yard, whooping and hollering. Raymond went up to the door and banged on it until Tobe came out, armed with a shotgun. Raymond stepped back while two men took the gun away and wrestled Tobe to the ground, dragged him into the yard, and made him kneel in the dirt. His wife and two of his sons came out on the porch.

Tobe yelled at them to go inside, but his wife stood there, sobbing, holding on to one of her sons while the other one broke away, jumped off the porch, and ran at the men. The boy took a blow to the head and went down.

"Stop it!" Tobe's wife screamed. "Tobe ain't done nothing!"

"I ain't," Tobe said, on all fours now like a dog. "God knows, leave us alone!"

When Raymond gave the nod, the other fellows beat Tobe while his wife howled. They left him lying in the yard. Raymond rode up to the barn and set it alight. It caught fast, the livestock bawling and braying inside.

Raymond rode off from the Sanders place, leaving the burning and Tobe's crying wife behind him. Seeing Tobe in the dirt, seeing that barn go up in flames, energized Raymond like a shot of good whiskey.

It was getting dark by the time he rode out onto Pinson Road, split off from the other men, and headed home.

On the way, he saw Jesse walking down the road, carrying his dog. Raymond reined Belle in and rode alongside. "Well, look here," he said. "What're you doing out so late, Jesse? Why you carrying your dog?"

"He...he ran off. He's got a hurt paw."

Raymond got down off his horse. "Let me take a look."

"No, sir. He'll be all right." Jesse stepped back. "I'm gon' take him home now."

"That's good. You ought not to let your dog run loose. Never can tell what might happen to him." Raymond wrested the dog away from Jesse and held it up by the scruff of the neck. "He's a boy dog."

"Yes, sir."

"Maybe we ought to fix him so he don't roam. We don't want him making more mongrel dogs like your mama made you. Can't have a whore dog, can we?"

Jesse shifted from one foot to the other. "He don't roam. Just this one time."

Raymond took out his pocketknife. "All it would take is a swipe of the knife, and he won't be a nuisance no more. How about it?"

Tears rolled down Jesse's face. "Give him back. He don't bother nobody."

Raymond studied the dog like he was figuring out what to do. After a moment, he put his knife away and gave the dog to Jesse. "Go on home. Keep that mongrel out of my sight."

Laughing, Raymond got back on his horse. He rode off at a full gallop.

33

Jesse ran all the way home, carrying his dog, looking over his shoulder to see if Raymond was coming after him. When he got to the house, he hid with the dog in the shed out back. Maybe Raymond would still come and cut on his dog. Maybe he would cut Jesse. The shed was dark and hot and smelled of manure and mold. A rat ran across Jesse's foot. The dog growled. Jesse couldn't hold his pee any longer.

What had he done to make Raymond mad? Pa had told Jesse over and over to be polite, no matter what Raymond said or did. "He's a white man, and we ain't. Ain't nothing gon' change that," Pa had said. When Raymond came up on Jesse on the road, Jesse had said yes sir and no sir, but Raymond acted like he don't care, he was gon' put his knife to the dog anyway, didn't matter if Jesse was polite.

Jesse didn't know what to do with the feelings boiling up inside him, but he knew one thing. He had wanted to take that knife away from Raymond and stick it in his neck.

It was after dark when Pa came home, calling Jesse's name. Pa didn't like it when Jesse went off down the road by himself, but Jesse's dog had run off, and he had to find him, he had to. Jesse liked walking on the road. He liked how the gravel crunched under his feet and the trees swayed over his head. Sometimes he pretended to be a bird. If he were a bird, he could go anywhere he pleased.

His pa's footsteps stopped at the shed door. The dog whined and yelped.

"Jesse? You in there?" Pa opened the door, held up his lantern, and looked inside.

Jesse let the dog go. It ran out, wagging and peeing.

Pa said, "Come on out, son."

He didn't ask Jesse what he was doing in there, and Jesse was glad. He stood up and looked down at his wet overalls. "I'm sorry, Pa. I'm sorry."

"No mind. Let's get you cleaned up."

Jesse wondered if he might get a whipping for going off, but his pa heated up some ham and greens for their supper and they ate and then they sat on the porch. Jesse's dog lay at his feet, asleep.

Pa said, "Why were you hiding?"

If he told Pa what Raymond had done, would Jesse get in trouble? Or would Pa go tell Raymond to leave Jesse alone? Pa weren't afraid of nobody.

Jesse took a shaky breath. "Had to hide my dog. Raymond was gon' hurt him. He said he's gon' take a knife to him."

Luther sat forward. "Where did you see Raymond?"

"The dog ran off. I had to go find him, and we was—"

"You went off after I told you not to."

"Yes, sir." Now Pa would be mad. "But we was coming back and Raymond rode up on his horse and he took out his knife and he said he was gon' fix my dog so we don't have no more whore dogs around here. Like Ma, he said." Jesse started to rock. "My ma weren't a bad woman, was she?"

"No. Your ma was a good woman."

His pa got up and walked to the edge of the porch. He stood there for a while and then he turned. "Jesse, I'm gon' tell you something about men like Raymond Pinson. He ain't a big man, so he tries to act like one. He ain't gon' hurt you or your dog. He's mean, but he's mostly words. From now on, when you go down there to work, do what he says. You say yes sir and no sir. Don't never argue, you hear me? You'll be all right."

Jesse had done those things, and Raymond had threatened to cut his dog anyway. Jesse shook his head. "No, sir."

"What you mean, no?"

"I ain't going down there no more."

"All right. I don't blame you." Pa put his arm around Jesse. His arm felt good and strong. He said, "Come on inside. It's getting late."

Lying in bed, Jesse remembered the night last summer when there was a racket outside the house, and he had looked out and seen white shapes riding up on horses. They shone in the moonlight. They had black holes for eyes.

Jesse had said, "Pa, are they ghosts?"

"No," Pa said, "they're just men, dressed up in them white robes and hoods."

"What's a hood?"

"A hood's something that covers your face so nobody sees who you are. Cowards, that's what they are."

"What's a coward?"

"A man scared of his own shadow."

Some of the men got off their horses, whooping and hollering. They threw rope over a big limb of the beau d'arc tree and hung a man up there and set fire to him. When the man started to burn, Jesse set up a howl, but Pa said, "That's a straw man, Jesse. It ain't real, it can't feel nothing." He told Jesse to stay inside, but he went out on the porch. Jesse hid that night, too, till he heard the men ride off, and Pa came inside.

"It's all right," Pa had said. "They won't bother us no more." But Pa had bolted the door and sat all night with his shotgun in his lap.

After the straw man, Jesse had dreamed about white hoods coming back to make Jesse and Pa dead. When you're dead, they put you in the ground, like Ma and Mr. Herbert and Miss Rose. Sometimes Jesse lay on his belly and put his ear to the ground to see if he could hear the dead.

34

Sheriff Taylor came to the Pinson place Monday morning and asked to speak to Raymond.

Leona said, "Why, Mr. Bobby? What's he done?"

"A bunch of hooligans almost killed Tobe Sanders Saturday night. Beat him up real bad and burned his barn to the ground." The sheriff mopped his face with a handkerchief. "Raymond's been after Tobe one way or another ever since your daddy died. Tell him to come see me, or I'll be back to get him."

"Yes, sir. I will."

Leona told Raymond when he came home. She was surprised when he didn't argue. He rode into town the next day. She wondered if the sheriff would hold him, but Raymond came back not the least bit subdued.

"Did you have anything to do with Tobe Sanders' beating and the barn burning?" Leona asked him. "Tell me the truth."

Raymond sat down and took off his boots, worked his toes. "The sheriff's looking for somebody to blame. You think I'd do such a fool thing?"

On the third day that Jesse didn't show up for work, Leona and Luther were in the barn tending a calf when Raymond came in and dragged Luther up and shoved him against the stall. "Why ain't Jesse coming to work?"

Luther looked Raymond right in the eyes. "He don't want to come down here no more."

Leona said, "Why is that?" What had Raymond done now?

"You stay out of it, Leona."

"You tell me, Mr. Raymond. I expect you know."

Raymond let Luther go, stepped away, and spat. "Don't talk in riddles, old man. Tell Jesse to come tomorrow, or you're both gone."

"Your granddaddy gave that land to me. I ain't going no-where."

Raymond stabbed at the dirt with the toe of his boot. "Don't push me, Luther. You'll go if I say so."

After that day, Luther worked with hardly a word to anybody. Raymond groused about how he was going to have to hire an-other man if Jesse wouldn't work.

"Give him time," Leona told Raymond, but she worried.

One afternoon, she went out to the garden where Luther was on his knees, pulling weeds. Raymond was out on the place somewhere, so she hoped she had time to talk to Luther. For a while she watched him work, but he didn't look up.

"Luther? Would you talk to me, please?"

"Ain't nothing to talk about. Got work to do." He yanked a stubborn weed out by its roots.

"Something's wrong. I know it. Tell me."

Sweat glistened on his face. With some effort he struggled to his feet. "All right. What you want to know?"

"I want to know what Raymond has done to Jesse."

Luther sighed. "You can't do nothing about it. Jesse says Raymond threatened to cut his dog. He called Varna a whore. When I got home that day, Jesse and the dog were hiding in the shed. He was scared to death. That's why he don't want to come down here no more. Because of Raymond's meanness." Luther wiped his face with his kerchief.

Leona shook her head in dismay. "Raymond has gotten this crazy notion. After Mama died, we were talking about how sad she was, and how strange, and he said— Oh, it's too awful. I can't even say it out loud."

"He thinks Jesse is your daddy's child."

Leona nodded. "Because of Jesse's light skin." She took Luther in, head to toe. "But you're lighter than most of the Negroes I know."

"Black people got different skin, different color eyes. Just the way God made them."

"I know, but Raymond is like that when he gets a thing in his head. He won't let it go."

"Well, there ain't no truth to what he said. Varna was the best woman ever lived."

She saw tears in Luther's eyes. "I'll talk to Raymond. I'll put a stop to it."

Luther got back on his knees. "You can talk all you want, but it won't do no good."

After supper, Leona followed Raymond out to the front porch.

"Luther says Jesse won't come to work because you threatened his dog. He says you called Varna a whore."

Raymond took a swig from the bottle in his hand. "Well, ain't she?"

"It's an awful thing to say, Ray. You want Jesse to work? Leave him alone. I won't have you treating him that way. It's not right."

Raymond stood. He towered over Leona. "You won't have it? We'll see about that."

35

Raymond was tied to the field work, so Leona was the one to go to town when they needed things. Sometimes she took Isaiah. He was a beautiful child who should have caught even the most hardhearted person's attention, but when she passed other mothers on the street, they gathered their little girls closer to their skirts or turned the girls' faces away, as if the sight of Leona was enough to bring a curse upon their daughters.

On a Saturday in late August, the heat was stifling, and Leona went to town alone. She stopped off at the Pratts' wagon on the square before she ran her errands. She wanted some of Mr. Carl's tomatoes. Leona's garden was already burning up in the heat.

Bertie pulled her aside. "Have you met Walker Broom's wife?"

Leona looked away. "I have. Back in the spring."

"She was here just now. We got to talking, and she told me she's expecting."

"She is?" Leona registered the full force of the word. Walker and Edith would have a child, maybe many children. Why hadn't Leona considered that?

Bertie fussed over the tomatoes, rearranging them in the basket. "Edith doesn't look well, if you ask me. Isn't she a lot older than Walker? Well, anyway, she asked me if I know of anybody who does nice handsewing. She said she never learned to sew. She wants to pay somebody to make baby clothes. I told her you do the nicest handwork of anybody I know."

"Oh, Bertie. You didn't." Leona's mind flashed to that last day at Hawks Creek, the cold sun overhead, the cold ground underneath.

"Why not? Don't tell me you couldn't use the money."

"When do you think I would sew? After midnight?" Leona needed to get away from Bertie before she said something she shouldn't. "I need tomatoes." She walked around to the front of the wagon and braced herself against it.

Bertie followed her. "I thought I was doing you a favor."

"No favors. All right? I have all I can do."

Leona paid for three tomatoes and put them in her bag. She walked away without saying goodbye. Why couldn't Bertie mind her own business? But Bertie had no idea why Leona wouldn't be pleased or at least curious to know the new Mrs. Broom. Bertie was probably flattered by Edith's attention.

Mercifully, Leona hadn't seen Walker or his wife since the day she ran into them, coming out of the drugstore. But when she went to the drugstore that day, Edith was standing at the counter. Leona turned to go, hoping not to be seen, but Edith called her name.

"Leona! Hello." Edith came over. "How are you? Where's your beautiful little boy?"

"He's at home. He's a handful these days."

"I can imagine. Well, I can't imagine, but soon I'll know." Edith rested her hand on her waistline, lowered her voice. "Walker and I are expecting a child."

Leona was thankful Bertie had told her. How could she have stood it otherwise? She forced a smile. "That's good news. I'm happy for you and Walker."

"Thank you." Edith cocked her head as though she were studying Leona. "It must be very hard, raising your boy without a father."

Leona had heard Yankee women were brash. Edith certainly seemed to be. "I manage."

The druggist came back to the counter with a dark glass bottle and handed it to Edith, who showed it to Leona. "Vitamin tonic. We ordered it from New York."

Enough. Leona said, "It's nice seeing you. I have to go."

"Please wait." Edith turned back to the counter and paid for the medicine. She said to Leona, "I met your friend today.

Bertie. She told me you do lovely hand sewing. I want to have some baby clothes made. Would you be interested?"

Could Leona bring herself to put needle and thread to a garment Walker's child would wear?

"No. Thank you. I'm sure Walker's mother can recommend someone."

Edith grasped her arm. "I don't want to ask his mother, and I really don't know anyone in Sully." Tears came to Edith's eyes. "It's very hard."

"I'm sorry. I can't."

Edith let her go. She took a white card out of her bag and pressed it into Leona's hand. "In case you change your mind."

Leona put the card in the pocket of her dress without looking at it. She hurried out of the store and crossed the road to the Pratts' wagon. Bertie was busy with a customer, and Leona paced beside the wagon until Bertie finished.

The second Bertie was free, she said, "What in the world is wrong with you? You look like you saw a ghost."

"No ghost." Leona sat down on the grass, and Bertie got her a cup of water.

"Want to tell me what happened?"

"Nothing. I'm sorry for the way I acted before. I know you didn't mean any harm."

"Harm? Goodness, no. But there's more to it than that. Don't tell me there isn't. What's got you so upset?"

Leona didn't want to tell Bertie she had run into Edith Broom and had turned her down. "I told you, nothing. It's the heat. It's enough to make anybody cross."

Two young men walked past, and one of them tipped his cap at Bertie.

"Who is that?" Leona said.

Bertie rolled her eyes. "A new fellow in town. His name is Brian Bedingfield. That's a mouthful, isn't it? He seems nice enough."

So that's the way it would be. Bertie would marry. She would have babies. She would be happy.

"I need to go," Leona said. "Raymond will throw a fit if I'm late."

When she got to the wagon, she looked at the card.

Mrs. Walker Hollis Broom
At Home
3 Water Street, Sully, Mississippi

Leona had never seen such a thing. She put it back in her pocket. By the time she was halfway home, her head throbbed. She had gone to the drugstore to buy headache powders, and she'd forgotten them.

The image of Edith Broom's glowing face burned into her mind.

Over the coming days, Leona tried to forget about the child growing inside Edith's body. She felt imprisoned on the farm, consigned to hard work and loneliness. She wrote a letter to Walker and tore it up. She considered taking Isaiah into the store when she thought Walker would be there. She fantasized about meeting him at Hawks Creek and being intimate with him. Surely that would bring him to his senses.

None of it would do. Walker must have figured out by now that Isaiah was his, but she hadn't heard from him since his return. By his own lights, he had come to his senses. He had chosen Edith.

But Edith had teared up. She had said was hard for her in Sully. If she was unhappy—

Leona could go and see Edith Broom. If Edith were ordering tonic from New York, why wouldn't she order a fancy layette? It seemed there was money to do so. What did Edith want? What did she know? What had Walker told her?

Leona wished for nice paper, but she didn't have any. She wrote to Edith on a piece of lined paper left over from her school days: *I would like to come and visit you a week from this Saturday, if it's all right. Leona Pinson.*

Her mother had always kept a few envelopes and stamps in the top drawer of the pie safe in the kitchen. Leona put the last stamp on a yellowing envelope, took it to the mailbox, tucked it inside, and raised the flag.

What was she setting in motion? At each step, she could have changed course, and later that day, after the postal carrier had come by, she wished she could take the note back, but it was already on its way to Edith.

Within the week, Leona received a reply.

36

Walker was tired of losing sleep. Edith was well along, but she was still sick in the mornings and often sick during the night. He should be ashamed. Edith was the one carrying the child and enduring the sickness, not he.

He was supposed to open the store on Saturdays. Even though he had overslept, Edith prepared eggs and toast for him, and she would be hurt if he didn't sit down and eat. He took a piece of toast—he loved biscuits, not toast, but Edith had yet to master the art of biscuits—and she poured his coffee and sat across from him.

"I'm meeting with someone about sewing a layette."

Walker looked puzzled. "What's a layette?"

Edith laughed. "You never heard of it? It's clothes for the baby. You know, little dresses and gowns and shirts, caps, blankets. I hear she's a fine seamstress."

"All right, if it's what you want." Walker lifted his pocket watch, a wedding gift from Edith. "I should go."

Edith leaned forward and rested her chin on her hands. Her eyes were brighter than Walker had seen them lately. She said, "Don't you want to know who it is?"

He took a bite of the eggs. "Who is what?"

"Sewing the baby clothes."

"All right. Who?"

"The Pinson girl. We ran into her, remember? She has that handsome little boy? Her friend, one of those women who sells things on the square, told me Leona does beautiful hand sewing, and that's what I want for our child. Leona agreed to come by today and talk about it."

Walker hoped he hadn't blanched. He set his cup down carefully. "No."

"What do you mean, no?"

"You don't understand how things are around here. Leona isn't—she isn't somebody we can associate with. I'm surprised you would suggest it."

"I won't be having tea with her, Walker. She'll be doing work for me." There was the smell of something burning. Edith took more toast off the stove, but it was ruined. She tossed it away "I have to say I'm surprised. I didn't know you were a snob. I thought you would like the idea of doing her a kindness."

"I'm not a snob. But people talk."

Edith got up from the table. From the side, the swell of her belly was noticeable, something he had not been able to see when it happened to Leona. "Let them talk, then," Edith said. "I want handmade baby clothes, and I intend to have them."

Walker stormed out, as much to hide his panic as anything else. How could things have taken such an absurd turn? He would put a stop to it. He would send word to Leona not to come. But what would that accomplish except to make Edith more set in her ways? Let it alone, he told himself. Leona's sewing probably wouldn't please Edith, and she would tire of Leona soon enough. It was a gamble, but one Walker felt compelled to take.

37

Leona left the baby at home when she went to see Walker's wife. She would not share Isaiah with Edith Broom. September now, but still in the full heat of summer; anything Leona wore would be soaked with sweat by the time she got to town. She chose a plain light-blue dress, one she had made after Isaiah was born, and a straw hat, her best, that would shield her from the sun. Raymond refused to let her take the buggy and Belle, so she took the wagon. By the time she reached Sully, her hair stuck to her head beneath the hat, and her dress was wrinkled and damp with sweat.

She had confessed to Bertie that she'd decided to visit Edith. "Once Edith sees my handwork," Leona had said, "I doubt she'll hire me. She'll want to order something fine. Apparently, she can afford it."

Leona left the wagon on the square and walked to the little white clapboard house with a porch and a tin roof. The house needed painting. The flowers in the front beds were dying for lack of water.

Leona straightened her dress and bit her lips. She took off the ridiculous hat, tucked up her damp hair as best she could, shifted the satchel she carried to her other arm. She had packed patterns and some of the baby clothes she had made for Isaiah. She rang the bell and wiped her sweating palms on her skirt. What if Walker were at home?

Edith opened the door. "Leona. I'm so glad you came."

She stepped inside and followed Edith into a small parlor off the front hall. The velvet curtains were closed—against the heat of the day, Leona supposed—but the house felt gloomy and smelled of dust.

Edith looked Leona up and down. "Oh, you poor thing! The heat is miserable, isn't it? Sit. What may I get you? Tea? Water?"

"A glass of water would be nice, thank you." Wishing she had not come.

Edith left, and Leona took in the details of the room: a settee and one chair; a table with a stack of books on it. Edith's books or Walker's? A lamp with a shade made from pieces of colored glass. Leona wanted some sign of his presence, but she saw none. Edith returned with water with ice in it, unheard of out in the country. The cold water made Leona's head hurt. Edith sat down and arranged her skirt, a lovely print material the likes of which Leona had never seen in Sully.

"Well, we should get right to it," Edith said, a little too brightly, Leona thought. Was her being there as awkward for Edith as it was for her? "I haven't bought any fabric yet. I haven't seen much at the store that I like—all too coarse for an infant's skin, don't you think?"

"I used their best batiste for a couple of dresses, but I had little use for fancy things. I bought nice cotton flannel for gowns and shirts, since Isaiah was born in cold weather. I made diapers, too, but you may want to buy those." Leona set her glass on the doily on the side table. "Your baby will be born in the winter?"

Edith nodded. "The end of December, we believe."

"I brought a few things for you to see." Leona reached in the satchel and took out a dress, a couple of gowns, a blanket edged with even stitching.

Edith turned the gowns and blanket in her hands and held one of the little dresses to the light. "Look at these tiny stitches." She smiled. "You do nice work." She passed everything back to Leona. "Do you embroider?"

"I do, but not very well." She rummaged in the satchel. "I brought patterns. I guess there are newer ones, but these are the ones I used."

Edith studied each one and gave them back. "I would like to engage you. Tell me how much batiste to buy, and I'll order it from a shop back home."

"It depends on how many dresses you want."

"Oh, several!"

Leona did a quick calculation in her head. "I'd say three, four yards then, to start."

"I'll order it. You can buy whatever else you need here. Will you excuse me for a moment?" Edith left the room again and came back with money in her hand. She held out two twenty-dollar bills. "Will this be enough for now? Keep track of how much time you spend, and I'll pay you for the labor when you finish the clothes."

Leona had never held bills that large. "It's too much."

Edith held out the money again. "Here. Take it." Was there irritation in her voice?

Leona took in Edith Broom's severe hair, her pale skin, her abrupt ways. What had Walker seen in her to love that had changed him so? Or had Leona simply not known him?

"All right," Leona said. "When do you want them?"

"We have plenty of time, but as you finish things, would you bring them to me? It's exciting, you know." Edith sat back down, clasping her hands in her lap. "I hope you were able to feel excitement over your baby." She picked at a thread on her skirt. "Do you see him?"

Leona's hands went cold. "Who?"

"Your son's father. Does he live near you? Or here in Sully?"

"No." Leona's eyes fell on a photograph on the mantel: Edith wearing an ankle-length white dress with an overlay of lace and tulle, carrying a bouquet of flowers. Walker beside her, dressed in a dark suit. They were smiling.

Leona gathered up the baby clothes and put them in her bag. "I'd rather not talk about it."

"I'm sorry," Edith said. "I didn't mean to be rude."

Didn't she? Leona picked up the satchel.

Edith followed her to the door. "Do come back soon and show me your progress."

Leona was relieved when the door closed behind her. She was all in a sweat, but it wasn't because of the heat. She stopped to catch her breath before she headed back to the wagon. She would have to walk right past the mercantile store. She didn't want to run into Walker, but if she didn't go in the store now, she would need to make another trip to town before she could begin sewing. Dealing with Raymond's questioning would be worse.

When she went into Broom's, Walker was with a customer at the back of the store. He glanced in her direction and turned away without the least sign of recognition. Undone, she hastily chose some white flannel and a yard of pale-yellow cotton that felt silky in her hand. That would be enough to get started.

When she handed the clerk a twenty-dollar bill, he looked askance at her, as though she might have stolen it. She wanted to say, "I'm sewing for Mrs. Broom," but thought better of it. She pocketed her change and the receipt and picked up the bundle. She glanced again toward the back of the store, but Walker was no longer there.

All the way home, Leona worried. If Edith had told Walker she was hiring Leona to make baby clothes, he must not have given anything away. But Edith's comment about Isaiah's father had shaken her. Leona was curious, but Edith was dangerously so.

When Leona arrived at home, Sally turned from the pot of greens she was stirring and pointed the spoon at the package Leona carried. "What's that?"

"I bought some material."

"My land. What did you use for money?"

"Walker Broom's wife, Edith, is paying me to make clothes for their baby." Leona was proud of the steadiness of her voice while her heart was racing so. "Edith met Bertie, and Bertie told her I make beautiful baby clothes. Edith hired me."

"Didn't know they were expecting." Sally climbed down from the stool. "Let me see." Leona opened the package, and Sally fingered the yellow cotton. "This is right pretty."

"She wants lots of clothes." Leona took one of the baby

gowns she had shown Edith out of her bag and handed it to Sally. "She liked this one, and the dresses too."

Sally had seen the baby gown many times, but now she held it up to the light and shook her head. "Look at this, Leona." She turned the garment wrong side out and fingered the seam. "It would be nicer if you made a closed seam. You stitch the seam as if it were on the outside, and then you fold it, so." Sally demonstrated, enclosing the raw seam in the fold. "And you stitch it again." Sally handed the baby gown back to Leona.

"That is nice. I'll try it."

"Why would that woman want homemade clothes? Can't she buy whatever she wants?"

"I have no idea, Aunt Sally. Their house is modest."

Sally's eyebrows arched. "You went to their house?"

Leona nodded. "I did. Edith was nice enough." She almost said, I think she's lonely.

"Don't put yourself where you got no business, Leona."

Her aunt couldn't imagine how complicated things were. "Don't worry. I won't."

38

Leona was home alone the following Wednesday, laying out patterns and cutting out baby gowns on the dining room table, when she heard a car out on the road. Cars seldom came by their house, especially on weekdays. Whoever it was either knew exactly where he was going, or he was lost.

She picked Isaiah up and carried him out to the front porch just as the car rounded the last curve in a spray of gravel and turned into their yard, heaving and bouncing almost to the front steps before the driver cut the engine. The door creaked open and a man climbed out, took off his hat, and held it below his heart, against his big belly.

"Morning, ma'am. How're you this morning?"

"I'm all right," Leona said. "May I help you? Are you lost?"

"No, ma'am. I'm not lost." He climbed the porch steps. His shirt clung to him, wet with sweat. "What a fine boy you got there." He tweaked Isaiah's cheek. Isaiah rubbed the spot. "Let me introduce myself. My name's James Rutherford. I take pictures. I been traveling all over north Mississippi, going house to house. If you can spare the time, I'd like to get my case out of the car and show you some of my work."

He handed her a worn business card: *James Rutherford Photography. Reasonable Prices. Tinted Extra.* She looked from the card to his red face. Whether he was flushed from the heat or from something else, she couldn't say, but she didn't smell liquor.

She handed the card back. "We don't need any pictures."

"Well, that's a shame. You got such a handsome little fellow. If I could show you my pictures, you might change your mind. Wouldn't you like to have a good likeness of the boy? He'll be a grown man before you can turn around."

He put his hat back on, went to the car, and got a black case out of the back seat. He struggled up the steps. "Let me show you a few. It won't take but a minute."

Leona had no idea how much photographs might cost. She had hidden the money Edith paid her in a coin purse in her bureau drawer. The pictures Walker had taken of her were hidden there too. Leona had intended to burn them, but she hadn't done it. Not yet.

She looked to the northwest, in the direction of the pastures where Raymond had gone. He had said he wouldn't be home till late. Sally had gone to a sewing circle and wouldn't be back until late afternoon. This man seemed nice enough. He had clear eyes, his hair was neatly barbered, and his clothes, though threadbare, looked clean. They had allowed worse folks in the house, folks whose cars had broken down, traveling seed salesmen, itinerant workers.

What could it hurt to look? "Come on in," she said.

She went ahead of the man into the house. The parlor was cooler, but it wasn't bright. Leona pointed to the settee. "Over there, where the best light is."

The man set the case down. He took off his hat and tossed it in a chair. He rubbed his reddened hands together, opened the case, brought out a large velvet-bound album, and laid it on the table beside the settee.

She sat Isaiah on the floor and gave him the fire engine, hoping it would keep him occupied. She sat down. The man walked to the window and stood with his back to her.

So many pictures, mostly black and white, some with a brown tone, some tinted with a little bit of color: girls in pretty dresses with big bows in their hair; boys in suits and slicked-back hair, looking out with solemn eyes; young women in wedding dresses; mothers with babies in christening gowns; unsmiling mothers and fathers surrounded by children; severe old women alone, dressed in black. Leona savored them all like chocolate that left a bitter aftertaste. She closed the book and ran her hand across the velvet cover against its weave, watching it change color.

Why had this man come so far back in these hills? Why had he come to her?

Mr. Rutherford said, "We can set up in this room. I'll go get my equipment out of the car. Won't take but a minute."

Leona's mouth went dry. "I need to know how much it costs."

He tapped his forehead as though he couldn't believe he had forgotten such a thing. "Yes, you do." He took a little ledger out of his pocket and ran one blunt, ink-stained finger down the page. "I can photograph the boy, three poses, for three dollars. Tint's extra."

Would she dare to spend the sewing money on something so frivolous? What if the sewing didn't please Edith, and she wanted her money back?

"I'm sorry. I can't." Leona stood as a signal for him to leave. Out the window she saw a cloudbank closing in from the north-west. If it rained, Raymond would come in from the field early. "You'd better go before my husband gets home." Why she had lied, she couldn't say. Why would this stranger care whether she was married or not?

Mr. Rutherford took a pencil out of his pocket and wrote in the ledger. "Times is hard. I can see how much you want it. I'll do it for two dollars. You won't find a bargain like that nowhere else."

She had never imagined having a photograph of Isaiah. Now, she couldn't imagine not having one. What better use for Edith's money? "All right. I need to change his clothes."

The photographer smiled. "Yes, ma'am. You go right ahead. I'll be setting up."

Leona changed Isaiah into a sailor suit Sally had made. She washed his face and combed his hair, which he tolerated fairly well. By the time she got back, the man had set up his camera, a painted landscape background, and a little velvet-covered bench. "Set him down right there," he said, but Isaiah threw his arms around her neck and wouldn't let go. The photographer made funny faces and squeezed a rubber toy that squealed.

Nothing worked. Finally, he said, "Take a seat and hold the boy on your lap."

Was this a trick? "Won't you charge me more?"

He smiled, and she saw his crooked, tobacco-stained teeth. "No, ma'am. Don't mind a bit, such a pretty mother and son."

She had not wanted to be in the photograph, but she tucked loose strands of hair up as best she could, straightened her dress, pinched her cheeks, and licked her lips.

"That's right," Mr. Rutherford said. "You look nice."

No matter what the photographer did, though, Isaiah wouldn't smile. And then Leona started singing a song he loved, "Ride a little horsey," bouncing him, and Isaiah giggled. Mr. Rutherford disappeared under the black drape once, twice, three times. Flashes of light.

He snapped the last shiny black box out of the camera and dropped them all in his case. "These ought to be real good. That'll be two dollars."

Spots of light danced before Leona's eyes. Isaiah was rubbing his. "How will I get the photographs?"

"I'll bring them to you. Be about a month." He grinned. "Couldn't ask for better service than that, can you?"

Leona shook her head. "No. I'm sorry."

"Lady, I took them. You got to buy them."

"That's not what I meant. I'd rather you not bring them here. Could you leave them at Mr. Carl Pratt's place, just up the road?"

The man shrugged. "Sure. I know of the Pratts. Sad what happened to them, ain't it? The influenza."

"Yes, it is."

She left the man packing his case and went to her room. She put Isaiah in his crib and got the money. When she returned, all of Mr. Rutherford's equipment was gone, as though he had never been there. He stood by the front door, hat in hand, mopping his face with a handkerchief. When she gave him the money, she had a sinking feeling she would never see any pictures.

"Thank you, ma'am." He pocketed the bills, put on his hat, and started out the door.

"Shouldn't you write down my name?"

He tapped his forehead. "I sure should." He fished the ledger and a pencil out and licked the pencil lead. "Spell it for me."

She spelled out her name. He wrote "Mrs." in front of it.

Leona waited until she heard the car head off down the dirt lane before she looked out. The car disappeared, leaving a cloud of red dust that quickly dissolved in the hot wind.

Leona imagined how Isaiah would look in the photograph. It occurred to her that if she saw a striking likeness, others might too. What a shame if the pictures had to be hidden away, like so much else.

39

Raymond walked the rows of green, lush corn, the stalks a foot taller than he. He picked an ear here and there and peeled back the husks to see the plump kernels. Nearing the end of September; another week, maybe two, and this crop, the best one ever, would be ready to harvest.

He squinted up at the bright sky. "There, Father. See what I can do?" As soon as the crop came in, he would make Tobe Sanders an offer on the ridge land. Tobe wouldn't refuse, no matter how paltry the offer.

A week later, Raymond pulled a few ears and noticed tunneling damage. Armyworms. "Well, I'll be damned," he said. Unless he harvested right away, those little devils could do a lot of damage. He hired the colored boys who had worked on the barn roof to help bring the crop in. They came to work for a day but didn't show up the next. Raymond paced and swore.

Leona asked if she could help.

"Naw," Raymond said. "It's men's work. But you can take the mule to Sully and get that sore hoof looked at. Can't haul corn without the mule. Take Luther with you. He'll know what to tell the blacksmith. And y'all stop by the Pratts' and the Caldwells' on the way and see if they can spare any hands down here."

It seemed to Leona the mule could wait, but she did as she was told, and she and Luther headed off to Sully. The Caldwells weren't at home, but Mr. Pratt said he would go down to the place later.

"I'll talk to Raymond," he said. "See what I can do."

In the back field, Raymond pulled bad ears and tossed them on the ground. After an hour in the heat, he walked out of the field and sat in the shade. He'd give a nickel for a jar of water, but he didn't want to go all the way to the house. He stretched out on the grass. He was dozing when he heard movement in the woods behind him. No animal would be moving around in the midday heat. When he heard it again, he scrambled up off the ground.

"Hold up!" he shouted. "Come on out!" Whoever it was stood still, out of Raymond's view. "Who's there?"

Jesse stepped out of the woods, looking at the ground as he walked.

"Jesse? Damn, boy. What're you doing here? You taken to coming to the place through the woods? You sneaking up on me?"

"No, sir. I was looking for Pa. He say he would be here."

"He's gone to town. What you need him for?"

Jesse shrugged. "I just need to find him. That's all."

Raymond took in the boy's height, his slender build, his light eyes and skin. "Come over here, Jesse. I want to take a look at you in good daylight."

Jesse didn't move.

Raymond waved him over with both arms. "Come on now. I don't bite."

Jesse stepped closer, and Raymond tilted Jesse's face toward the sun. "You ever see yourself in a mirror?"

"No, sir. I never did."

"You don't know the color of your eyes, do you?"

"Yes, sir. They dark brown. Like Pa's."

"Oh no. You got what they call hazel eyes. Almost green in this bright light, got some gold in them. You know what that means?"

"No. No, sir."

Raymond released his hold and Jesse rubbed his chin. "It means you got a white daddy. Some white man laid with your mama. Big boy like you, you know what it means to lay with a woman?" Raymond snickered. "Or maybe you don't."

Jesse shifted his feet, started to rock a little.

"Well, do you?"

"Yes, sir. I know." Jesse took a couple of steps back. "I got to go. Got to find Pa."

"Don't go yet. We ain't finished talking. You got to use your imagination a little bit. Imagine a white man on top of your mama, pumping away." Raymond poked a finger at Jesse's chest. "And that's how she got you. Ask your pa. Ask him if it ain't true."

Jesse raised his head and his eyes met Raymond's. "Don't you say that about my mama."

Raymond cupped a hand to his ear. "What did you say? You talking back to me?"

Jesse clenched and unclenched his fists. "No."

"You mean no, sir."

Jesse looked at the ground. "No, sir."

Raymond clapped his hands. "Get out of here!" When Jesse didn't move, Raymond shoved him, and Jesse stumbled backward. "I said get on!" Raymond swung a punch at Jesse and then another, but neither of them landed. Raymond's punches were more like shadow boxing, but then he landed a right to Jesse's stomach and doubled him over. Jesse coughed and straightened and came at Raymond with a roar.

The blows to Raymond's jaw and stomach staggered him. The next took him to his knees and down, and Jesse was pummeling his gut and face and head. Jesse's wild eyes, his distorted face, tears streaming down, were the last things Raymond would remember.

❧

Returning home that afternoon, Leona and Luther topped the last rise where the Pinson house came into view. Dr. Dunlap's automobile was parked in the yard. Before Luther could halt the mule, Leona climbed out of the wagon and ran across the yard and into the house, calling Isaiah's name. The baby came toddling out of the kitchen with Sally right behind him.

Leona scooped him up. "What's the matter, Aunt Sally? What happened?"

"Ray's been beat up real bad," Sally said. "Carl Pratt found him in the field and brought him to the house. Mr. Carl went for Dr. Dunlap."

"Who beat him up?"

There was a knock at the back door. "Miss Leona? Miss Sally?"

Luther, with the box of groceries. Leona started toward the door to let him in.

"Wait." Sally lowered her voice. "Raymond says Jesse did it."

Leona shook her head. "I don't believe that."

"Raymond swears it was Jesse."

"Raymond used to make moonshine. He owes people money. God only knows what else. It could have been just about anybody around here." Except maybe Tobe Sanders. Leona had heard he was still laid up from the beating he took.

She opened the kitchen door. Luther said, "What's the matter?"

"It's Raymond," Leona said. "Come in." She held the door open for him.

He set the box on the kitchen table. "He sick?"

A moan came from the back of the house.

Sally said, "His face is beat to a pulp. Lord, you ought to see it."

Leona saw Luther's expression change. "Let's go out on the porch," she said. "Aunt Sally, can you watch Isaiah?"

Sally nodded. Leona sat Isaiah on the kitchen floor, and Luther followed her out the door. How to tell him? Straight out. "Raymond says Jesse did this."

Leona had never seen Luther's eyes so bright and hard. He shook his head as if to clear it. "No. Jesse ain't got that kind of meanness in him. No matter what somebody might've done to him, he wouldn't never do such a thing. Besides, he's scared of Raymond." Luther turned and started down the steps. "I got to go home."

"Luther—"

"No. I got to go see about Jesse." He was already crossing

the yard. Leona wanted to go after him, but she didn't. She went to the bedroom where her brother lay. Dr. Dunlap was closing a cut over Raymond's right cheekbone, below his eye. "Not going to be perfect," he told Leona. With every stitch, Raymond grunted. His face was battered, already swelling and bruising.

"Oh my Lord," Leona whispered. She couldn't stand to watch.

She sat in the kitchen and fed Isaiah while she waited for the doctor to finish. An hour later, he came and washed up at the kitchen sink. He gave Leona a vial of medicine.

"Give Raymond a few drops in water whenever he needs it for the pain. It won't taste good, but make him drink it anyway. It'll help some."

"What about whiskey?"

"Let him have his whiskey. Can't hurt. I've never seen anybody beat up worse than he is. His nose is broken, both cheekbones, ribs on each side. I wrapped his ribs up good. Can't do much about his face. As long as he's not bleeding on the inside, he'll be all right."

Leona said, "Tell me how much we owe."

He closed the catch on his bag. "You got a dollar? That's enough."

She went and got a dollar out of her coin purse.

He put the bill in his pocket. "I'll let the sheriff know about Raymond."

"No. Please don't tell the sheriff."

"Leona, Jesse almost killed your brother. You understand that?"

She turned away. Out the window the heat shimmered, the corn in the distance still as could be, no breeze. "Yes, sir. I know."

"You know about anything between Raymond and Jesse?"

There was that awful business Raymond had raised about Jesse being Herbert's son, and the way Raymond had taunted Jesse. But she couldn't tell the doctor.

"No, sir. I don't."

Dr. Dunlap raised an eyebrow. "You sure?" She nodded. "I'll be going, then. Check Raymond for fever and send for me if you need me."

After he was gone, Leona considered that Dr. Dunlap might be right about telling the sheriff. She remembered the night of the white-hooded men, the burned effigy. What might Raymond's cronies do to Jesse when they heard he had nearly beaten Raymond to death?

What would their father do if he were alive? She believed she knew. Sheriff Bobby Taylor was a friend, a good man. Leona would talk to Luther. She would persuade him to take Jesse to town to turn himself in. Mr. Bobby would take care of Jesse.

ॐ

Luther's temples throbbed, his chest hurt, and the humid air smothered him, or maybe it was the thoughts running through his head that cut off his breath like an iron trap. Leona was wrong, wrong to say Jesse might have done such a thing. Jesse would be waiting at home, a little hot, a little hungry, but all right. Luther had given him chores to do that day: slop the hogs, put out hay for the mule and cow, gather eggs, sweep the porch. Jesse had repeated them back to him. Luther had told him not to leave the house after his trouble with Raymond over the dog. Since then, Jesse had started at the least sound and sat for hours in that straight chair, rocking. He mumbled in his sleep, but Luther hadn't been able to make out a single word.

Within earshot of the house, Luther called Jesse's name. The house was empty except for Jesse's yellow hound asleep in a shadowy corner. Luther saw a smear of blood on a door facing. "God Almighty," he said. He sat to catch his breath and let his hammering heart calm down. He looked around: a tin plate of fried eggs left untouched on the table, a jug of milk spoiling in the heat, flies swarming. Luther got to his feet. A little unsteady, he walked out back.

"Jesse!" The air hot, so still, not even a bird calling. "Son? Where are you?"

Jesse wasn't in the barn or the shed. Luther was about to head back in the house when he heard a sound from the outhouse. He opened the door. Huddled there, Jesse blinked at the light.

"Oh sweet Jesus. Come on out. It's gon' be all right."

"You be mad at me, Pa. I got in a fight with Raymond. He—"

"It don't matter. We'll talk about it later."

Jesse started to cry.

Luther said, "None of that now."

He helped Jesse up. Jesse's shirt and overalls were spattered with blood, his knuckles bruised and cut. While Jesse washed, Luther heard shouts on the road and the sound of a wagon. He tried to think what to do, but his mind went off in all directions. He saw Herbert Pinson's bloodied head, imagined Raymond's beaten and bloody face. How the circle of life closes in, Luther thought, one man's blood for another's, a death for a death. Then Varna's face appeared, so pretty and young, and Rose Pinson's too. Together the women said, "You've come this far, Luther. Take care of the boy."

The women were right. If he and Jesse could get to Luna by morning, they might hitch a ride up to Alma's place in Memphis.

While Jesse put on clean clothes, Luther dug a hole in the hard-baked garden and buried the bloody ones. He was putting a couple of cold baked yams and biscuits in a knapsack when he heard a clatter in the front yard, the whinny of a horse. He pushed Jesse into the lean-to and closed the curtain.

A knock on the door. "Luther?" Leona's voice.

Luther opened the door. The girl was winded and drenched with sweat. "What you doing here, Leona? You got no—"

"Let me in."

"I ain't got time. I got to get Jesse out of here."

"You think you can hide him? They'll find him. You know they will." She glanced toward the road. "Please, let me in."

Luther stepped away from the door. Leona came inside and shut it.

"Let me take you and Jesse to town. Jesse can tell the sheriff what happened. Sheriff Taylor's a good man. He'll take care of Jesse. I can handle Raymond. Especially now."

Could Luther do that? Turn his own son over to the law? He shook his head. "No. They'll lock Jesse up."

"I don't think so. There's no telling what Raymond did to provoke Jesse." Leona put her hand on Luther's arm. "It'll be worse if Jesse runs away. You know that."

Luther wondered if she was right. If Jesse ran and got caught, things would go worse for him. Maybe Raymond wasn't as bad hurt as Sally had said. Maybe Leona could talk Raymond out of bringing a charge against Jesse. To depend on the mercy of the sheriff—Luther wasn't sure there was such a thing, although he thought Sheriff Taylor to be as good a white man as Luther had ever known besides Herbert Pinson. He let out a deep breath. His chest and arms ached from digging in the hard dirt. He heard Jesse in the lean-to, hiding like a rat.

"All right. But there ain't no need for you to go."

"There's every reason. I brought the buggy. It'll be faster."

❧

Leona told Luther and Jesse to stay out of sight in the buggy, although she reasoned that nobody would have heard about Raymond yet. All the way to town, above the noise of the buggy on the road, she heard Jesse's whimpering, Luther's soft cadence, soothing him.

The deputy at the desk in the sheriff's office didn't look up until she cleared her throat. "Yes, ma'am?"

"I'm Leona Pinson. I need to see the sheriff."

"Just a minute." The deputy disappeared down the hall and came back quickly. "This way," he said, and Leona followed.

The sheriff swiveled his chair around to face her. "Leona. What brings you to town? Y'all got trouble?"

She waited until the deputy had closed the office door. "Luther and Jesse are outside in the buggy. Jesse and Raymond got into a fight, and Raymond's bad off."

The sheriff sat forward. "Jesse beat Raymond up?"

"It seems that way."

Sheriff Taylor sighed. "They're outside?" She nodded. "All right. I'll talk to Jesse. Pull the buggy around back. No need for everybody in town to see."

She did as he said. It took some persuading on Luther's part to get Jesse out of the buggy. The sheriff led them into a bare room next to his office. He pulled up a chair for Jesse and gave him a cup of water. Luther stood off to the side with Leona while the sheriff questioned Jesse. He admitted he had beaten Raymond up but he wouldn't say why. Leona was glad to see Mr. Bobby's patience with Jesse.

Finally, the sheriff stood. "What do you know about all this, Luther? Anything going on between those two boys?"

Leona watched Luther's face. He didn't blink. "No, sir. Not that I know of."

Jesse sat, head down, hands dangling, rocking. The sheriff paced the little room, frowning, rubbing his chin. He stopped and said, "I want to keep Jesse here for a night or two."

Luther twisted his hat in his hands. "No, Mr. Bobby. Please don't do that. Jesse don't deserve to be in the jail. He'll be scared to death."

The sheriff turned to Leona. "Is Raymond in any shape to talk to me?"

"I don't believe he is."

The sheriff laid a hand on Luther's shoulder. "I'll go see Raymond in a couple of days. If he wants to bring a charge against Jesse, there's not much I can do about it. Meanwhile, Jesse's safer in the jail than he would be at home."

"I'm staying too, then," Luther said. "Jesse's gon' need me close by."

Sheriff Taylor said, "You can't stay, Luther. Go home. I'll take good care of him." To Jesse he said, "Come along with me now."

"But—"

"Let me handle it, Luther."

Jesse's eyes went wide and fearful. "Pa?"

Luther gathered the boy into his arms and held him for a full minute before he let him go. "It's all right, Jesse. Go with Sheriff Taylor. He's gon' give you a place to sleep. Bring you a good supper too."

The sheriff gestured for Jesse to go ahead of him. Jesse took a couple of steps and stopped. "Go on, Jesse," the sheriff said, but Leona heard no irritation or anger in his voice. Leona looked from Jesse to Luther and felt a flutter of uneasiness. Had she done the wrong thing, bringing Jesse here? The sheriff put his arm around Jesse's shoulders and led him away.

"Let's go home, Luther," Leona said.

"I ain't going nowhere. I'll stay here."

"You can't. The sheriff said—"

"I can and I will. I'll be home soon as they let Jesse go." He walked down the hall in the direction the sheriff had gone. Leona saw the deputy step out and stop him.

What could she do? Nothing that she could think of. She would come back to town in a day or two, and if the sheriff wasn't ready to release Jesse, she would make Luther go home with her. Somehow, she would.

Sundown by the time Leona got back to the house. Raymond was sleeping, and the baby was playing in a tub of water in the kitchen. Isaiah stood up, dripping and laughing, when Leona walked in, and she picked him up, never mind that he was wet. She didn't want to let him go.

"You were gone long enough," Sally said.

Leona told Sally what she had done.

Sally said, "Well, thank the Lord. Jail's the right place for Jesse. Half dumb, half crazy, I don't know which. That boy gives me the willies."

40

Overnight, Raymond developed a fever. All day and into the night, Leona kept his wounds clean as best she could. She put cool cloths on his forehead and neck and gave him sips of a tea made from yarrow for the fever and nips of the pain medicine. Every time he moved, he cried out.

When neighbors came the following day to harvest the corn, Leona knew the word had gotten out about Raymond. By late afternoon the healthy corn had been loaded into the crib behind the barn. It wouldn't all be lost. Leona and Sally thanked them, and they piled back in their wagons and left.

Leona hoped the sheriff had let Jesse go. She vowed she would go to Luther's as soon as she could to see if he had brought Jesse home. If they weren't there, she would go to town.

That evening, Mr. Pratt brought the news that he had seen Luther sitting on the steps of the jail. "Right about noon today," Mr. Pratt said. "Luther told me he wasn't leaving Jesse, but then a gang of men and boys, friends of Raymond's, I guess, came up and started spitting on Luther and pushing him around. It was awful, no matter what Jesse might have done. I told the bunch of them to get, and I talked Luther into coming with me. I told him y'all needed him here. He's in pitiful shape. All the way home, he kept saying they'll kill Jesse. I told him Jesse's safe in the jail."

Leona hoped Carl Pratt was right. She wanted to go and see Luther, but Sally balked at cleaning Raymond's wounds. Leona worried aloud to Sally about Luther.

"Luther's got neighbors and friends," Sally reminded her. "They'll take care of him."

When the sheriff drove into the yard the following afternoon, Leona was sitting on the porch with the baby. There was something about the man's slumped posture—he was tall and dignified looking—that made her heart pause.

He took off his hat as he came up on the porch. She figured he had come to question Raymond, but he said, "Mind if I sit?"

"No, sir. Of course not."

He took the rocker next to hers. It seemed the lines around his eyes had deepened since the other day. "I have bad news, Leona. There's no easy way to say it. Jesse Biggs is dead."

She bolted up, clutching Isaiah so tightly that the baby struggled and cried out. "But how can that be? Jesse's in the jail."

The sheriff passed his hands over his face. "Some men took him during the night. They strung him up at Hawks Creek. We found him this morning."

Isaiah felt too heavy in her arms. Her precious son, just as Jesse was Luther's. How would Luther bear it? "It's my fault. If I hadn't talked Luther into bringing Jesse to you—"

"Don't blame yourself. If anybody's to blame, I am. I thought I could keep that boy safe. I was wrong."

Isaiah gave her kisses as though he knew she needed loving. But loving wouldn't fix this. She had stepped in where she had no business, and now Jesse was dead. She couldn't get her mind around it. Who would do such a thing? She knew the answer. Raymond was laid up from the beating, but he had friends who would do it for revenge.

"Oh no. Oh no, no, no." She started to cry. "I don't understand. How could somebody just take Jesse from the jail?"

"I figure it was some of the Ridge Rider boys, but they had to have help. I wouldn't have thought my deputy on duty last night would do such a thing, but— Well, anyway." He cleared his throat. "I have to tell Luther. I wondered if you would go with me."

How could she face Luther? How could she not? "Yes, sir, I'll go. Let me get the baby settled with Aunt Sally."

"Thank you. I appreciate it."

She carried Isaiah inside and told Sally what had happened. "Can you keep him a while? The sheriff wants me to go to Luther's with him."

"I can," Sally said. "Lord. I knew it would all come to no good."

Leona rode with the sheriff in his car. The weather had turned cooler overnight, a hint of fall in the air, but the trees were still heavy with the green of summer. As they got closer to Luther's place, she wanted to turn back time and make things right. Or she wanted to tell the sheriff to let her out, and she would run and run across the fields and through the woods until she was back at home with Isaiah. When they came in sight of the house, Leona saw Luther standing on his porch, as though he were waiting for Jesse to come home or for the news she and Sheriff Taylor were bringing. The band of hurt around Leona's heart tightened. She got out of the car and let the sheriff lead the way across Luther's yard.

Luther stared out at the yard while Sheriff Taylor told him, and then Luther went in the house and brought out a piece of paper with something written on it. He gave it to the sheriff. "It's the telephone number of the grocery store where Alma works," Luther said. "Would you call her, Mr. Bobby?"

After the sheriff left, Luther sat down on the porch steps. When Leona sat beside him, he didn't object, but the distance between them might as well have been miles. What could she say to him? Finally, she gathered her courage. She had willed herself not to cry again, but the tears came anyway. "I'm so sorry, Luther. I didn't know—"

"I know you didn't." He didn't look at her. "Just go home."

"No. I'm not leaving you." Her words echoed what Luther had said to Jesse at the jail.

Luther closed his eyes. "I'd rather not look at you right now, Leona."

Leona got up and stood for a minute, watching Luther. He sat very still. She walked home, weeping all the way.

"He blames me," she told Sally.

Sally enfolded Leona in her short arms as best she could. "You did what you thought was best. Sometimes it's all we can do, but it don't always turn out right."

Leona dreaded telling Raymond that Jesse was dead and hearing him rant, but when she told him, Raymond only nodded. She supposed he was still in too much pain to care.

All morning and into the afternoon, Leona saw Negroes pass by on the road, headed in the direction of Luther's house. They came on foot and in wagons and riding on mules, young and old, women in hats and dresses, men in overalls. Jesse would be buried quickly because of the heat.

Leona missed her father, and she was angry with him. She thought she had divined what he would do about Jesse. She had been wrong. She considered going to her father's grave to talk to him but decided against it. Would her father hear her? Would God? Leona saw little evidence in the world of a God who listened, let alone one who was just.

She waited until the next day to go back to Luther's. Colored men, women, and children milled about in the yard. They parted and made a path for Leona. Most of them stared at her stonily.

His daughter, Alma, met Leona on the porch. Alma was taller and darker than Luther. Leona reckoned Alma to be not much more than thirty, but her hair was already scattered with gray, and she was too thin.

Alma nodded gravely. "Miss Leona. What're you doing here?"

"I couldn't stay away."

Alma crossed her arms. "You done enough, don't you think?"

Leona winced. She felt the eyes of Luther's people on her. "Could we—could I come inside, just for a minute?"

"Daddy don't want to see you." Alma's eyes scanned the mourners. "Let's walk around back." Alma walked down the porch steps and made her way through the crowd. Leona followed, jostled more than once by an elbow, a shoulder. She was relieved when she and Alma rounded the corner of the house. Had they all heard? Did they know she had talked Luther into taking Jesse to town?

The back yard was as bare and clean-swept as the front. Luther's garden, scorching in the heat. The privy. A shed, Luther's mule tethered to it. The ramshackle barn. Where would Luther have hidden Jesse? No wonder he had wanted to run.

Alma stopped, her hands on her hips. "What is it you come to say?"

What could Leona say? "Just that—I'm so sorry. I guess Luther told you I convinced him to take Jesse to the sheriff. Sheriff Taylor is a good man. I thought—"

"Maybe he is," Alma said, "but he didn't do nothing to stop it."

"If he had known, he would have."

"So he didn't know, I guess."

Why couldn't Alma see? It hadn't mattered where Jesse was, in the jail or at home. Jesse's fate had been sealed when he hit Raymond.

Leona said, "Do you think things would have been any different if Luther had run off with Jesse instead? That's what he was going to do. Did he tell you that? How far do you think they would have gotten?"

"Maybe far enough, if he hadn't listened to you. You ought to see my daddy. Hardly speaks a word, won't eat nothing. If I could stay, I would, but I got to go back to Memphis. I'll lose my job if I'm gone too long. And I got my kids. I'd take him back with me, but he says he won't go. Says this is where he was born and this is where he'll die."

Leona said, "I'll look after him, if he'll let me." If Luther would rather stay, maybe he could forgive her. Maybe she could hope for it.

Alma picked a morning glory flower off the vine growing on the fence. "Daddy helped me plant this vine. And it's still here." She started to cry. "You know what else he told me? He says his vision is failing him. I thought he meant his eyesight, and I told him, I says, 'Daddy, come home with me, and we'll get you some eyeglasses.' He says, 'It ain't my eyes I'm talking about.'"

"Luther sees visions."

Alma tossed the flower on the ground. "You knew that?"

Leona nodded, but had she known it, really? Had she ever given much thought to Luther other than what he could do for her?

"I was so scared when Isaiah was born. I believed if Luther was there, he would know what to do. I willed him to come, and he did."

"Well, he thinks the sight has left him. He says he should've seen what would happen to Jesse. If he had, he could've saved him." Alma took a handkerchief out of her dress pocket and wiped her eyes. "You want to know what you can do for my daddy? Pay him off and tell him to leave. Make him come to Memphis and live with me."

"No, Alma. Luther belongs here. Leaving here would kill him."

Alma shook her head. "You couldn't be more wrong. If Daddy stays here, one Pinson or another will be the death of him."

Leona started to protest, but what Alma said was true. How would Leona live without Luther? She couldn't begin to imagine it.

Alma came to the house a couple of days later and told Leona she was going back to Memphis. "Daddy won't leave with me. He says things ain't finished here."

"If I go to see him, will he talk to me?"

"Can't say." She looked away, then back at Leona. "He's angry at you, and oh Lord, how he hurts. But it's you he's hanging on for. If it weren't for you and your boy, he would lay right down and die. You know how that makes me feel?" Alma turned and went down the porch steps and headed back toward the road, her back ramrod straight, her fists clenched at her sides.

Luther had said things weren't finished.

That was true. Things were not finished at all.

Leona would not force her presence on Luther. She waited and hoped he would show up at the house, but he did not. Raymond was a little better and no longer needed her constant attention, although he was restless and demanding as a sulky child. He had asked her more than once to relate the story of Jesse's death. He seemed to delight in it. She refused to tell it again.

She tried to turn her attention to the layette she was making for Walker's baby. It didn't help to ease her mind about what had happened to Jesse, but by the end of the week, she had sewn a couple of long gowns that drew together at the bottom with ribbon and three tiny shirts that tied on the side. She had begun work on a simple long dress made from the yellow cotton. She would embellish it with white lace. A pretty dress for a boy or a girl child.

She decided she had enough finished work to show Edith. Maybe the batiste Edith ordered had arrived, and Leona could get started on a finer dress. She would make a cap too. Isaiah had not needed a cap since he wasn't baptized. She knew that had troubled her mother. Leona wondered where Walker's family went to church. She had never thought to ask him.

Saturday morning early, she dressed in her best white shirtwaist and a dark skirt and coiled her unruly hair into a knot at the base of her neck. She stood at the glass, dismayed by her appearance. Edith Broom wasn't pretty, but she had an air of elegance and refinement Leona would never have.

She had sworn she wouldn't allow the baby around Edith, but she couldn't leave Sally to tend to both Isaiah and Raymond. Raymond was up and about that morning, and all the way to the barn, she could hear his ranting refrain from the back porch: "Where you going, Leona! Come back here!"

41

When Leona got to Sully, she pinched her cheeks for color and dabbed Vaseline over her lips. It was the best she could do.

She rang Edith and Walker's doorbell at ten o'clock. Was she too early? She had no idea about the habits of city folk like Edith, but Leona figured Walker surely would have gone to the store by now.

When Walker answered the door, his eyes shifted from Leona to the boy and back. The color drained from his face. "Leona. What are you doing here?"

Stunned to see him, she stumbled over her words. "I— Edith said— She asked to see the baby clothes as I finish them, so I thought I would stop by." She held out the satchel. "I can leave them, if it isn't a good time."

"No. It's all right. Come in. I'll get her."

He walked down the hall. Isaiah pointed and said, "Man."

That's your father. Say Father, Leona wanted to say. She heard Walker's voice and then Edith's, rising. Was she crying? Were they fighting?

She shouldn't have come. She turned to go, but Edith came down the hall.

"Leona! What a surprise. And look, you've brought your boy." Edith swept toward Leona with her hand extended, but Leona didn't have a free hand to offer her. Edith dabbed at her reddened eyes. "I'm sorry. I'm a little undone this morning. You have something to show me? Come in here."

She led Leona into the parlor. Today, the velvet curtains were open, the windows too. A door slammed at the back of the house, and Edith startled. She said, "Please excuse Walker. He's running late for work."

Leona stood in the center of the room, the satchel growing heavier, Isaiah bouncing. "Isa down," he said.

Edith clapped her hands. "Listen to him. How dear is that?"

"Is it all right if I put him down? I didn't want to bring him, but—"

"Oh, I'm so thoughtless. Yes. In fact— I'll be right back." Edith hurried out of the room and came back with a quilt and a little wooden train engine. "This was Walker's. His grandfather carved it."

She spread the quilt on the floor and put the toy down. Fighting tears, Leona sat Isaiah on the quilt. He ran the engine back and forth making a humming sound, as though he were thoroughly familiar with trains, although he had only seen a freight train pass through Sully once when they were in town.

The buttons of Edith's dress pulled over her bosom and waist. Her body seemed to be changing rapidly now. "Let me see what you've done so far," she said.

Leona laid the baby clothes out on the settee.

Edith said, "They're so tiny. What's this?" She picked up the yellow dress and held it to the light. "It's a pretty color, like pale sunshine." Her smile turned to a frown. "Oh, but look here." She sat beside Leona and folded the dress so a seam was visible. She picked at the stitching with a fingernail. "This won't do." She picked up a shirt. "And this. You call this fine sewing?" She tossed the dress and shirt on the settee, picked up another shirt and tossed it too. "You'll have to do it over. I won't have such shoddy workmanship."

Leona's face burned. She folded the clothes and stacked them neatly on the settee. "They're the best I know how to do. I'll leave them with you. If you aren't happy with them, you should find someone else to do your sewing."

She scooped Isaiah and her satchel up and was halfway to the door when Edith said, "Please don't go. Why is it that carrying a child makes me so fragile? Walker says I cry all the time."

Leona took in Edith's growing belly, her puffy face and

eyes and hands, and her own anger eased. Maybe Edith Broom hadn't known Walker well enough, either. Leona settled Isaiah back on the floor and sat. "I guess babies do that to us," she said.

Edith nodded. "I'd always heard it." She took a deep, shuddering breath. "I don't have anybody I can talk to. You can understand that, can't you? Nobody, not even Walker, can understand how hard moving here has been. Maybe especially Walker. And his mother—dear God, what a pain she is. I want to go home to New York to have the baby. Walker says women give birth here every day, and they do, but I'm terrified."

Leona didn't want to know the details of Edith and Walker's arguments. "I managed to have Isaiah," she said.

"Yes, you did. Way out in the country. Who attended his birth?"

"My aunt." Leona left off the fact that her aunt was a dwarf, but she wondered, half amused, what Edith would think of that. "My mother was there, but she wasn't a help."

"No doctor? What would have happened if you or the child were in danger?"

"I was in danger. I bled a lot, but Luther was there. He helped me."

"Who is Luther?"

"A man who lives on our place. His wife was the midwife who birthed me."

Isaiah babbled. Somewhere outside the open window a blue jay called, and down the street Isaiah's father was most likely engaged with a customer by now, but he would come home tonight and he and Edith would sit down together for a meal and talk about their respective days, and later, they would go to bed together. The thought of Walker and Edith spooned together in bed made Leona's heart hurt, a physical pain.

How dare Edith talk to Leona about a hard life? "I'm sure you'll be fine, Edith."

Isaiah rolled the toy engine across Leona's lap. "Mama, train," he said, and Edith burst into tears again.

Leona stood. "It's not a good time for me to be here."

"I'm sorry. It isn't like me to talk about such intimate things." Edith's voice was out of kilter.

"You should rest. I'll bring the other pieces I've already cut and the extra material to you the next time I come to town. I'll return your money."

"You don't need to do that. I was all out of sorts. The sewing is fine."

"Are you sure?"

Edith pressed a handkerchief to her face and nodded.

Leona remembered the material Edith had ordered. "Has the batiste come in at the store?"

"No. I'll let you know when it does."

Leona picked up Isaiah and shouldered the satchel. "I'll let myself out."

She walked back to the buggy, thinking it was the weight of Isaiah and the satchel that drained her strength. Or maybe it was the charged, unhappy air inside that house. Leona chided herself. Edith Broom had just revealed how discontented she was; shouldn't Leona be pleased? But she wasn't. All she felt was a growing sense of loss.

That evening, Leona rocked Isaiah to sleep early, and she went to bed before the sun was down. The following day she didn't get out of bed, leaving Sally to take care of Isaiah and Raymond.

At noon Raymond hobbled into her room, holding his side. "Sister? You sick?"

She turned her back and didn't answer, and he went away. Late in the afternoon, Sally came in. "What's the matter with you, girl? Get out of that bed. I can't do everything around this place by myself."

Leona got up, washed, and dressed. It was her heart that was sick: over Edith Broom's discontent and by extension, Walker's; Luther's grief for which she felt responsible; and her own unhappiness for which she believed there could be no cure.

She remembered something her father had told her long

ago: when you're in doubt, he'd said, and you don't know what to do, do something. What could she do?

She could finish the baby clothes and be done with Edith Broom. She could beg Luther's forgiveness. She would not give up.

42

The Sunday afternoon after Leona's latest trip to town, Raymond's cronies came to visit him. Raymond sat with them out on the porch. "I been thinking about paying Tobe Sanders a visit," he said, "when I can get around better."

"You ain't heard?" Silas Warren said. "Tobe's gone. Packed up his family and left. There was an auction. Land, house, everything, down to the last spoon and hammer. The land went for a pretty penny, I heard."

Raymond tasted bile. That land, gone. "Who bought it?"

"Leonard Barnes."

Anger rose in Raymond like a boil. Even if he had been well, he could never have outbid the likes of Leonard Barnes, who owned a thousand acres already. He rubbed his throbbing jaw. "Well, ain't that a hell of a note," Raymond said. "I guess the joke's on me."

After the men left, Raymond's anger turned to despair. He squeezed his eyes shut. All his dreams shot to hell. It seemed like he was always out of the running, like an old horse. His breath caught in a sob. He sniffed, blinked away the tears.

"Y'all heard about Tobe Sanders?" Raymond asked that evening at supper.

Leona's first thought was that Tobe had died. "What about him?"

"He's gone. Picked up and left. The place got auctioned off. Leonard Barnes bought it. The ridge is gone." Raymond's eyes looked sunken and blank. "Just when I thought I had him."

43

Leona woke the next morning before dawn with a sense that something was terribly wrong. Isaiah was sleeping, and his forehead was cool. She could hear Sally in the kitchen and Raymond moving about the house, the sounds of an ordinary morning. The uneasiness remained, and suddenly she knew: something was wrong with Luther.

She finished her chores early, left Isaiah with Sally, and set out for Luther's house. He was unable to get out of bed, his eyes glassy with fever. He turned his back on her, but she stayed anyway. She killed a chicken and plucked it and put it on to cook, and when it was ready, she gave him the broth, and he drank a little of it. She didn't want to leave him, but he insisted.

When she went back the following day, Jesse's dog whined at the door like he was waiting for her. She found Luther on the floor in a pool of vomit. She cleaned him up and got him into bed. She left him long enough to walk home and get Isaiah and gather up clothes for herself and the baby and his few toys. Her mother's Bible caught her eye. She tucked it into her satchel. Luther might like for her to read to him. When he was better, she would show him the marked-out name. Luther had known them all longer than anyone else. If anybody alive would know the story of that name, Luther might. She packed the sewing too. She would work on the baby clothes if she had time.

When she told her aunt she was going to take care of Luther, Sally's mouth drew down in a tight line. "You're making a mistake, girl."

Raymond stepped into the hall and blocked her way. "You going somewhere?"

"I'm going to Luther's. I don't know when I'll be home. I think he's dying. Seems like none of the Negroes come around anymore. Wonder why that is?" She hoisted the baby and the satchel and walked out the door.

She didn't look back at her brother, but she felt his hard gaze. The loss of the ridge land had upset Raymond, but he seemed to draw strength from the sorrow surrounding Luther. What was it Raymond wanted?

Back at Luther's, Leona shoved the empty wood box into the lean-to where Jesse had slept and padded it with quilts to make a bed for Isaiah. She had not thought about how demanding it would be to take care of Isaiah and tend to Luther at the same time, but Isaiah seemed to sense that she needed him to be good. He played quietly with his toys on the floor of Luther's room. He only cried when he wanted "Loo," and Luther didn't respond to him.

The rales in Luther's chest reminded Leona of her mother when she was near death. Leona made a poultice of lard and baking soda for his chest, the way he had taught her, the way she had done for the Pratts, although it hadn't seemed to do much good. She took down Varna's basket of herbs and brewed elderberry tea and gave it to him throughout the day. He had lost so much weight that he was light as a shadow. She bathed him with the sheet pulled up and lifted him and put a pan under him so he could relieve himself. He objected, but then he closed his eyes and turned his face away and allowed it. When the bed became soaked with sweat, she changed the coarse muslin sheet the way Sally had done during Isaiah's birth. Luther owned only two sheets, but he had ample quilts stored in the wardrobe, and she piled them on him when he was wracked with chills.

At night she slid the bolts on the doors before dark, put Isaiah to bed in the lean-to, and kept vigil beside Luther. Sometimes she slept an hour or two on a pallet by his bed. All night, she listened for the sound of horses. That became the pattern.

One night, into the second week of Luther's illness, he was especially fitful. He looked at Leona, his gaze intense as a flame,

and reached for her hand. She gave it to him, and he squeezed
it so tightly that it hurt. He muttered something she couldn't
understand.

She leaned closer. "What is it? Do you want something?"

"Rose?" He ran a finger down Leona's cheek.

Her impulse was to withdraw, but she remained still. "No.
I'm Leona." She thought it must be the fever. Yet it was unnerv-
ing to be mistaken for the dead.

Over the following days, Luther's fever came down. He took
some broth and sat up for short periods of time, but the cough
and the bloody sputum hadn't gone away, and his skin held the
ashen cast of sickness. Or was it grief?

Slowly, he got better. Soon he was able to walk to the porch
and sit for a while. Isaiah pulled at his pants legs and begged to
be picked up. Sometimes Leona sat Isaiah in Luther's lap, and
he and the boy took naps together in Luther's old chair.

One afternoon, she and Luther were sitting on the porch
while Isaiah played and she sewed. After a cool spell, the weather had turned hot again, as mercurial as Leona's feelings. Some
days, her heart ached, and time stood still. Other days, time flew
by, when moments of joy with Isaiah turned her mind away
from the things that hurt her. She remembered a line she had
read in school: time heals all things. She didn't believe it. Not yet.

When Luther asked what she was making, she held up the
baby gown. "I'm getting paid to sew baby clothes."

"Your mama was a fine seamstress."

"She was. I wish I had paid attention. I wish I'd paid attention to a lot of things."

So many questions burdened her. Raymond might show up
any day and drag her and Isaiah home, or something might happen to Luther. She feared Luther was fragile in body and mind.
He had come close to dying. Did he know the answers? Now
might be the time to ask. If not now, when?

"The other night, when you were out of your head with the
fever, you called me Rose." Leona kept right on stitching, but
she felt Luther's eyes on her.

"I did?"

She looked up, expectant. "Yes."

"You look like your mama at your age. I knew her a lot longer than I've known you."

She couldn't read his expression. "I want to show you something. I'll be right back." She got the Bible out of her satchel and pulled a chair close to Luther. She turned to the page with the scratched-out name. "What do you make of this?"

He held the page close to his eyes, squinted at it, and handed the Bible back to Leona. "Looks to me like an ink blot."

"It is that. Somebody went to the trouble of marking out a name so completely that the pen tore through the paper." She closed the book and ran her hand over the cover. "I believe my mother had another child."

Luther looked out across the yard and the road to the fields of cotton beyond. It was a minute before he spoke. "She did."

"It died?"

Luther nodded. "Yes, he died."

He. "The child was a boy?"

Luther's brow knotted up. "I didn't say he."

"Yes, you did."

"All right, then. It was a boy." He shifted in his seat. "Boy, girl. What difference does it make?"

"But why would Mama blot out the name? It must have been awful for her, to have a child die. For Father too." She tapped the Bible. "Maybe somebody else marked it out. But that child's name ought to be here."

Luther's gaze was as feverish as the other night. With difficulty he stood. "I'm gon' walk a bit. It's time I get up and about, get my strength back."

"We'll go with you."

"No. I rather be by myself."

He took his walking stick and headed down the steps and made his way across the yard and out into the road.

❧

Luther's breath came shallow. He leaned on his stick and walked a little ways up the road, but he couldn't go far. Sweat ran down his face. It had been dry all of September, and the road had turned to dust. Dust coated the leaves of the trees and sifted down with the slightest breeze. The colored cemetery where Jesse was buried was half a mile up the road, but he wasn't strong enough to walk there.

He was about to turn back toward the house when a flock of buzzards lifted and settled over a mound on the side of the road. When he got closer, he saw the carcass of a young doe. What was that little thing doing out on the road? And what had killed her? Might have been an automobile. Might have been a gunshot. Hard to tell because there weren't much left of her—her forelegs, her back haunches, her head, though flies had settled on the one eye Luther could see. Her midsection had been eaten away, only a few entrails left, and the birds were fighting over those.

"Shoo! Get on! Get away!" One of the ugly birds made a hissing sound, flapped its broad wings, and ran at Luther. He stepped back and nearly lost his balance. The other birds lifted and flew in a circle but came right back. He ought to drag the animal off into the woods, make a shallow grave for it, at least cover it with leaves, but he didn't have the strength. Something else would probably come along and dig it right up.

Death everywhere, everywhere he looked.

He thought of Jesse in the ground. He wanted to go to the cemetery and fall on his knees and claw at the soil that covered his boy. He wanted to crawl in that grave with him and die. No use living any more.

If only Luther hadn't gone to town for Raymond that day to take care of that damn mule.

If only he hadn't listened to Leona and taken Jesse to the sheriff.

That girl ought to go home where she belonged. What was she thinking, bringing Rose's Bible here, showing him that blotted-out name? He knew what the name was. He knew the secret it held, the one he had sworn to keep to his grave, but he was tired, so tired of keeping secrets. He was tired of lying. Lies catch up with a man, if he lives long enough.

He heard Leona calling his name. He turned toward home.

44

That evening, Carl Pratt stopped by Luther's house with a package for Leona. "Fellow brought this by our house. He said you told him to leave it there. I went by your place, and Sally said you were staying here." Mr. Pratt didn't look pleased.

Leona took the package from him. She didn't explain why she was at Luther's.

Stamped on the outside of the package was *James Rutherford Photography*. The photographer had kept his word. Leona smiled. "I got a picture made of Isaiah."

"Well, that's nice," Mr. Pratt said. He stood there, like he was hoping to see, but Leona waited until he left to open it.

Three small photographs. Her own likeness shocked her, so different from the picture taken at her graduation from the Pinson Road School not even three years before. Older, her face thinner, her hair pulled back, her dress plain and faded. The pictures confirmed that Isaiah was a beautiful child. He looked solemn in two of them, but in the third, he was smiling. His eyes were like hers, but his brow line, the cleft in his chin, his coloring were all like Walker. The likeness was stunning. Couldn't Edith see it? Surely Walker must have.

Leona was about to put the pictures away when she became aware of Luther's eyes on her. He wouldn't see the likeness she had both feared and hoped for. Even if he knew who Walker Broom was—and she doubted it—there was no reason for him to make the connection.

"Come to the window, Luther. Look at these."

He turned the photographs this way and that. "Ain't he handsome. Looks like Mr. Herbert, don't you think?" Luther looked at the three photos again before he gave them back to

Leona. "Isaiah's a fine boy. He'll grow up to be a good man. You'll see."

"I hope so." It hadn't occurred to her until right then that she could give Luther one of the photographs. It seemed the least she could do, the way he had always looked out for her and now for Isaiah.

"Would you like to keep a picture?"

"No. You only got those three."

"But I want you to have one."

She chose one and handed it to him. Luther looked at it for a full minute before he propped it on the mantel.

She put the other pictures in her bag and went about the business of preparing supper. Luther dozed. Isaiah's little cars rumbled over the bare floor. They might have been father and daughter, grandfather and grandchild, if the world were a fair and decent place.

After she put Isaiah to bed, she sat with Luther by the hearth. He rocked back and forth in his chair. It reminded her of Jesse.

"Bring me Varna's basket," he said.

She set the basket beside him. He rummaged through it and brought out a small, roughly carved figure of a woman. "I made this for Varna. She believed it brought good luck with healing. Birthing babies too. Had it with me the night Isaiah was born." He pressed it into her hand. "I got no more use for it."

She had no need for a talisman, but she slipped the doll in her pocket. "Thank you."

"It's time for you to go home."

"But I don't want to."

He nodded in the direction of the room where Isaiah was sleeping. "If you hold on and be strong, that farm gon' be Isaiah's one day. If your daddy had lived, things might have turned out different. But he didn't. And Jesse didn't. You and me, we're still in the world whether we want to be or not."

Leona sat on the floor beside him. "I'm so sorry. About everything."

"We all got things to be sorry for." Tears traced the creases of his face. He stood, unsteady on his feet. "I'm worn out. I'm going to bed."

She knew he was right. She had moved the pallet out of Luther's room days ago, a sign that he was well enough for her and Isaiah to leave. Now she unrolled the pallet and lay down near the hearth. The night was unseasonably warm. She opened a window and lay awake, listening to the call of an owl in the woods, the occasional rumble of wheels on the road, the clop of horses' hooves. Who would be out that time of the night? Somebody up to no good, like her brother. And then she heard the unearthly wail of a panther, like the one she had heard in the woods with her father years ago. Was it giving birth, or was it dying? Either way, it was frightening. She wondered if it was an omen.

Isaiah woke her just after dawn. She took him out to the porch to keep from waking Luther. An hour later, they went inside and she made breakfast. When Luther didn't come out of his room, she knocked on his door. "Come," he said.

He was still in his clothes from yesterday, sitting on the side of his bed. "Luther? Are you not well?"

"I'll be out in a while." He had the most mournful expression she had ever seen.

"But—"

"Go on."

She left him alone all day. She tried his door later and found it bolted. Knocked, and got no answer.

ༀ

All night, Luther had lain awake. Those ugly buzzards with their stink of death had not let him close his eyes. Death had come for Luther the week before when his fever raged and a terrible weight had sat on his chest and nearly stopped his breathing. Death had stood at the foot of Luther's bed with a hand outstretched and waiting, and Luther had almost taken that hand and crossed over. But Luther wasn't done yet.

Last evening, he had admitted to Leona that he knew Rose had given birth to a third child. He had almost slipped and said the name. He had lied and said the child died, and that was wrong, wrong.

Now, in the light of day, he would have to decide what to do.

He opened the wardrobe, reached behind the quilts, and took out a little wooden box. Its edges were worn down, the brass catch tarnished. He sat on the side of his bed nearest the lamp, opened the box, and took out a small packet of carefully folded white tissue paper tied with faded satin ribbon. His fingers fumbled at the knot, and it took a while to untie it. Inside, a white handkerchief edged with handmade tatting, a lock of blond hair. In one corner of the handkerchief, the embroidered initials RTP. He pressed Rose Pinson's handkerchief to his face. Surely no scent of her left there, but he could imagine it, could close his eyes and see Rose as a young woman, tall and shapely and fine, her green eyes, her light hair, her smooth fair skin, not like Varna's, dried out by the sun. He fingered the lock of hair, and it came apart in his hands. He remembered how Rose had cut off all her hair after the birth of that child.

Caught up in the complicated maze of lies, Luther had watched it all unfold. What if he had been man enough then to tell the truth? But he knew. If he had, he would have been a dead man. Luther regretted the hurt then, and he regretted the hurt that telling the truth now would bring Leona. But it had to be done, for Jesse's sake. Jesse had not lived a lie because he had not known. Jesse had been the real and physical embodiment of a lie.

Luther put the things back in the box, closed it, and hid it away. He had thought that someday he would give them to Jesse, when he was old enough. He'd meant to tell Jesse who he really was. But he never had, and now it was too late.

❧

It was after dark when Luther finally came out of his room. Isaiah ran to him, shouting, "Loo!" but Luther didn't pay him any mind.

Leona set a plate of food in front of him. "I saved you some supper."

He pushed the plate away. "I ain't hungry." His voice was hoarse and unsteady. "Sit."

Her stomach clenched. Why such strange behavior? Something was terribly wrong. She said, "All right, but I need to put Isaiah to bed first."

He nodded, but he didn't look up.

She carried Isaiah to the makeshift bed. He protested, but she sat with him and sang the songs he loved. All the while, her heart and mind raced. After Isaiah fell sleep, she went out and sat across from Luther. She waited for him to speak. He spread his hands flat on the table and stared at them for a long time. They were the hands of a much older man, gnarled like the roots of an old tree and callused by work. Sad hands.

He looked across at her. "The ink blot in that Bible."

"You know, don't you." She felt a chill, as though a ghost had brushed past her.

"I do. It's Jesse's name."

"But why would Mama record Jesse's name in the Bible?" Leona got up and went to the window. Her mouth had gone dry as paper. A drizzle of rain, no moon, no stars, only the watery reflection of Luther, sitting behind her. She said, "Or maybe Mama didn't do it. Maybe Father did, and Mama blotted it out. If Jesse was Father's and Varna's child, and Mama knew—"

"No."

What did he mean, no?

He said, "Come over here and sit down."

She had thought she wanted to know the truth, but now she wasn't sure. She could take Isaiah and walk out, but something held her there. She sat.

"Long time ago, when your daddy used to go off to cut

timber, I'd go to the house and stay with you and your brother and your mama. You remember that."

She nodded. She remembered how she used to cry when dark came, and Luther would take his lantern and go out and walk all around the place. She would run from window to window in the house, watching his lantern bob in the darkness, until he came back and told her everything was all right. She was safe for the night.

"Rose was unhappy back then, when Herbert would go away. She would say she was gon' leave, but Herbert, he wouldn't have it, he told her if she went, he was keeping you two children with him, and she couldn't leave you behind. Sometimes when Herbert was gone, she would sit with me, and we'd talk late at night, until the fire died down and the room got cold." Luther stared out the window, as if the dark held the words he needed. "It went on like that until Rose took sick, and there weren't nobody to help her. I told Varna to go on down there, but she was promised to tend another woman when her time come. So I went." He paused, rocking in the chair like Jesse used to. Closed his eyes. "One night, Rose got the chills, and she couldn't stop shaking. She begged me keep her warm." He stopped, and in that moment Leona's world as she knew it stopped too.

What was he saying? And then she understood. "Stop. I don't want to hear any more."

"Leona." The way he said her name nearly broke her heart. He reached across the table and took her hands in his. "It's the truth. Rose was lonesome and sick at heart. It was my fault, what happened. It never should have, but it did. Jesse was Rose's child, not Herbert's. He was mine."

She pulled her hands away and wiped them on her skirt. "I don't believe you. Why should I believe you?"

"I swear to God it's true." He told her how he took Varna to tend Rose the night the child was born, how he waited there and prayed the child wasn't his, but he never prayed for it to be dead. He was waiting on the porch when Herbert came out of the house and dropped to his knees in the yard and wailed. In

a while Varna came out with the little baby, wrapped up like a
bundle. She folded the blanket back and showed him to Luther.
The child wasn't dark, Luther said, but he had a dusty cast to his
skin and ringlets of black hair. He said, "My shame and guilt lay
right there in Varna's arms."

Leona tried to imagine it: the ash-colored, unwanted baby,
her mother's fear and shame, her father's anguish. And Luther—what was it Luther had felt? What did a man feel after he
had betrayed his best friend in the world by lying with his wife?

Besides her father, Luther Biggs had been the only person
Leona trusted. If what Luther said was true, what would ever
be right in her world again? What would hold her together now?

She moved about the room, touching things: the mantel,
Varna's basket, a chipped pitcher on the table. "If it's true, why
didn't Father—"

"Rose made up a tale. She told Herbert she'd gone to the
orchard one day the winter before, picking up late apples off
the ground, and a man come up on her and overpowered her.
Said she never seen his face, but she knew he was a colored man
because she seen his hands. Your daddy, he raged and cried, said
why didn't she tell him when it happened. Said he'd a gone after
that man and found him and killed him. He told Varna to take
the baby away, said he didn't care what she did with it, long as
she got it out of his sight. I brought Varna and the child back to
this house, and Varna, she was already talking about keeping the
boy. Didn't matter to her if he was black or white or if he was
conceived in the darkest sin. Varna was with child five times
after Alma was born. Two times, she gave birth, and the babies
died. The others, she cramped and bled long before they could
live in the world."

"Mama had a living child. You couldn't just take him. Surely
people knew."

"Herbert sent out word that their child had died. Told the
preacher, and he came and said words over a little mound of
dirt at the back of the garden. Varna kept the baby close, and
after a little while, she claimed to have given birth to him. Said

she had stopped her bleeding and didn't even know she was with child. I don't believe she ever knew Jesse was mine, but even if she had, it wouldn't have mattered. She loved him like her own. She told everybody Jesse was a miracle." Luther looked smaller somehow, as though the telling had aged and withered him. He said, "All so tangled up, you see, there weren't no escaping it, ever."

"People believed that baby was Varna's."

"They did."

"And Father? He believed what Mama told him? Father wasn't a stupid man."

"If he hadn't, he would have killed me."

"And you've lived with that lie all these years."

"You think I ain't paid for what I done? Maybe Jesse weren't quite right because of it, and that was my punishment. You think every time I laid eyes on Herbert or Rose or Varna that I weren't sorry? But I weren't sorry to have Jesse."

"I remember Mama taking to her bed. I must have been three or four years old. I remember going into her room one day, and she was cutting off all her hair." Leona had often thought she might have dreamed it.

"Your mama about lost her mind, she grieved so. She wouldn't sleep, wouldn't eat. And later on, she would bring Jesse things. A blanket she had made, some applesauce, a little toy that had belonged to Raymond. She was always asking to hold the baby, but Varna, she weren't gon' have it. I had to tell Rose not to come here. She was gon' spoil everything."

Luther stopped, and Leona waited.

What more could there be?

Then, "I want you to know, Leona. I loved your mama, and she loved me. God knows I tried to make it up to Herbert."

She tried for a deep breath that wouldn't come. She glanced around that poor little room, imagining Jesse as a baby, playing on the hearth, and her mother sent away in despair. She said, "You should leave. Go to Memphis and live with Alma. You can't stay here. Not now."

He got up. "Baby girl." He rested his hand on her shoulder. She flinched away. "Don't touch me."

He stood there for a minute and then he went to his room, holding on to the chair, the table, the door frame as though he had to feel his way.

Leona's mind was in a fury. Her mother had borne Luther's child?

To think how Rose had condemned Leona, how she had scolded and quoted the Bible and told Leona she would burn in Hell because of Isaiah.

You don't know me, Rose had said when she was dying.

"Oh, Mama," Leona said aloud.

She went outside. Her stomach heaved, but nothing came up. She walked the yard barefoot, looking up at the overcast sky as dark as her thoughts. She heard a noise inside the house and turned to look. A light moved from window to window; Luther was up. That light brought back the memory of Luther's care when she was little, ruined now by what he had confessed. She hoped he wouldn't come looking for her. When she could no longer see his light, she went back inside and curled up on the pallet.

Toward morning, she slept a little, and when she woke, Luther was gone from the house. It was her habit to worry about him, but she told herself she would not. Luther Biggs had betrayed her. He had betrayed them all, and she would have no more to do with him.

She fed Isaiah a few bites of biscuit, collected their things, and walked home, Isaiah looking back over her shoulder, crying and calling, "Loo, Loo." She was almost home when she remembered the little doll Luther had given her. She took it out of her pocket, turned it over in her hand. A crude thing, a reminder. She considered throwing it into the woods, but she couldn't bring herself to do it. She put it back in her pocket and walked on.

45

When Leona got home, Raymond was shut away in their mother's room, and Sally wasn't in the kitchen or her bedroom or the parlor. Leona's door was bolted from the inside.

"Aunt Sally? Are you in there?"

"Coming." Sally opened the door. One side of her face was purple shading to yellow, her bottom lip scabbed over.

Leona's hurt was all on the inside. She touched her aunt's face, and Sally winced. "Oh, Aunt Sally. What happened?"

Sally closed the door and bolted it. "What does it look like? One night last week, Raymond didn't like the cornbread. Said it was too salty. He ordered me to make him some more, and I told him to make it himself. He hauled off and hit me."

"I'm sorry. I shouldn't have left you alone with him."

"That's the truth. You shouldn't have."

When Leona put Isaiah down, he buried his face in Sally's skirt.

Sally stroked his curls. "I've been locking myself in here at night. I can't go back to that other room."

Leona put her arms around her aunt. "You can stay here with me."

Sally climbed the step she had set by Leona's bed. She patted the mattress. "Sit down. I got to tell you something."

What could Sally possibly have to tell her? Some bit of neighborhood gossip? Leona wondered if she could tell Sally what Luther had revealed. What might Sally have known? Probably nothing, Leona decided. Sally had left home at twenty and hadn't returned until after Leona's father died. No, there was no point in telling Sally.

She sat beside her aunt on the bed. "All right. What is it?"

"I'm leaving." Sally tucked her head, and when she looked up, she was smiling. "I met somebody. Somebody nice."

"You mean a man?" Leona almost laughed, but when she saw the look on Sally's face, she knew it wasn't anything to laugh about.

"You remember that day at the circus, when the clown came up and sat on my lap?" Sally covered her face with her hands, peeked through her fingers. "It's him."

"The clown."

Sally nodded. "He had the influenza, and he was sick longer than the rest. He wound up staying in town after the troupe moved on. I saw him later, when I went to town while you were at the Pratts', and a few more times after that, like the time I told you I was going to the sewing circle." She blushed furiously. "There wasn't no sewing circle that day. I got Luther to take me to town." She glanced at Leona. "Fred Sams is his name. He went off with the circus again, but now he's back. He wants me to go away with him."

Isaiah crawled onto Sally's lap. She played pat-a-cake with him. Leona couldn't take her eyes off Sally's misshapen hands.

"So you're going away with this, this—man—you hardly know."

"I do know Freddy. He's got a place down in Florida where he stays when he ain't on the road. He showed me pictures. We'll stay there in the winter, and then I'll travel with him. With the circus." She leaned closer to Leona. "He wants to marry me."

"You can't be serious."

"I never been more serious in my life." She touched the bruise on her face. "Even if there wasn't no Fred Sams, I can't stay here." She moved Isaiah off her lap and slid down off the bed.

There had been a time when Leona might have been glad to see Sally go. Not now. "When are you leaving?"

"Soon." Sally laid her hand on Leona's. "Don't hate me, Leona."

Leona shook her head. "I could never hate you. Why would you say such a thing?"

Raymond banged on the door. "Sally? Get on out here."

When Leona opened it, he said, "Well. It's about time."

"We'll be out in a minute." She closed the door in his face.

"See?" Sally said. "Ain't no end to it." She stood on tiptoe and retrieved an envelope from Leona's dresser. "There's a letter for you. Came about a week ago."

Leona opened it. She recognized Edith Broom's handwriting. The batiste and lace had arrived. Leona should pick them up at the store.

At the store, not at their house. Edith must have thought better of having Leona come there. Or maybe Walker had.

That night, she helped Sally cook supper, and then they locked themselves in Leona's room. Long after Sally slept, Leona went over and over Luther's story, which was as unbelievable as a fairy tale but most likely true. Raymond had sensed something awry. He had simply put the wrong pieces together.

46

Leona waited a week to pick up the material. Raymond wasn't up to driving the buggy yet; his ribs still hurt, so she drove him to the feed store, and she went to Broom's. She told the clerk that the younger Mrs. Broom had left a package there for her.

The clerk brought the box out and gave it to Leona. She didn't open it until she was back at the buggy. The batiste was light as air and silky, so fine that she wondered if she dared put scissors to it, but that night, after Isaiah was asleep, she cut out the pieces of a dress Walker and Edith's child would wear with Leona's brand upon it. She would be glad to get back to the sewing. It helped occupy her hands and her thoughts so she wouldn't dwell so much on what Luther had confided. Her parents gone. Varna, too. Leona had nobody to verify his story, but deep down, she felt the truth of it.

For weeks Leona heard nothing from Luther. She was surprised when Raymond didn't question his absence. He hired a couple of older Black men he paid mostly with whiskey. Leona mentioned Luther only once to Raymond, and he said, "Good riddance."

In mid-October Bertie told Leona she had seen Luther in town. "He don't look well," she said. "Looks like an old, old man." Leona hoped he had gone to Memphis. Even in her anger and hurt, Leona fought the urge to go and see him. She pictured him lying dead in his house with nobody to find him.

On a cold morning in late October, Leona went to wash her face at the bureau and found a small box wrapped in brown paper and tied with string and a note scrawled on the back of a

feed store receipt. Leona recognized Sally's awkward hand, like
a child's first attempts at script. *I'm gone. Please forgive me.* What
was it Sally had said the day Leona came home? *Don't hate me.*
Leona felt the chill and wrapped her shawl closer. She untied
the string and tore away the brown paper. Inside the box, a
white card and a blue velvet box. Leona read the note on the
card: *Wear this and think of me. Love, Walker. July 12, 1917.* She
sat down and read it again. *Love.* The date, a few days after the
Caldwells' party. In the velvet box, a gold heart-shaped locket
on a delicate chain. On the back of the locket, engraved in fine
script, the letters LRP and WHB. Inside it, a photograph of
Walker, wearing a hat at a rakish angle.

So Walker hadn't gone off to the war without a thought of
her.

How had Sally gotten her hands on this? She had no right.
No right at all.

Leona imagined Sally slipping the package in the pocket of
that old apron she wore. Maybe she had put it away and forgotten about it until now, but Leona doubted it was a matter
of forgetting. Sally's deception must have been deliberate. How
could she have wished Leona so much unhappiness?

Isaiah turned restlessly in his sleep. He would be awake
soon. Leona fumbled at the clasp and put the locket on. She
looked at herself in the mirror, her red eyes, her flushed face,
the locket catching and reflecting the morning light. She was
surprised that it felt cold and hard as a small stone against her
skin. A pretty thing, but meaningless. She could never show it
to anyone.

If only she could have had the satisfaction of telling Sally to
leave, but Sally had cheated her of that too. Leona wondered if
Sally was still in town with the man. Even if she were, it would
do no good to confront her.

Leona wore the locket under her dress all day long. Now and
then she touched it, warmed by the heat of her skin, but she
found no comfort in it.

She was sitting at the window, making tiny stitches in a shirt for Walker and Edith's baby, when it occurred to her that now she could explain to Walker what had happened. It had been a mistake, a cruel joke on her, on both of them, that Sally had kept Walker's gift. Telling him wouldn't threaten his marriage. Edith had already revealed that the marriage was troubled. Telling Walker would simply be honest. But how would she do it? She couldn't think of a way.

She hid Walker's card and the velvet box in the drawer with her other keepsakes. She fed the cardboard box, the brown paper, even the string to the kitchen stove and watched them catch, flare up, and burn.

With Sally gone, Leona and Raymond lived together as though each occupied a different world within the house. Leona avoided looking at her brother. His nose had healed crooked, as had the cut over one eye, leaving an ugly, livid scar. There was still a yellowish bruise where his jaw had been broken. He complained of terrible headaches. The first time Isaiah had cried in his presence after they came home from Luther's, Raymond had pressed his hands to his temples and shouted, "Get him away from me!" After that, if Isaiah fussed when Raymond was around, Leona swept her son out of the room. She woke Isaiah before dawn and took him with her to the barn. Besides the barn chores, Leona did all the cooking that Sally had done. Raymond and the two older Negroes tended to the larger work of the farm.

After the baby went to sleep at night, she took all the things Walker had given her out of the bureau and held them to the light of Luther's lamp, turned them over in her hands. The wildflowers were crumbling, but the stone from the creek bed was still a stone; it wouldn't change over time. Maybe it was a trick of the light, but it seemed the photographs Walker had taken of her were already fading.

One night, she took out the two remaining pictures of her and Isaiah. His likeness to Walker was unmistakable. How could he not see it?

"That's it," she said, so loud that Isaiah sat up in his crib. Why hadn't she thought of it before?

The burden of lies and betrayals—Sally's, Walker's, her mother's, Luther's, and even her own, she had lied, too—were more than she could bear. The photograph of her and Isaiah didn't lie. It was time she confronted Walker with the truth. She couldn't predict the outcome. Maybe he wouldn't believe her. He was married, after all; what could he do to remedy things? But when Raymond went off somewhere—sooner or later, he would; he was restless and tired of being cooped up in the house—she would go to Luna and mail a photograph to Walker. Luna was quite a trek from home, but she dared not mail it at the Sully post office, where the postmaster knew her. She imagined his raised eyebrow when she handed him the envelope with Walker's name on it.

A few days after Sally left, Raymond took one look at his supper and said, "What is this?"

"Eggs. What do you think it is?"

He swept his plate to the floor. "I don't want eggs for supper. What's the matter with you?" He stormed out.

Leona sat down and ate her eggs and fed some to Isaiah. Raymond came back through the kitchen carrying a knapsack and his shotgun and slammed out the back door. When he didn't come home that night, Leona took the baby the next morning and drove the wagon to Luna, where she didn't know a soul. She went to the post office, bought an envelope and a stamp, and sent the photograph on its way.

47

Walker stayed late at the store most days, volunteering to be the one to lock up, even though Edith complained of being bored, lonely, and homesick. Now it seemed she had formed an alliance of sorts with Leona. What did they talk about when Leona came to the house? Couldn't Edith look at the boy and see Walker? His heart went wild at the thought, but if she had, he would have caught hell about it before now. And, he reasoned, if Leona were going to tell Edith, she would have done it already. Unless she were playing a reckless game.

At the store Walker sometimes gazed out the window, hoping for a glimpse of Leona and the boy. Occasionally, it happened: across the square, or at a block's distance, but she never came in the store when Walker was there.

The first of November, a letter arrived for Walker at the store. It was postmarked Luna, but he didn't know anybody in Luna who would write him a letter. He went into the office before he opened it. A folded piece of ruled paper and a photograph fell out. He picked them up. The paper had one line written on it: *You should have this.* In the photograph, Leona and the boy are sitting in front of a crudely painted backdrop of trees. Leona's hair is mussed, tendrils clinging to her face and neck as though she'd pinned it up in a hurry or the photograph had been taken in the heat of the day. It reminded Walker of their first outing in the car when she'd taken the pins out of her hair and let the wind tangle it. He had wanted to comb it out with his fingers. Isaiah—such a grave name for a little fellow—is looking at the camera, his bottom lip curled out like he's about to cry. Walker turned the photograph over. On the back, in Leona's handwriting: *Isaiah ~ Age one year and five months.*

Feeling sick to his stomach, Walker got up and locked the

office door. What did Leona hope to accomplish—getting close to Edith, sending him this picture? He held it in his left hand and gripped the right corner, but he couldn't bring himself to tear it.

"Walker?" His father rattled the doorknob.

"Yes, sir. Coming." Walker stuffed the photo and the note back in the envelope and shoved it to the back of the top desk drawer before he opened the door.

His father frowned. "What are you doing, locking the door?" His expression changed, and he laughed. "You got something secret going on in here?"

"No, sir." Walker gripped the edge of the desk to steady himself.

"Well, get on out there, then. We got customers." He frowned. "You sure you're all right? You don't look too good."

"I'll be right there."

After his father left, Walker locked the door again. He took the photograph out of the drawer. He couldn't take it home, but his father and the bookkeeper also used this office, so he would need to hide it well.

A framed picture of his grandfather Broom hung on one wall. He took off the back and slipped the note and the photograph behind his grandfather's picture. He secured the back and hung the picture where it belonged.

"Walker!"

"Coming." Every time Walker looked at the picture of his grandfather, he would feel Leona looking down at him. And the boy's eyes too. His son's eyes.

Walker was sweating and cold at the same time. He straightened his tie and walked out into the store.

48

Ten days after Leona mailed the photograph, she left Raymond sleeping off a drunk and took Isaiah into Sully. She didn't care if Raymond woke and found her gone. She would take the consequences. Sending the photograph had unleashed a fervor in her.

She went to Broom's mid-morning, thinking Walker would be there, and he was. When Mrs. Harmon offered to help Leona, she said, "No, thank you. I'm just looking." She walked around the store and bounced Isaiah, who was cranky.

Thankfully, another woman came in, and Mrs. Harmon turned her attention to her. After what seemed a long while, Walker came over and offered to help Leona.

She pointed to a bolt of sturdy dark blue cotton. "I'd like a piece of that."

"I'll get it for you." Walker took the bolt to the cutting table. "How many yards?"

"Just one."

Isaiah wriggled. "Get down!"

"No, Isaiah. You can't get down in the store." He started to cry. "I'm sorry," she said to Walker. "If you could please hurry?"

Walker glanced over his shoulder. "I got your letter." His voice was tense, barely above a whisper. "What do you want from me?"

She felt the blood rush to her face and neck. "I don't want anything."

Isaiah sobbed and she paced with him, aware of people turning to look at them. Walker cut the fabric, the scissors unsteady in his hand. He wrote out a receipt, she paid him, tucked the receipt in her pocket, picked up the package, and headed for the door, her face burning.

What had she expected? Not this.

"Wait," Walker said. She stopped and turned. He went behind the candy counter and brought out a lollipop. "For the boy."

Isaiah reached for the candy. "How much does it cost?" Leona asked.

"No charge. I want him to have it."

He was offering Isaiah candy? "No, thank you."

She walked out the door. Isaiah wailed, reaching over her shoulder toward Walker and the lollipop. When she got back to the buggy, she tossed the bundle of fabric she didn't really need on the floor and climbed up. She dropped the receipt, and when she picked it up, she saw he had written something on the back. No time to read it; she had to tend to Isaiah, who bucked and screamed. She tucked the receipt inside her dress and popped Isaiah on his leg. He cried harder, and she was sorry.

"Yup," she said to the mule. In a while, the motion of the wagon soothed the baby. He snuggled against her and slept. She took the receipt out.

We need to talk. Meet me Sunday, two o'clock, Hawks Creek. Stay away from Edith.

Leona crumpled the paper and tucked it away. Her temples throbbed with a sudden headache. If only she could take the photograph and the note back, but she couldn't. "Foolish, foolish," she said aloud. What good was talking?

Her mind still reeled when she drove into the yard. This was Wednesday. She had four days to make up her mind.

49

Walking home after work, Walker hoped the crisp air would clear his head. Had he done a terrible thing, asking Leona to meet him? But he needed to settle things with her once and for all. He might make a mess of his life with Edith, but he would not let Leona interfere. Was he happy with Edith? No. And there was the boy, Isaiah. There was no mistaking the likeness, but what could he do about it? Not a damn thing.

What a mess he had made.

He squared his shoulders and prepared himself for whatever might be in store with his wife. Over breakfast that morning, Edith had again brought up her desire to go home. "I don't want to have the baby here," she'd said. "You could come with me."

"It's the busiest time of the year. I can't leave."

He had taken her to see Dr. Dunlap last week, hoping he would talk sense into her, but Edith was determined to go. Women up East traveled all the time when they were expecting, she said. She wouldn't be treated like a hothouse flower. "I'm going, and I want to go now."

He wondered sometimes if Edith was losing her mind. He had heard of that happening to women after they had babies, but not before.

He let himself in the back door. "Edith?" He walked through the kitchen. No sign of supper underway. "Edith!" He went to the bedroom and then to the parlor. The fire in the fireplace had died to embers. Edith was sitting in the dark.

"There you are." He lit the lamp with the colored glass shade. "There. That's better."

Edith sat, her back straight, her belly prominent. She still wore her dressing gown. She clutched something in her hands.

Paper, cloth, he couldn't tell. Walker knelt beside her and pushed a strand of hair away from her face. She turned away.

His gut tightened. "What's wrong?"

"This." She held out a bent photograph and a packet of letters. "This is what's wrong." All the breath went out of Walker when he saw the picture of Leona at the river, wearing her mother's coat, all that bright hair around her face. He didn't have to see the letters to know they were the ones he had written to Leona while he was away. Edith must have been searching in earnest to find them.

He stood. "You went through my trunk. You ought not to have done that."

"You said you didn't really know her." Edith's voice was cold and level. "You had seen her around town, you said." Edith ripped the picture in half. "Is the boy yours?"

"No, I swear."

"Don't lie, Walker. That cleft in his chin, his coloring. Dear God in heaven. To think I let her come in this house. And you let it happen." Edith tossed the photograph and the letters on the floor, got up clumsily, and walked out. The bedroom door slammed, and Walker heard her sobs, louder than his heart. He picked up the torn photograph and the letters. He sat down and pieced the picture back together on the table. He read the letters, one by one. They were the sentimental words of a boy far away from home, full of clichés about love.

After a while, Edith's crying stopped. Walker left her alone. What could he possibly say to her? He felt ashamed when his mind strayed to Leona. Would she meet him at Hawks Creek? He was both hopeful and afraid that she would.

50

When Leona got home, she was relieved Raymond wasn't there. She fed Isaiah his supper and put him to bed. She tried to read, but Walker's face kept appearing before her. She bolted the bedroom door as she did every night, extinguished the lamp, and lay awake.

Was mailing the photograph a mistake? She had told herself she only wanted Walker to know the truth, but if that was all, she could have written him a letter. If she were honest, she had to admit she wanted him to see the truth in that picture. She wanted to sear the image of Isaiah and her on his heart, to imprint in his mind the likeness he couldn't deny. As for the details of Sally's deceit, did they matter now? Not a whit.

How awful and confusing things had gotten.

Stay away from Edith, his note said. Surely, he must know that Edith had sought her out, not the other way around. Leona hadn't meant sending the picture as a threat. He had misunderstood her intent and turned it into something sinister.

She didn't have to meet him, but if she didn't, she was keeping the lies and misunderstandings alive. If she did talk to him, could she clear it all up? Probably not, but even if she never laid eyes on him again, she would have had her moment of truth, like Luther had wanted to have with her.

She would go.

She would have to ask Bertie to keep Isaiah. What excuse she would give Bertie she didn't yet know, but she would think of something. Finally, she fell asleep. She didn't know what time it was when she woke to the back door slamming. She held her breath until she heard Raymond's door close and his boots drop one by one.

෮

Sunday afternoon, Raymond stood on the back porch, out of the heavy rain. It had started the morning before and hadn't let up. He still had cotton in the fields that should have been picked already. He needed a drink bad.

Leona came out the back door, wearing their father's old rain slicker and carrying the boy and a bag. She seemed flustered when she saw him.

"What're you doing out here, Ray? You're soaking wet."

He glanced at his clothes. "Watching the cotton get ruined." He noticed Leona was wearing a nice dress under the slicker. "Where you going?"

"I got to go to Bertie's."

"In this weather? What're you going up there for? You crazy?"

"She's making her wedding dress. I promised I would help. She's worried about getting it done in time."

Bertie was getting married? First he'd heard of it. "It can't wait till tomorrow?"

"She's teaching. She doesn't have a lot of time. You mind if I take the buggy?"

He waved her on. "Naw. I ain't going nowhere. I got better sense."

"All right, then. I won't be gone long."

Raymond went inside and put on dry clothes. He got a bottle of whiskey and sat in his mother's chair in the parlor, taking a drink now and then. Out the window, the rain blurred the road, the woods, and the hills beyond. What could be so important that Leona would go out in a pouring rain and take Isaiah with her?

He sat up straight. Odd that she was dressed up. Maybe she wasn't going to the Pratts'. Maybe she was going somewhere else. To Luther's? He thought not. She seemed to be done with Luther.

"God damn," he said. Leona must have thought she had

pulled the wool over his eyes. Well, he was not so easily fooled. He would go after her and find out.

He shouldn't have let her take the buggy and Belle. He would have to walk. A flash of lightning, too close, followed by a thunderclap. Another wall of rain coming. The longer he waited, the angrier he got. He looked everywhere for his father's old slicker before he remembered Leona had been wearing it. He slapped his forehead with the palm of his hand. He put on a coat and his father's oilskin hat, went to the barn and found an old piece of a tarpaulin, wrapped up in it, and set out.

❧

Leona had gotten halfway to Bertie's before the rain picked up again. The horse stumbled in the mud and tossed her head, and the buggy lurched along. Which would be better—to stop and wait out the storm or to go on in the downpour and risk running off the road? She decided she shouldn't stop. She and Isaiah huddled under the slicker and she whipped the horse on.

When Leona pulled in at the Pratts', she looked at her mother's watch. Quarter to two. She climbed out of the buggy with Isaiah and grabbed the bag with his diapers and a biscuit. She slipped going up the steps and almost fell.

Bertie came to the door before Leona could knock. "Leona, look at you! Come on in here and let me get you something dry."

Leona's dress was wet and spattered with mud in spite of the slicker. "I don't have time." She handed over Isaiah and the bag and glanced back the way she had come. The rain had slacked. "I've got to go."

Bertie looked miffed. "What if I won't keep Isaiah unless you tell me where you're going?"

"But you said you would."

Bertie crossed her arms. "Maybe I won't."

It was easier to lie. "All right, I'll tell you. I'm going to Hawks Creek to meet somebody. I can't have him coming to the house."

"Is it Isaiah's daddy?"

Leona shook her head. "He's just a boy I met. He doesn't know about Isaiah." She shrugged. "He's nice. Real nice."

"But you won't tell me who he is? Oh, Leona. Don't do this."

"I have to. I'll be back in a little while."

Leona got in the buggy and drove off. She looked back once at Bertie and Isaiah standing on the porch. Isaiah waved. Bertie didn't.

She drove as far down the lane at Hawks Creek as she could. Fifty yards from Pinson Road, the creek had overflowed its banks. She turned the buggy around and pulled into a clearing, hoping she was out of sight. She let up on the reins, and the horse slowed and dropped her head. Leona worried the sound of the automobile might spook Belle, so she got out and found a sturdy sapling to tie her to. She got back in the buggy. A little past two now.

She waited half an hour. She hadn't considered that Walker might not come. The rain had slowed to a drizzle, but she was wet and cold. She decided not to wait any longer. There was nothing either of them could say or do to make things right. He had asked her what she wanted, and she hadn't answered. The answers weren't simple.

She could still write to him, but better to let well enough alone. Better for Walker, certainly, and maybe even for her and for Isaiah, who would only know his father as the friendly merchant they saw in town who would give him candy, if his mother allowed it.

She was untying Belle when she heard the car laboring over the mud and ruts, the engine sputtering like it might die. Walker pulled near the buggy and stopped. The wheels and running board were coated in thick mud. He got out and walked toward her. He was as soaked as she and muddy to his knees. She must look a sight, she thought, wearing her father's slicker, her skirt muddy, her shoes ruined, her hair wet and sticking to her scalp. They stood with some distance between them.

"I thought you weren't coming," Leona said.

"I got stuck. If some colored boys hadn't come along and pulled me out, I wouldn't be here." He looked inside the buggy. "Where's the boy?"

Could he not bring himself to say Isaiah's name? "He's with Bertie."

The rain picked up. He said, "Let's sit in the car." He opened the door and helped her in.

She sat against the passenger door, hugging herself against the chill. Walker offered her a lap robe that had somehow remained dry. There was so much to say, but she couldn't find the words to begin.

After a long silence, he said, "What were you thinking, sending that picture to the store?"

"I wanted you to have it. And I guess I thought sending it would get your attention."

"It got my attention, all right. What if my father had opened it?"

"I'm sorry. I didn't think about that."

"I guess you weren't thinking when you tried to get close to Edith, either."

Leona faced him. "That's just plain wrong, Walker. Edith asked me to sew for the baby. Maybe she was the curious one."

"Well, you don't have to worry about her. She's leaving."

Edith gone? Was it too much to hope for?

Leona said, "She told me she didn't want to have the baby here. She was afraid."

"It's more than that. The day you came in the store—I got home that night, and she had gone through my trunk and found the picture of you I'd kept, the one I took at the river. She found letters too."

"What letters? I never—"

"They're my letters. I wrote to you while I was at Camp Pike and aboard the ship. Even after I arrived in France. I never mailed them." Walker gripped the steering wheel with both hands, his knuckles white. "Edith believes Isaiah is mine. She says any fool can see the likeness. That's why she's leaving. She's taking the train on Wednesday."

Tears welled in Leona's eyes. She looked out at the trees, their leaves gone brown now, and falling. They had never come here in the rain. "I want to tell you what happened, how things went wrong. It wasn't all our fault that we made a mess of things."

&

By the time Raymond was a hundred yards from the house, the wind blew the tarp off. Just as well; it slowed him down, so he threw it away. Lightning struck a tree in the woods nearby, and it fell with a crash like the thunder. He took a flask out of his pocket and drank. Once, he almost turned back, but no, he had started this thing; he would finish it. He slogged along, stumbling in the muddy ruts.

He'd had enough of Leona's foolishness. The way she'd gone off to nurse Luther rather than staying home and taking care of him like she ought to have. That had about driven Raymond crazy. Well, he would find out if she was at Bertie's, and if she wasn't, he would find her and bring her home. She couldn't have gone far.

When Raymond got to the Pratts' yard, there was no sign of the buggy. "I knew it," he said. He stomped up the front porch steps and banged on the door. He could hear the sound of children laughing.

Bertie opened the door with Isaiah in her arms, but she was talking to somebody in the hall behind her. When she turned and saw Raymond, she moved to close the door, but he shoved it open. "Where's my sister?"

51

When I saw you at the Caldwells'," Leona told Walker, "I didn't know about the baby. Aunt Sally figured it out before I did. I didn't know anything about having babies."

"Why didn't you write and tell me?"

"I couldn't figure out how or where to write to you, and I was so mad at you and hurt and afraid. Raymond went crazy, trying to figure out who the baby's daddy was. Besides, if I'd told you, I don't know what we could have done. You were gone by then."

"When I never heard from you, I didn't know what to think." He pushed wet hair back from her face.

She moved his hand away. "I should've known that something happened or somebody got in the way. Now I know. I don't know how Aunt Sally got the locket and the card, but she did, and she kept them from me. She's gone now, for good. She left the package on my dresser the morning she left."

Walker struck the steering wheel. "I came to your house. I wanted to say goodbye. There was something odd about the way your aunt talked to me, but when I asked her to give them to you, she said she would."

Their little comedy of errors was worse than she had imagined. She'd learned that phrase in school, but she'd never understood it until now. She unbuttoned the top two buttons of her dress and showed him the locket.

He fingered the locket where it lay on her skin. "Are you staying there with Raymond?"

"What would you have me do? You know a place I could go?"

"You could stay with Bertie, couldn't you?"

"You think he would leave me alone there?" Leona looked out the window. Nothing to see but rain.

"I don't know what to do. Do you need money? I could send you some every month."

"Oh, Walker, no. I don't want money from you." She looked at her watch. Nearly three o'clock. "I have to go. I told Bertie I'd be back in an hour. She was suspicious, but I made up a story about a boy I met." She forced a smile, but he didn't smile back.

"Don't go." He pulled her closer to him. "What can we do?"

"We can't do anything. And you have to promise you'll never tell anybody you're Isaiah's father."

"I can't promise you that."

"You have to. Nobody can ever know. I mean it." Her voice gave way. "I have to go. I won't—" She pulled away and looked past him out the car window. There was a blur of movement down the lane. A man wearing a hat and coat, carrying something in his arms. For a moment she thought it was her father, and then she saw clearly.

"Oh Lord. It's Raymond. He's got Isaiah."

"What the hell?" Walker opened the car door, but Leona gripped his arm.

"Stay here. Let me talk to him." She was out of the car and running, the mud dragging at her feet. One of her shoes came off. She slowed when she got close enough to see Raymond's face. His expression took her breath away. She tried to keep her voice calm. "Raymond, give Isaiah to me. Let's go home."

"Well," he said. "Look who we got here, son. It's your mama, the tramp." Isaiah was crying and reaching for her.

"Let me have him."

Raymond slipped and went to his knees. Isaiah wriggled out of his grasp, tottered over the muddy ruts, and fell. Leona picked him up and backed away, not taking her eyes off her brother. If she could get to the buggy, she could drive off, but Raymond was back on his feet, and she knew he was not going to let her do that.

Walker moved past Leona and stood between her and her brother. "Go home, Raymond," Walker said. "Take the buggy. I'll bring Leona and Isaiah in the car. This isn't any of your business."

Raymond struggled to his feet. "So you're the one. You're the brat's daddy." He tossed off his father's hat, ran at Walker, and threw the first wild punches, landing one on Walker's jaw that staggered him. Walker rallied with a blow that knocked Raymond down.

"Leona, take the baby and go!" Walker shouted.

"No, Leona! You're not going anywhere but home with me!" Raymond had a cut above his eye, blood streaming down his face. Neither man could move fast, their feet mired in mud. They grappled and fell and thrashed about. Finally, Raymond pinned Walker down, and Walker was getting the worst of it. Leona sat Isaiah on a grassy bank, away from the mud and water and the fighting men. "It's all right, Isaiah," she said. "Stay here."

She waded into the fray and tried to pull her brother off Walker. "Stop it, Ray! You'll kill him!" Raymond knocked Leona backward. She was crying now, Isaiah crying too, and the rain coming down heavier. She crawled to where Isaiah was and gathered him to her.

Walker and Raymond were on their feet again. More slamming blows to Walker's face and gut, and he fell. He no longer fought back. Raymond kicked him in the stomach, groin, and head, Leona begging him to stop.

Walker was still. Raymond stepped back, wiped his bloody mouth on his sleeve, and spat. "He won't come near you again, that's for sure."

She put Isaiah down and waded through the muck. She dropped to her knees beside Walker. Her hands wavered in the air: where to touch him? His face was a bloody mess. She touched his hair.

Raymond pulled her up. "You and the boy get in the buggy."

"But we can't leave him here."

"We can, and we will. Let the bastard crawl back to town, for all I care."

She went back to where Isaiah was and picked him up. Raymond dragged her to the buggy. "Climb in. Let's go."

In the seconds it took Raymond to untie Belle, Leona thought about jumping out and running, but she wouldn't get far, carrying the baby. Raymond got in, whipped the horse, and they drove away. Leona looked back at Walker lying in the mud. He had not moved, but she told herself he would be all right. He would get up and follow them, or better still, he'd go for the sheriff, and the sheriff would come to the house and take Raymond away. Out on the road, Leona listened for the sound of the automobile.

52

Searing pain in Walker's head and chest, gut and groin. Through a bloody haze he saw trees rise around him into a wavering mist of rain and fog. Or was it smoke? He was back in France, lying in a trench surrounded by earth walls and blood and death, the sky above punctuated by showers of rocket fire and stars. But it wasn't night; it was day, and it was raining. He heard the whinny of a horse and voices, a man, a woman, a crying child. Something on wheels—a caisson?—lumbered past and showered him with cold, muddy water.

He was not in France; he was at Hawks Creek. He had come to blows with Raymond Pinson, and Leona and her baby were there. His son.

Walker raised his head, spat out broken teeth and blood, rolled onto his stomach, edged forward, crawled until he couldn't go any farther. He slipped into darkness, into a vision of Leona bending over him, her hair a halo around her face.

53

Raymond whipped Belle, driving her hard through deep mud and around the places where the road had washed out. Didn't Leona know he had done it for her? Their father would have done the same. He would have hunted down the bastard who gave her that illegitimate child and killed him. But she was crying and carrying on.

"Go back, Ray. Please. He'll die."

"He ain't that bad off. Now hush!"

One of Raymond's eyes was swelling shut. His head hurt bad. He had to hand it to Walker. He had fought damn hard at first, but then he'd pretty much laid himself down and let Raymond beat him senseless. That had surprised Raymond, but he figured Walker knew he deserved it. He would leave Leona alone now, no doubt about it. The question was what to do about Leona and the boy, who had hardly shut up since he took him from Bertie.

They were just past the Pratts' farm when Leona jumped out of the buggy with Isaiah, scrambled down the bank, and ran off into the field.

"Damn it, Leona!" Raymond jerked the reins and pulled Belle up short. The horse reared and bolted sideways, and the buggy slid down the washed-out bank, taking the horse and Raymond with it.

The buggy lay on its side. He climbed out. The horse whinnied and strained against the weight of the buggy that had landed on her rear flank, the wheels still turning. He shoved and tugged at the buggy and managed to move it enough to see that Belle's back leg was shattered. The horse's eyes were wild, her nostrils flared, her sides heaving.

"Aw, Jesus," he said. "Aw, Belle."

He turned away from the horse and vomited. Emptied out,

he straightened, wiped his mouth. The horse whinnied and
thrashed. He would have to put her out of her misery, but first,
he had to find Leona. She had gone into a cornfield where the
old stalks were tall enough to hide her, but she wouldn't get far
in the mud, carrying the boy. Raymond remembered she was
wearing only one shoe. He pushed through the corn, following the sound of the baby's crying. He caught up with them,
grabbed for Leona's dress, and brought her and the child down.
Leona fought him, but one good slap, and she crumpled. The
boy sat in the mud, bawling. Raymond hauled Leona up. Blood
poured from her nose. She went limp against him.

He picked Isaiah up and half carried Leona back to the road
where the turned-over buggy and the injured horse were.

He grabbed her hair and forced her to look at Belle. "See
what you did? You see?"

"Oh, Belle," she said.

"Come on! Let's go."

They walked the rest of the way home. When they got to the
house, Raymond steered Leona inside and down the hall to her
room. He put Isaiah in his crib and shoved Leona into the rocking chair. "Don't you move." When she made for the door, he
grabbed her and struck her on the jaw. She fell against the table
by the bed, and the lamp Luther had given her crashed to the
floor, the glass chimney scattering like sparks. Leona dropped
to her knees and picked up the pieces.

Raymond got his father's tools and ripped the bolt from the
inside of her door and screwed it to the outside. "There. You
ain't going nowhere. Now I got to tend to Belle." He closed the
door and slid the bolt.

He wished for the pistol he had bought not long after he
moved to Sully. A pistol would be an easier, cleaner shot, but he
had lost that gun in a poker game. His father's deer rifle would
have been better, too, but Raymond had sold it, along with the
twenty-gauge their father had given Leona, when he'd needed
money to clear up a gambling debt. He took his shotgun from
the rack over the kitchen door. It would be a messy, ugly end

to Belle, but this gun was all he had. It wasn't the one his father had given him when he was ten. After his father died, Raymond could hardly bear to touch that gun. He had traded it for this one.

He walked back up the road, sliding and stumbling in the mud. He tried again to move the buggy off Belle, but he couldn't. He considered going for help, but the end would be the same. Belle would have to be shot. The horse lay as he'd left her, but she was still now. He squatted down, let her nuzzle his hand. He stood, shouldered the gun, aimed at a spot at the center of the white blaze above Belle's eyes. He had seen his father take down a mule once. He heard his father's voice. *Take good aim. You don't want to have to shoot twice.* He stepped closer to Belle, took a breath, shouldered the gun again. He blinked back tears, aimed, and fired.

54

Locked in Leona's face hurt. A sliver of glass from the lamp's chimney lodged in the palm of her hand. She pulled the sliver out, sucked away the blood, and gathered up the glass fragments. She mopped up the mineral spirits with a cloth, but the smell remained. The lamp's metal base was dented but otherwise unharmed. Maybe she could replace the chimney, but it wouldn't be the same.

That little light had carried her through many dark hours. Luther had called it a spirit light, and she'd asked if it had ghosts in it. He had explained that the mineral spirits burned and made the light; it had nothing to do with spirits or ghosts. In her childish misunderstanding, she had come close to the truth. The lamp had been both spirit and light, hers and Luther's.

A little water remained in the basin. She cleaned the baby up as best she could and dressed him in dry clothes. There wasn't enough water to wash herself, but she stripped off the soiled clothes and put on a clean dress and an old pair of shoes. She looked at her reflection and waited for it to settle and coalesce in the cloudy mirror. Her hair tangled and muddy, her nose and her right cheek bruised and swollen. She cleaned her face and hands as best she could and lifted Isaiah out of his crib and rocked him.

While he nursed, she tried to think how she could get to Walker. The one window in her room was eight feet off the ground; she couldn't risk climbing out with Isaiah. The baby fell asleep, and she put him back in his crib. She curled up on the bed and pulled a quilt over her. She could hear Raymond rambling about the house. Although she battled to stay awake, she slipped into sleep and dreamed her father drove up in a motorcar as fine as Walker's. She heard him coming from far off, ran to meet him, and thrust Isaiah into his arms.

The sound of the sliding bolt woke her. Raymond smelled of sweat and whiskey. He lay down beside her. "Hold me like you used to," he said. When she didn't move, he pulled her to him and wrapped his arms around her. "Now. That's better," he said.

She lay still and prayed that was all Raymond wanted. To be held.

55

The warmth of Leona's body sickened Raymond. The thought of her, giving herself to a man, like a common whore. But he was no better. He was tired, so tired. If he confessed what he had done, would it take away the weight so he could breathe again? He might as well tell her. If Walker died, Raymond's life would be shot to hell anyway.

"I been thinking about those kittens," he said. "You know the ones I mean."

"The ones you killed?"

"Yeah. I need to tell you what happened."

He felt the rise and fall of her breath. "It doesn't matter."

"But it does. I was mad at Father that day. He had whipped me for something, I don't remember what. And when I went out to the barn that morning, I was itching to get my hands on something and break it. Those sorry kittens were the first thing I saw, and I got to thinking about how easy it would be to wring their necks. A lot easier than a chicken's."

She struggled against him, but he tightened his hold. "Be still. I got to tell you. I twisted the runt's neck first. When I heard it snap, I felt sick, and I knew I ought to stop, but I didn't. What was wrong with me, Leona? They was just kittens."

He could barely make out her face in the dim light, but he could see it was bruised. Had he done that? There was dried blood on her cheek. He licked a finger and rubbed at the spot.

She turned her face away. "It was a long time ago," she said. "What's happened since— I don't have any answers."

"Well, I do. Maybe Father was no good, and I'm not either." His head hurt worse, his father's voice a pounding rhythm. *I don't trust you. Don't come around here anymore.*

"Let's not talk about it. Aren't you hungry? Let me make you some supper."

What was she trying to do, sweet-talk him? "Not yet. There's something else."

She sighed. "What's that?"

He had waited a long time to say the words out loud, although they had played in his head every hour of every day. "I shot him." Her body tensed, but he wouldn't let her go. She would listen, by God.

"Shot him? Who?"

"Father. I'm the one. I did it."

"You? I don't believe you. You're—"

"Hear me out, Leona. It was an accident, I swear to God. After Father sent me away and I got work at the timber camp north of Sully, sometimes on a Sunday, I would come back to the farm early in the morning or in the evening. I thought if I could see Father and talk to him, he might change his mind and let me come home. When I saw him head out that morning with his gun, I knew where he would go, and I followed him to the ridge. I imagined that if Tobe Sanders tried to run us off, I would stand up to him, and Father would be proud of me. He'd tell me to come on and hunt with him, and I'd kill a good bird or two, and we would shake hands and be done with it. It didn't go that way. I caught up with him just as it got light, near the top of the ridge. I asked him if I could come home, and he said no. Because of you, Leona. Luther, too, with his big mouth. Father said for me not to come around anymore. Said he didn't trust me."

"Let me go, Ray. I don't—"

"And then you know what he did? He told me to hand over my gun, the one he gave me when I was ten years old. Can you believe it? I told him no, I'd worked hard for that gun, and it was mine. He tried to take it from me, and then—" He remembered it clear as day. How could he ever forget? "I didn't think about the gun being loaded. I didn't realize I had pulled the trigger until I heard the blast, and I saw Father jolt backward against the big oak tree and slide to the ground and settle against that tree like he was resting there after a long day. I remember I said,

'Father?' but he didn't answer. He just sat there, looking at me with the one eye that was left." He relaxed his hold a little, and she pulled away.

She was shivering. "If it was an accident, why didn't you tell somebody?"

"Nobody would've believed me."

"Why are you telling me now?"

"Because it don't matter now. Nothing matters." He got out of bed. "You ought not to worry about that bastard Walker. He got what was coming to him."

Raymond went out and bolted the door.

He finished a bottle of whiskey in his room. Even with the whiskey, he didn't feel better. He had thought he might, after he told it. He heard the boy crying, and then quiet. What would Leona do? She wouldn't go to the sheriff because he wouldn't let her. Leona wasn't going anywhere.

He hadn't told her everything. How after the shot, he'd heard somebody call out, "Herbert? You got something?" He'd had a split second to decide whether to stay or to run, and he had run, past his father's body and into the undergrowth and down the hill on the back side, his heart stopping in his throat, behind him the shouts of men, aware that he passed something or somebody moving in the opposite direction—a man—and Raymond wondered if whoever it was had seen him. He veered off to the north and around to Hawks Creek from the back. There was Belle, right where he had tethered her. He bent double, gasping for breath. Blood on his coat, his trousers. His father's blood.

At the creek he stripped off his clothes and cleaned them as best he could. He would go back to the timber camp. He could get cleaned up and hide his stained clothes until he could burn them. His mother would know where to find him. Somebody would come looking for him, to tell him the news.

He searched his heart for some kind of feeling: regret, grief, fear. But all he thought was, he could go home now. His mother would have her son back. Wasn't that what she wanted?

At that thought he had felt something release in his chest: relief that his father was dead and out of his way. He had pushed that thought to the back of his mind, but he'd thought it. His father's torn face had loomed in his mind, that one open eye staring him down.

Dusk. When he moved, he felt the soreness. His head pounded. He sat on the side of his bed. No need to pull on his boots. He was still wearing them. He listened for the sounds of the house, heard nothing, remembered: he had locked Leona and the boy in her room. He retched and wiped his mouth on his sleeve crusted with dried mud.

"Mama?" he said, but his mother was dead. His father too. Sally gone away. Only Leona and the boy left.

56

Leona smelled Raymond on her skin and in her bed-clothes, a sweat-smell like rancid fat that turned her stomach. She didn't know whether to believe him, but why would he invent such a story? What he had said made sense. By the time their father died, Raymond wasn't living at home. Father had sent him away, and Leona had been the cause of it.

A month before her father was killed, Raymond had come upon Leona in the barn, alone. He'd pulled her up off the milking stool and slapped her.

She touched her lip. Blood. "What did I do, Ray? Tell me!"

"Nothing. That's the problem, Leona. You ain't never done nothing around here. Least of all for me. That's about to change."

She broke free and ran for the door, but he caught her and shoved her against the wall. She smelled whiskey. Had he been drinking so early in the morning, or was the stink still on him from the night before? He clamped one hand over her mouth. She struggled against it, tried to scream, and then he was pushing her skirt up and tugging at her drawers. His fumbling gave her the seconds she needed. She brought one knee up hard, and he stumbled backward.

Somebody was banging on the barn door. "Leona? Raymond? You in there?"

Luther. It took all Leona's strength to slide the bolt, and then she was outside in the light. She turned away from Luther, knowing what he would see. Her clothes mussed, her hair falling down, her lip bloodied.

Luther said, "What's happened here?"

She swiped her mouth with the back of her hand. "I fell." She brushed past him, but Luther put a hand on her arm.

"Hold on. Did Raymond hurt you?"

She shook her head. She was trembling.

"Don't lie to me. I looked in. I saw."

Raymond came out of the barn and walked over like he hadn't a care in the world. He gripped Luther's shoulder and gave it a shake. "You keep your mouth shut, old man." He walked on toward the house.

Luther rubbed his shoulder. "You gon' tell your daddy?"

"I can't. Ray was drunk. He didn't do any harm."

"Next time, he might. If you don't tell your daddy, I will." Luther started back to the barn, turned. "I mean it, Leona."

How could she tell? Raymond was already in trouble for building a still on Tobe Sanders's land. Whatever happened now, Raymond would blame her.

Leona didn't get a chance to tell. All that week, Raymond shadowed their father like they were chained together. The next Saturday afternoon, though, in spite of a cold rain, Raymond went to town. He hadn't been gone half an hour when Luther showed up at the back door. Leona was sitting at the kitchen table, mending her father's socks. She froze when she heard the knock and looked up and saw Luther through the glass.

Her mother said, "What's the matter with you, Leona? You're white as a sheet."

Rose opened the door, and Luther asked to see Herbert. Rose yelled, "Herbert? Luther needs to see you." Muttered, "Why in God's name on a Saturday, I don't know."

Leona stood behind her mother and mouthed, "Don't do it," but Luther looked away.

The two men walked out in the yard. Leona watched them deep in conversation. Her father took a step back and raised his voice, but she couldn't understand his words. Luther shook his head. Her father headed back to the house, his expression dark and furious. Leona escaped to her room and closed the door, hoping to avoid his questions. Let him talk to Raymond, let Raymond deny it, and the whole business would be over.

A tap on her door. "Leona? I need to talk to you."

She might as well get it over with. "Come."

She had never seen him so angry. "Is Luther telling me the truth?" When she looked away, he tilted her face up. "Look at me. Is what Luther told me about Raymond true? What he tried to do to you in the barn?"

She nodded.

He let her go. Under his breath, "Sweet God Almighty."

Leona's mother was standing in the doorway. "Herbert? What's this about?"

"I'll tell you later, Rose. Leave us."

"But—"

"Go, and close the door." Leona's mother scowled, but she did as he said.

Her father sat down on Leona's bed. "Come here." When she hesitated, he held out his arms to her, and she sat beside him. "Has anything like that ever happened before?"

Leona thought about all the times since they were children that Raymond had come to her in the night. "Hold me," he would say. Lately, he had touched her in ways she didn't like, but she had been afraid to tell. He had never put that part of him inside her, the way she'd seen the farm animals do. Never that. But he would have in the barn if Luther hadn't come along, wouldn't he?

She could spare her father that. "No, sir."

He sat with his head bowed, his arms braced on his legs. After a while he stood, rested his hand on her head for a moment, and then he was gone.

That night, Raymond came home after midnight, and Leona heard the men's raised voices and her mother's crying. When Leona rose at six, her father was sitting alone at the kitchen table, still wearing his clothes from the day before.

"Raymond's gone. You don't have to worry about him hurting you. Not as long as I'm around."

After Raymond left, her mother and father passed each other in the house like ghosts. They sat at the table without a word.

They entered their bedroom at night and snuffed out the light, but did they sleep? Did they talk? Leona didn't know. Would it have mattered? She thought not.

A month later, neighbor men brought her father's body to the house on a Sunday morning when Leona was home alone. She sat on the porch and cradled his bloody head in her lap until Luther convinced her to let the men move him inside and cover him before her mother got home.

At dawn the next morning, Leona and Luther were sitting with his body when she heard the whinny of a horse. She looked out and saw Raymond ride into the yard. Climbing down from his horse, he seemed unsteady, his shoulders slumped like he'd been beaten down. He removed his hat before he walked in the house.

"I came as soon as I could," he said. His eyes were sunken and bloodshot. He smelled bad but not of whiskey. "Does anybody know what happened? Was it a stray shot?"

"He was shot in the face," Leona said. "Close range. His face was half gone."

"I want to see him."

Luther said, "It's hard to look at, Mr. Raymond. You sure you want to see him like that?"

Raymond nodded. Luther slid the coffin lid down and moved away. Raymond stood for a while, looking down at their father. Leona turned her back. His ruined face would haunt her forever. She had no need to see it again in the flesh.

Their mother came down the hall then, calling Raymond's name. He crossed the room and took her in his arms. Leona had walked out into the yard, away from Rose's weeping.

She should have known. She should have figured it out. It was horrifying to think that Raymond had accidentally shot Father. It was worse—it was unthinkable—that he had murdered him. If Raymond was capable of that, he was capable of anything.

When Raymond came and demanded supper, she went to the

kitchen and warmed up mustard greens and cooked a skillet of cornbread. He propped his shotgun against the wall next to him, sat down at the table, and ate and drank whiskey like it was any other night. The sight of the gun made Leona ill.

Isaiah was crying. "He's hungry. Let me feed him."

"All right. Get him."

She got Isaiah out of his crib and considered the distance to the front door. She couldn't risk it. If Raymond kept drinking, he might eventually pass out. That would be her chance.

She took Isaiah in the kitchen. Raymond held the bottle of whiskey out to her. "Want a drink?" She shook her head. "You said he's hungry. Feed him." When she hesitated, Raymond sat forward, his hands spread flat on the table. How quickly those hands could become fists.

"Go on. Do it."

As modestly as she could, she opened her dress, and Isaiah nursed. Raymond watched. She was conscious of the locket. If he saw it, he would take it. She prayed he was already too drunk to notice. She expected him to press her for details about Walker, but he didn't. Isaiah fell asleep. She closed her dress, and still they sat there. Raymond hadn't eaten much. She needed him to keep drinking. She poured more whiskey into his glass.

He looked at her, one eyebrow raised, and grinned, his expression awful and frightening and sad at once. "What? You trying to get me drunk?"

"I would never do that. You know your drinking worries me. It worried Mama."

"Yeah." He ran a finger around the rim of the glass. "I know it did."

He downed that glass and poured himself another. And then he drank straight from the bottle. Once, he almost slipped out of the chair, but he righted himself. His head drooped. Finally, he crossed his arms on the table and rested his head. Leona waited a while to be sure he was out. Isaiah was sound asleep in her arms. She tiptoed out and put him in his bed.

She had to get the gun away from Raymond.

Was this the gun that had killed their father? The thought of touching it turned Leona's stomach, but she had no choice. It would be hard to walk the muddy road carrying Isaiah and the gun, but she couldn't leave it with Raymond.

Hide it. Her father's whisper, the smell of his pipe. Goosebumps rose on her arms. How many times had she listened for his voice, yearned for it, but had not heard it?

Yes, yes. Hiding it would do. She knew a place where Raymond might not think to look. At the very least, it would take him a while to find the gun, and she and the baby would be long gone. A gamble, but if he woke before she could take the gun, all would be lost.

In the fireplace in her bedroom, an iron bar supported a ledge just above the chimney opening. She felt for it and measured the ledge's width with her hand. It was wide enough to hold the gun if she could balance it against the chimney wall. First, she had to get her hands on it. Isaiah whimpered. She patted his back until he was quiet. She went to the kitchen.

Raymond was passed out at the table. She avoided the board that creaked and eased closer to him. She pressed her shaking hands against her sides until they were still, took a deep breath, let it out. She lifted the gun away from the wall. Careful, don't bump, don't touch him. She walked slowly to the bedroom and shut the door, winced at the click of the latch, stood still, listened. She pushed the gun up into the chimney, balancing it on the ledge. She took Isaiah out of his crib and smothered his face against her breast. Down the hall and out the front door. The porch, the steps, the yard, her breath coming hard, please don't let him come after us please.

The rain had let up, but the road was hard going. Soon it would be dark. She wished for the wagon, but it would have taken too much time to hitch the mule. If Walker was still at Hawks Creek and he needed to be carried to town to the doctor, how would she manage?

She would soon be at Luther's place. After what he had done, after he had confided his terrible secret to her, could she ask him for help? If she did, she would have to tell him the truth about Walker.

One hard truth exchanged for another. To save Walker's life, she would do it.

57

Luther was galled by his own weakness. The sight had failed him, and now his eyes were failing too. He saw no stars even on the clearest nights. Even in daylight, darkness narrowed his vision like curtains being drawn. Days, he sat on his porch with his shotgun across his lap, turning his head from side to side to see whatever or whomever came along that road. At night he slept with the gun beside him. In the dark, he didn't have to turn his head. All darkness was the same.

Last night, he dreamed Rose came to him and they lay together, her skin like moonlight. Herbert Pinson stood in the corner, pipe in his mouth, watching with his one good eye. Varna came to Luther, too, sweet, good Varna with her wide hips built for children that wouldn't come, and Jesse, burden in the flesh of Luther's sin. When Rose left him, he tried to follow her, but he couldn't. Somebody had piled stones on his chest.

He woke, gasping for breath. All his beloved dead, gathered together in that dream. Leona and her child were still on this earth, though.

After Jesse died, Alma had begged Luther to go back to Memphis with her.

"You could live here," he'd said.

Alma turned away. "No, Daddy. I ain't coming back to this godforsaken place. It'll kill you if you stay here long enough."

One evening, she was kneading biscuit dough with a vengeance. She had hardly spoken to Luther all day. He waited for her words to spill out. Like Varna, Alma had a way of speaking her mind. If he waited long enough, she would talk.

"It's Leona," Alma said. "She's the reason you won't leave, ain't she?"

"Memphis is a big city. I ain't suited to live in a place like that."

She brushed her hand across her brow and left a smear of flour. "That don't answer my question. No need to. I know." The look on her face had hurt Luther to his core. The next day, Alma had packed up and left.

Since Luther told Leona the truth about Rose and Jesse, he had not lost hope that she might forgive him as he had forgiven her for what happened to Jesse. And God help him, he *had* forgiven her, whether it was right or wrong to do so, because he loved that girl with his whole heart. He had prayed she might still come walking up the road, her little son in her arms. But she had not.

That Sunday afternoon, he waited out the storm and passed the time by putting things into cotton sacks and an old valise Herbert Pinson had given him: his few clothes, his mother's quilts, the little wooden box with Rose's handkerchief and lock of hair. He set Varna's basket aside. Maybe Alma would like to have it. Jesse's dog lay asleep on the hearth. Alma wouldn't want that dog. He would kill it before he would leave it behind. Free it to go and be with Jesse.

Luther looked out the window. He had never seen rain like this in all his life, turning the road into a river of mud. He put coffee on to boil. Rubbed his hands together and held them near the flame. A hint of winter in the air.

He took his coffee and sat on the porch. When the rain stopped, he would go to the Pinson place and tell Leona he was leaving, whether she cared to know it or not. He finished his coffee, went inside and washed his face, put on clean overalls. But the rain didn't end. Maybe it was a sign that he was supposed to stay.

When evening came, feeling out of sorts but not sure why, he put out the lantern and lay down on his bed in the dark. It was a miracle he heard the knock on his door, heard Leona's voice, calling his name.

58

When Leona got to Luther's house, she saw no lights, no sign of life. He could have gone away without telling her. Why would he want her to know, after the way she had reacted to the story he'd told? She tapped on the door, called his name, waited, knocked again. The door opened and Luther stood there with a lantern. "My good Lord. What happened to you, girl?"

She looked toward the road. "Raymond. He—"

"Come in, come in." Luther stepped aside to let her pass, closed the door, and latched it. He touched the side of her face, and she winced. "Let me tend to that."

"There's no time. I need your help. There's a—a man at Hawks Creek. He and Raymond had a fight this afternoon, and he's bad off. I need to go and see about him. Can I borrow your wagon to take Walker to town?"

She hadn't meant to say his name. After all this time, it had slipped out, the easiest thing in the world.

"That road? Ain't no way you can get the wagon to Hawks, let alone to town."

"Please, Luther. I have to try."

"All right. But I'm coming with you. You can't leave the boy here with me. This is the first place Raymond gon' look if he comes after you."

Leona hadn't thought about that. "You're right, he would. But are you able?"

"Able as I'll ever be. You gon' need help lifting that man."

He didn't ask her who Walker was to her, and she was grateful.

The rain had slowed to a drizzle. He brought the wagon around front, and Leona climbed in with the baby. She wrapped up as best she could with a tarpaulin Luther brought out. He put a couple of quilts under the wagon seat and hung two lanterns on their hooks. He threw two sturdy wood planks into the back. "In case we get stuck," he said.

They were halfway to Hawks Creek when Leona said, "I need to tell you something."

He stopped her with his raised hand. "This Walker. He's Isaiah's daddy."

"Yes."

Luther said, "Well, then. Let's see what we can do for him."

They got to the turnoff, and Luther halted the mule. "Can't take the wagon no farther. We'll get stuck for sure, won't be able to get back out. We gon' walk in from here."

She would have to leave Isaiah in the wagon. She made one of the quilts into a kind of nest in the back of the wagon and laid Isaiah there, willing him not to wake.

Holding one of the lanterns in front of her, Leona led the way, sinking into the mud with every step, her long skirt soon weighted down with it. She prayed the car would be gone, that Walker had been able to get in the car and drive himself to town. They were well out of sight of the wagon when she almost stumbled over him, lying face down not far from where she and Raymond had left him. He had moved; that was something. She set the lantern down and knelt beside him. She rolled him over as gently as she could, swallowed a cry. His face was covered in mud and blood, but she could tell that his nose was crushed to one side like Raymond's had been.

"I'm here," she said. "You'll be all right." She wished she had brought a quilt from the wagon.

"Lord, look at that," Luther said.

"Let's get him to the wagon. We'll take him to town."

"I don't know about that. I expect he's got broken bones, and maybe he's hurt bad on the inside. The wagon ride on that rough road all the way to town?" Luther shook his head. "That'd be mighty hard. I hate to pick him up and move him at all, but we got to. We can take him to my house, and you can go for the doctor first thing in the morning."

The lantern light threw shadows on Luther's deeply lined face. Would he tell her wrong? Could he see something she couldn't? "What if he doesn't live through the night? What then?"

He rested his hand on her shoulder. "We do the best we can. It's all we can do."

Her heart shrank at the thought of moving him. It was a job for two strong men, not an old man who had recently been near death and a slight woman.

The wind gusted the lantern out. Just as well. Neither of them would have a free hand to take the light back to the wagon. They would carry Walker in darkness.

Leona got hold of Walker under his arms, and Luther took his feet. They felt their way along the muddy track. Leona's arms and back cramped under the weight. When she thought she couldn't go another step, she saw the tiny flickering light of the other lantern on the wagon. Somehow, they made it the last few yards, and she and Luther lifted Walker up into the wagon bed. She wrapped him in a quilt as best she could and rode beside him. Isaiah slept on. The three of them together, but it wasn't the way she had dreamed it.

She wished she had taken the gun. She braced for the worst when they pulled into Luther's yard, expecting to find Raymond there, but there was no sign of him. Luther drove the wagon around back. Leona despaired of getting Walker into the house. They had carried him all that way in the dark, but she didn't see how they could carry him again.

She climbed down with the sleeping baby. What to do with him? As though Luther had read her mind, he said, "That old wood box still his bed. It's clean. Lay him down there."

Tears flooded Leona's eyes. Luther had kept a place for them, even though she had turned away. But she had known it all along, hadn't she—that she could turn to Luther? She put Isaiah to bed in the wood box and pulled the curtain.

Luther propped the back door open. This time, he took Walker's shoulders and Leona his feet. "We put him on my bed," Luther said. He was out of breath and sweating. Leona knew the effort was too much for him, that he had done it for her. Luther brought her basins of water, and she set about cleaning Walker's wounds. He moved and moaned when she touched his face, but he didn't wake. It was a blessing that he was unconscious; maybe he didn't feel the pain as much. She wondered if his face would be misshapen like Raymond's.

Luther came in. "How's he doing?"

"I don't know. There isn't much I can do."

Luther folded a quilt and placed it beside the narrow bed. "You lay down here. Call out if you need me."

"I will. Did you bolt the doors?"

"I did." He turned to go. "I'll be on the watch."

Leona sat the night beside Walker. He didn't wake or stir. More than once, she listened for his heartbeat. More than once, she got up and went to the window, thinking she heard somebody outside. When the morning light came, she saw that Walker's face had swollen and bruised beyond recognition.

Isaiah woke crying, poor little boy. She made breakfast for him and Luther and brewed a tea to help with Walker's pain once he woke. But he didn't wake. He didn't wake when, unable to find a spot on his face to kiss, she kissed his filthy hair. At seven o'clock, she set out for Sully in Luther's wagon.

Leona pushed the old mule hard, but it seemed to take forever to get to town. How would she explain to Dr. Dunlap what had happened? She could say she didn't know who had hurt Walker, that she had come along and found him. No. The lying was behind her now. If Dr. Dunlap knew Raymond had done this to Walker, Ray would be in terrible trouble. But why should she care what happened to her brother after the way he had treated her?

She couldn't, wouldn't think about Raymond. She would get help for Walker, no matter the cost to Raymond or to her.

She went around the side of the doctor's house to the office door and rang the bell. Dr. Dunlap opened the door and adjusted his glasses. "Leona? Good God. Your face."

"It's not about me, Dr. Dunlap. Walker Broom's been hurt out near our place. He's at Luther Biggs's house. You need to come."

The doctor's expression turned grim. "He's at Luther's, you say? How— Never mind. I'll be right along, but I'll need to stop and tell Hiram."

She hadn't thought of that. Of course, he would want to tell the Brooms. The questions would begin. What was Walker doing way out there? Who was this girl? Oh, they would nod and say, She's the one with the illegitimate son.

"Can't you take care of Walker first?"

"I'll decide that. You go on now."

Not far outside of Sully, the doctor's car passed Leona on the road and threw up a spray of mud that spattered the wagon and Leona. Hiram Broom sat in the passenger seat. By the time she got back to Luther's, the doctor and Mr. Broom were already in the house. She ran inside. Luther was sitting in his chair, holding Isaiah.

Luther nodded toward the open bedroom door. "They in there with him."

Leona looked in. Dr. Dunlap was bending over Walker, listening to his heart and chest, probing various parts of him. Walker didn't seem to respond. Hiram Broom stood on the other side of the bed, a handkerchief pressed to his mouth.

Leona stepped back into the other room to wait. Isaiah climbed down from Luther's lap and ran to her and buried his face in her skirt. She picked him up and he clung to her, his little arms tight around her neck. How much of the last day and night would he remember? If only things were different. If only she could say, "Your father is here," but Isaiah didn't know what a father was.

It seemed a long time before Dr. Dunlap came out, wiping his bloodied hands on a cloth.

"What do you know about all this, Luther?"

Why would he ask Luther, not her? Her anger flared, and she answered before Luther could. "Luther helped me bring Walker here. He had nothing to do with—"

"Leona," Luther said. "Tell Dr. Dunlap the truth."

She shot Luther a warning look.

"Don't you go looking at me like that. Tell him. You don't have no choice."

In her mind, the image of Raymond and Walker grappling on the ground, all that rain and mud and blood. Isaiah, crying and crying. What if he had been hurt too? He still could be.

She felt all the breath go out of her, as though she had been holding it for a very long time. "There was a fight," she said.

Hiram Broom had come into the room. "What? What did the girl say?"

She looked straight at him. "I said, Walker and my brother got into a fight." Isaiah was fidgeting to get down, and Luther took him.

"My God. What about?" Mr. Broom said.

She remembered the times she had been tempted to walk up to Hiram Broom and tell him Isaiah was his grandchild. Now, the man stood within six feet of her, but she couldn't say the words.

Luther said, "Tell them, Leona."

She shook her head. "It's not your business, Luther. Don't tell me—"

"Mr. Broom?" Luther hoisted Isaiah on his hip. "Your son is this boy's daddy. Mr. Raymond found it out, and that's why he beat him up so bad."

Hiram Broom took a step back. "I'll be damned if that's true."

Dr. Dunlap turned to Leona. "Is it?"

She nodded. There it was. The truth. Isaiah held out his arms to her, and she took him. Couldn't they look at Isaiah and see the resemblance?

"Well, I don't believe you," Mr. Broom said. He turned to

the doctor. "We're wasting time, Dunlap. Let's get Walker out of here." He went back in the room where Walker was.

So the truth floated briefly in the air of that little room and dissipated like smoke. Hiram Broom would never believe it unless Walker vowed it was true. Leona didn't know if Walker would ever do that, even if he lived. She had sworn him to secrecy.

Dr. Dunlap asked her where Raymond was.

"He was at home when I left last night. I haven't seen him since."

"I'll let the sheriff know. You understand I have to do that."

"Yes, sir."

"Do you have a place to go? You ought not to go home."

She touched her face. "I can't, not while Raymond's there."

The doctor brought a tin out of his bag. "Use this ointment on your face. It'll help it heal." He closed the bag.

Hiram Broom said, "Where's the car?"

Was that troubling him—the loss of his fine car? "At Hawks Creek," she said.

The doctor and Mr. Broom used a folded quilt to move Walker to the doctor's car. They laid him in the back seat, and when he cried out, Leona was glad to hear it. It was a sign of life. That was all she wanted: she wanted him to live. Nothing else mattered.

Isaiah watched it all with his thumb in his mouth. He pointed toward Walker and said, "Hurt?"

"Yes," Leona said, "but he'll be all right." She wished it with all her heart.

The doctor's car pulled away slowly as though not to hurt Walker any further. Trying not to cry, Leona bit her lip so hard she drew blood. She might never see him again.

Isaiah said, "Mama! You hurt?" He buried his head against her shoulder.

What to do? The Pratts would take her and Isaiah in for a few days, until things resolved with Raymond, but she felt dizzy and sick. She couldn't go another step.

"Is it all right if I stay here for a while?" she asked Luther.

"You know it is."

He set a basin of water and a wash cloth in the lean-to. He offered her a skirt and shirtwaist that had belonged to Varna. "They'll be big on you, but they'll do till you can get back to the house."

Leona thanked him.

Had she judged Luther too harshly? Here was a man who had been so tormented by secrecy and grief and guilt that he hadn't been able to hold it in any longer. She knew what that was like. What people did for love.

He pulled the curtain and she heard him say to Isaiah, "Come on now. Let's you and me go outside."

She washed up as best she could. Varna's neatly pressed clothes smelled of lavender. They were too large, but she knotted the skirt at the waist and made do.

She helped Luther remove the soiled, bloody bedclothes from his bed. Luther spread a clean quilt over it. "You lie down for a while. I'll watch Isaiah."

"I don't need to rest."

"Hush now. Yes, you do."

The room still reeked of blood and mud. She lay down, but every time she closed her eyes, she saw Walker's face. She had not thought she would sleep, but she did. She woke to a clatter in Luther's yard. Raymond? Her heart seized. She got up and looked out the window and saw Sheriff Taylor getting out of his car. Wincing with every movement, Leona pinned up her hair and straightened her clothes. Her body hurt all over. By the time she got to the front room, Luther and the sheriff were already sitting down. Isaiah played at their feet.

Sheriff Taylor looked at Leona's face and blanched. "Did Raymond do that to you?"

She wondered what Luther had already told the sheriff. Luther said, "Tell him everything."

She told him about the fight. She didn't tell him that Raymond had confessed to killing their father. She hadn't told Luther, either. Some things she would keep to herself.

Sheriff Taylor listened, his head down. In spite of what had happened to Jesse, Leona told herself Mr. Bobby was a good man. He would do what was fair and right.

When she finished, he took a deep breath, let it out. He said, "Raymond's at the house?"

"I don't know. He was there when I left last night."

"I'll have to take him in."

She nodded.

What did she owe her brother? That morning, after she had seen in the light of day what Raymond had done to Walker, she would have said nothing. But what would her father do if he were alive? She had asked that question about Jesse, and she'd made the wrong choice. She didn't want to be wrong again. Her father had sent Raymond away because of her, and Raymond had nursed that hurt and anger until it poisoned him. If her father were here now, and there was a chance to help Raymond, wouldn't he do it? She didn't think Raymond would go quietly with the sheriff. The state he had been in, he might do something to himself.

She said, "I'll go with you."

Sheriff Taylor slapped his thighs and stood. "That's not a good idea."

"Mr. Bobby's right," Luther said.

She kissed Isaiah and gave him to Luther. "I'll be back in a while."

59

In his dream Raymond's father is telling him how to dig a grave.

"Dig it right," he says. "Make it six feet deep by eight feet long by four feet wide."

The earth is hard-baked. Raymond is drenched in sweat, his hands blistered. He's in the pit of it, the hole's depth as tall as he, the walls of red clay steep, precarious and trembling as though they might cave in any minute and bury him alive. He has brought a lantern into the hole, but its light casts his misshapen shadow against the grave's wall like a magic lantern show. He wipes the sweat from his eyes and looks up at the sky, racing clouds obscuring the moon. The shovel strikes something hard. He scrapes away the dirt and there's his father, grinning up at him, flesh still clinging to bone. "Son," his father says, grasping Raymond's hand and pulling him down. "I thought you'd never come."

Raymond startled out of sleep. The lantern gone out, the kitchen dark. He had fallen asleep at the table? He was all cramped up and sore as hell. Why was that? It took a minute to remember: he and Walker Broom had had a fight. A fine war hero Walker was. Couldn't even hold his own. Walker had gone awful still at the end. Raymond hadn't meant to kill him. He'd wanted to make his point: stay away from Leona.

The whiskey bottle was empty. He had no more stashed at the house, and he couldn't go to the bootlegger's because he didn't have Belle. Shit.

He got up from the table and stumbled over a chair. Found the matches and lit the lantern. The house was dead quiet. He went all over, calling for Leona, but he already knew she was gone.

He would have sworn he'd left his gun leaning against the

wall in the kitchen. Leona must have taken it. God damn it, how could he have drunk himself into a stupor?

Dark now; no point in going after Leona tonight. Where would she go? To Luther's, or Bertie's. Not far. He could wait until morning. He lay down in his mother's room, but he feared closing his eyes. Finally, he slept in spite of himself, a drunken sleep devoid now of dreams.

When Raymond woke, the sun was high. He lifted himself up and groaned. He hurt all over, his mouth dry as cotton. Dread rose up in him like bile when he remembered what he had done to Walker Broom. Somebody might have found him by now, dead or alive. If Walker was dead, Raymond would be in deep trouble. Even if he was alive, the sheriff would come after Raymond, and he'd have hell to pay.

He would have to leave, but where would he go, and how, without Belle? How far would he get on foot? He didn't know, but he wouldn't sit here and wait to be hauled off to jail.

He packed a sack with a change of clothes, the little bit of money that was left in the jar in the kitchen, a square of cold cornbread wrapped in a napkin. Damn it, he needed his gun. He searched the house but didn't find it. He walked through the rooms one last time, taking in every detail so he would remember. The portrait of William Pinson hanging over the mantel. His mother's rocking chair. Where was her Bible? Leona must have taken it. Well, hell, he would say goodbye to it all. Nothing left for him here anyway.

It occurred to him then that if he had to go, by damn, he wouldn't leave nothing behind. His great-grandfather had built this house. The old wood would be a tinderbox. Raymond went to the barn and got a can of kerosene. Nearly full; that should do it. He started at the front of the house, splashing it over the rugs and furniture, down the hall, and into the kitchen. He spilled a little on his pants and wiped it off with his hands. The smell turned his stomach.

He got the tin of matches from the shelf above the stove.

He lit one and dropped it on the trail of kerosene in the hall-way. The flames flickered small and blue and then yellow, lick-ing their way along the path. He tossed another match in the kitchen. The flames caught the bottom edge of the tablecloth, and within seconds the cloth was burning and the fire climbed there too. When Raymond went to put the tin of matches in his sack—they would be handy to have on the road—he dropped the tin, and matches spilled across the floor and into the burn-ing kerosene. They caught quickly. Raymond stood there, fas-cinated by how fast the fire spread. He almost wanted to stay and watch, but he had better get out fast. He turned to go and knocked over the can of kerosene. The kerosene pooled on the floor, and in a split second met the fire.

Get out get out get out—

60

Pinson Road between Luther's house and Leona's was still a mess of mud and standing water. Along the roadside, the trees had lost their leaves and turned to bare skeletons against the blue sky. All that rain must have signaled them it was time. The passage of time was a mysterious thing. Isaiah would grow up to be smart and curious. When he was old enough to ask about his father, what could she tell him? That Walker had abandoned them? That he had been killed in a brawl by Leona's brother? Or, if he survived, that he had married somebody else, and he had another family? She touched the locket with his photograph. She was glad to have it to pass on. She would show the picture to Isaiah when the time came. "You look like him," she would say.

Not far from her house, the sheriff said, "Look. Over there."

A plume of smoke rising. Leona's stomach clenched. They topped the last hill, and there it was: the Pinson house going up in flames.

As the car rolled to a stop, she jumped out and ran. The sheriff caught up with her and held her back from the fire, but she kept calling and calling Raymond's name.

One wagon and then another pulled up on the road and neighbors got out. Some gawked, some offered to help, but there was no helping now. Carl Pratt was there. He offered to take Leona to his house. They would stop at Luther's and get Isaiah. Sheriff Taylor and his men would comb the burnt wreckage as soon as the ashes cooled.

"I expect Raymond took off," the sheriff said to Leona.

She said, "I expect so," but in her heart she felt it: her brother lay in the midst of those smoldering ruins.

61

Luther had taken Isaiah outside to play and had seen the smoke off to the south in the direction of the Pinson place. Nothing to do but wait, but his heart was sick. One sin leads to another, he thought, and blooms like a fire.

In a little while, the Pratt wagon came into the yard. Leona climbed down, and Mr. Pratt tipped his hat at Luther, but he didn't leave. Leona came around the wagon and scooped Isaiah up. Tears ran down her bruised cheeks.

"The house is gone, Luther. Burned to the ground."

She told him how she and the sheriff had discovered the house in flames. "The roof fell in not five minutes after we got there. We don't know where Raymond is."

"Gone, I bet. Somewhere far away." Luther hoped it was true. "What're you gon' do, Leona?"

"I'm going to the Pratts for now. The sheriff said his men will go through the rubble." Her voice trailed off to a whisper. "After that, I don't know."

Although Luther had been planning to go to Alma's, his resolve was not complete until that moment. Nothing left for him here except sad memories and a pile of regrets and this girl and her child. Their lives had been tangled up together for so long. She might not realize it yet, but she and the boy were free now too.

"I been meaning to tell you. I'm going up to Memphis soon. Alma's kept after me. Maybe she's right. Maybe it's the best thing."

"Oh," Leona said. "I don't blame you. Lord knows, we've caused you enough trouble."

"It ain't that. I hate to leave you. I hate to leave this place, but it's time." He would leave Herbert, Jesse, Varna, and Rose in the red clay earth here. A hard, hard thing to think about.

Seized by the urge to take Leona in his arms, he shoved his hands in the pockets of his overalls. The space between them felt like when the creek flooded, and he dared not cross for fear of drowning. But then he gathered the girl and her boy to him and held them both. Luther was aware of Carl Pratt watching, but he didn't care.

Then Isaiah struggled, said, "Isa get down," and Leona stepped away and set the child on his feet. He toddled off, said, "Mama, go."

"You go on now," Luther said. How many times had he said those words during her lifetime? Now, they meant something different. Get on with living, don't look back, don't let anything get in your way.

62

At Bertie's house Leona fed Isaiah, rocked him, and put him down in the crib little Sarah Pratt had lain in, struggling to breathe. Bertie gave Leona a bowl of soup, but she refused it, so Bertie helped her bathe and put her to bed in Bertie's room. "You try to sleep," she said. "I'll listen for Isaiah." Bertie turned to go, then turned back. "The doors are locked up tight, and Pa will keep watch. Don't worry."

As though Raymond could rise from those ashes and come after Leona again.

She was exhausted, but she couldn't sleep. The only home she had ever known was gone, and she couldn't quite take it in. Her great-grandfather had built the house when Mississippi was still wilderness, and now it was gone, in the space of an hour.

She tried to piece together how things might have been different. If she hadn't gone to meet Walker that day, Raymond wouldn't have had reason to pursue her, there would have been no fight, and the house wouldn't have burned down. All of it, her fault. She walked through the place in her mind, trying to reconstruct her memories before they faded: the kitchen paneled with pine off the place, the wood stove, the table her grandfather had built, the open shelves. In the parlor, her grandmother Pinson's settee, the mantelpiece carved from a solid slab of oak, her grandfather's portrait hanging above it. The beadboard ceilings, the pine floors waxed to a sheen. Her room: the bed, the broken spirit lamp, the bureau drawer with the one remaining photograph of her and Isaiah and her mementos of Walker. All ashes.

Luther was leaving. She had pushed him to go, and there was nothing left for him here except the people he had loved who were all in the ground, including her own mother. In spite of

what he had confessed, in spite of what he had done, Leona
loved Luther more than anybody else in the world except Isaiah. What would she do without him?

Sometime toward morning she fell asleep and dreamed that
Raymond was calling to her from the burning house, but all
the doors and windows were boarded up and she couldn't get
to him. She cried out, and Bertie came. "It's over," she said.
"Raymond can't hurt you again."

"Oh, Bertie. It's about so much more than Ray."

Word would spread quickly about Walker and the fight with
Raymond, and Bertie would hear the gossip soon enough. It
was better if Leona told her the truth. So she told Bertie about
Walker, and after she finished, Bertie threw her arms around
her.

"What's done is done," Bertie said. "You're better than the
lot of those haughty Brooms. However it turns out, you and
Isaiah will be all right."

Leona wanted to believe it.

She didn't want to see the house in ruins, and she would have
stayed away except that the barn still stood, and the livestock
needed tending. A couple of days after the fire, she asked Mr.
Pratt to take her to the barn to take care of the animals. When
she offered him the two cows, a couple dozen chickens, and the
young sow, he seemed grateful. He didn't protest, and he didn't
ask her any questions. She kept the wagon and mule. A plan
was forming in her mind, regardless of whether Raymond was
alive or dead.

Bertie had heard in town that Walker was better, but he still
wasn't out of the woods. Mrs. Harmon had told Bertie at the
store that when he was well enough, he would go north to join
his wife. Edith's child was due any day. Leona didn't ask Bertie
if Mrs. Harmon had connected what happened to Walker with
Leona and Isaiah. It was better not to know.

Ten days after the fire, the sheriff came to see Leona. It was raining and cold, the landscape transforming to a stark palette of grays and browns. Leona and Sheriff Taylor sat in the kitchen where it was warm. He sat quietly, turning his hat in his hands. Finally, he tossed his hat on the table.

"If Raymond was in the house when it burned, we ought to have found evidence of it. We combed the place. We didn't find him, but we found this." He took a little box out of the satchel he'd brought and gave it to her. Inside it, a blackened disk. Leona rubbed a spot with her thumb and the black came off, revealing the gold, the engraving. Her father's pocket watch. Rose had given it to Raymond after their father died. Leona had been surprised that Raymond hadn't sold it or gambled it away, but he had kept it on him always.

She found the catch and opened it. The inside was pristine, untouched by the fire. "Raymond would never have left Father's watch behind."

"He must have dropped it. You should keep it for your boy."

Something of her father's for Isaiah. She closed the case and rubbed a little more of the black off it. "I will."

"I never assumed Raymond died in the fire. I've had men out looking for him, and I notified the sheriffs in the neighboring counties. My guess is, he's long gone."

"He wrecked the buggy, and he had to put Belle down. He doesn't have a horse. How far can he get?"

The sheriff shrugged. "I don't know. He could have hitched a ride with somebody, gone in any direction. He could be anywhere by now." He picked up his hat and stood, as if to say, That's all there is. "There's one other thing you should know. We found a tin inside the house, the kind you might keep kerosene in."

Leona's thoughts reeled. "Are you saying Raymond started the fire? He loved the place, Mr. Bobby. He was always saying it was rightfully his."

"There's no way to know for sure." He turned to go. "I'll let you know if there's anything else. And you let me know if Raymond gets in touch with you."

"Oh, I will." The thought of Raymond showing up sent chills through her.

After the sheriff left, she sat alone in the Pratts' kitchen. She needed to get hold of her wild feelings. She knew she should be ashamed, but she wasn't at all relieved to hear Raymond was alive. She had felt something close to joy when she'd thought he was gone for good. She didn't want to think he was out there somewhere. She would never be free of him, never free of the fear that he might turn up and ruin whatever life she was able to shape for herself and for Isaiah. Raymond would come back, or he would find her wherever she went.

She resolved not to think about her brother or about Walker, who was there every time she looked at their son, or about Luther, who had sent word by a colored man who worked for Carl Pratt that he had made it to Memphis just fine, and he was staying with Alma.

63

Leona and Isaiah stayed with the Pratts through Christmas. On the last day of December, she carried Isaiah to the clearing where her father had first taken her to see the turkeys. It was a long trek, and the day was overcast and cold. She spread a quilt Bertie's mother had given her and sat on the ground. She let Isaiah toddle around. "This is a special place," she told him. "I want you to remember it." Isaiah picked up pinecones and threw them at the squirrels. Found a stick and began to dig. Brought her a blue jay's feather.

Leona imagined her father walking out of the woods to sit beside her and take Isaiah on his lap. "So much has happened, Father," she said aloud, "but surely you know." She waited, heard the chatter of squirrels, caught a whiff of wood smoke. The wind picked up and stirred the trees overhead, but there was no sense of her father's presence.

The following day, Leona drove the wagon into town early and left it hitched near the depot where a southbound train stopped through every three days. She carried Isaiah, a carpetbag she had borrowed from Bertie, and a basket of food. The neighbors had given them clothes, and Mr. Pratt had given her money for the train ticket.

Nobody paid much mind to the empty wagon until late in the afternoon. Only then did people gather around it. It was the Pinsons' wagon and mule, all right, with no belongings inside. People shrugged and went about their business. Somebody remembered that the house burned down, that the brother might have died in the fire, or did he? Somebody else remembered seeing Leona board a train, but nobody knew which direction she had gone.

64

Leona had never been on a train before. She took a seat facing backward, toward home, and when the train moved, the world passed her in reverse. She didn't recognize anybody on the train, and she was glad. After a while, she fed Isaiah a little cold potato, bites of ham, which he loved, some biscuit. But she didn't feel like eating.

The hills of home receded, a blur in the early morning haze. The train sped south toward Moriah, a little town near Natchez, where nobody would know Leona except Bertie's cousin who had found her a room in a boarding house. Leona had invented a tale to tell: her young husband lost in the war, her family gone, she was looking to start her life over. She would miss Bertie's wedding in the spring. That made her sad. Carl Pratt would tend to the land until there could be some disposition of it. That couldn't happen as long as Raymond was missing.

The train rocked and lulled Isaiah to sleep. Leona slept, too, a calm and dreamless void. When she woke, the sky was blue, the sun high and bright. The train moved past unfamiliar fields and towns. Isaiah pressed his face against the window and named what he saw: cow, barn, tree, house. "Yes," Leona said. The train slowed and climbed among high hills, much like the red clay hills she had left behind. Around a curve, she could see the end of the train and beyond, where the tracks converged at a point and disappeared.

AUTHOR'S NOTE

This novel's journey has been a long one. I took an early draft to Jane Hamilton's novel workshop at the Writers in Paradise Conference, Eckerd College (St. Petersburg, Florida), back in 2010. Those pages won a "Best of Workshop" award, but over the years since, I set this book aside more times than I can count. In the summer of 2021, when I was restless and stalled on another project, I pulled the novel out again, still dissatisfied with it and yet still believing in its possibilities.

My utmost thanks to Jaynie Royal at Regal House Publishing, who read *That Pinson Girl* in the fall of 2021 and believed in it too.

To early readers Marion Barnwell and Gale Massey, who nurtured this book from the beginning, thank you. Thanks, too, to writer friends here and far away who offered sound advice, held me accountable, and, at times, kept me from burning everything!

My sincere thanks also to fellow participants and workshop leaders over the years who shared crucial insights, told me things I didn't want to hear, and inspired me to write beyond what I thought possible: the Nebraska Summer Writers Conference, Ron Hansen; Miami-Dade Writers Institute, Connie May Fowler and Dorothy Allison; Writers in Paradise, Jane Hamilton and Ann Hood; The Lighthouse/Denver, Antonya Nelson, Andre Dubus III, and Jennifer Wortman; and the Key West Writers Workshop, Claire Messud.

Special thanks to Kevin Morgan Watson, Editor and Publisher at Press 53, for publishing my debut story collection, *Crosscurrents and Other Stories*.

Residencies at the Rivendell Writers Colony, the Hambidge Center, and Ragdale afforded much-needed solitude and time for uninterrupted work.

To my "bookgroup" of many years now, as savvy a gathering of women readers as you could ever hope to meet—thank you for believing, too.

I am most grateful to my people, especially my maternal grandmother, whose stories inform this one. I'm also grateful to the place where I was born, a seventh-generation child of this complicated, messy Mississippi I call home. The harsh, beautiful landscape of the north Mississippi hill country provides the backdrop for *That Pinson Girl.*

Finally, thanks to our children and grandchildren, who encouraged the dream. My deepest gratitude goes to my husband, Austin, my best and toughest reader. Without him *That Pinson Girl* would not exist.

ACKNOWLEDGEMENTS

The author wishes to thank the editors of *Sabal: A Review Featuring the Best Writing of the Eckerd College Writers' Conference: Writers in Paradise, Volume 6, 2011* (Eckerd College, St. Petersburg, Florida), for inclusion of an excerpt from an early version of *That Pinson Girl*, winner of the Best of Workshop Award in Jane Hamilton's Fiction Workshop, 2010.